THE GATHERING OF SOULS

The Gathering
of Souls

Erica Darnell

For my husband, Amos,
who supported the adventurous
heart of an author
even though he hates to read.
That's love.

Chapter 1

Molly Gregory stared at the pistol in her hand. She had no experience with guns. Aside from corny cop television shows, Molly had never even seen a gun in her life. Her small veterinary practice proved adventurous enough.

"Has it really come to this?" she thought out loud. She could feel nervousness take over her body. Sweat trickled down the back of her neck as she allowed an outward shiver. Her friend and mentor, Ashley, put a loving arm around her shaking shoulders.

"You know we've talked about this. It's the most important decision you're ever going to make, Molly, and I'm here to make it with you." Ashley pulled open her handbag and plucked another gun from its contents. She had her dark hair pulled back in a ponytail and flipped it over her shoulder. "Don't fear what is to come. This is your ticket out of here. You don't have to feel the pain anymore. No one should live a life filled with depression and darkness. Think of all our brothers and sisters who have gone before. They wait for us now." Ashley placed both hands on Molly's shoulders. "Are you ready?"

Molly closed her eyes, her dark lashes standing out against her pale skin. "I'm only cutting in line to board the train a little early."

"That's right. Okay, did you leave the note where we planned?" Her friend eyed her. Molly nodded her head and slowly placed the pistol on her temple. She and her mentor lowered themselves to their knees. Ashley began to count as she mirrored Molly, placing her gun against her own temple, "One, two..."

"Three," Molly said. She heard her mentor's gun go off, and she flinched. Sadly, she felt a wave of relief to finally be free of her mentor.

~~~~~

Kate rolled to her side and peeked through one eye. Jake, her 3-year-old golden retriever, sat with his head propped on the side of her bed. She heard his morning greeting as his tail swept anxiously across

1

the floor. She groaned and looked up at the clock, 5:45. She switched off the alarm set for 15 minutes later and grabbed her gym shorts.

Jake bounded a few yards ahead on the trail behind her home and through the woods. She loved the sanctuary-like setting the trees provided. The morning sun broke through the canopy overhead, creating beams of light landing in the thicket around her. Kate owed the discovery of the trail to Jake's mischievousness. Jake brought in ticks and burs on his fur frequently, which led to her decision to fence in the yard. She noticed the path while laying the perimeter. After exploring the path, she and Jake agreed to keep the yard open and instead, she invested in a groomer.

She lived behind the town high school, not far off of Wild Cat Drive. If she took the trail far enough, she would run into Crab Orchard Creek, but instead, she cut through to dump out onto Carbon Street. She emerged from the thicket just three blocks from her home. Her feet hit the pavement in their regular rhythm, begging to go further. She pressed her lips into a smile and decided on a 5-mile day. Before long, she hoped fall would bring cooler mornings for her to accomplish longer runs.

Kate ticked through the day's events in her mind. Three meetings with clients would take up the majority of her time. Two years ago, she became an assistant to the CPO for Browning & Connor Associates in hopes of eventually achieving a higher status within the company. Unfortunately, her superiors kept her as an assistant, citing that she was "just so good at administrative work." It wasn't a job she loved, but it paid the bills.

Her cell phone vibrated on her hip. She glanced at the caller ID. Marcy. She answered, "Hey, girl! What's up?"

"Not much. Listen, I'm gonna have to take a rain check for lunch today. I've got some real problems with a nasty glitch in the system." Marcy owned an online business aiding other people in starting online businesses. She tried explaining the process too many times to count, yet Kate still had no idea how it worked.

"That's fine. Don't worry about it. We still on for the pool party next weekend?"

"Yeah. My little man can't wait."

"Alright, I'll see you then. Tell Brendon I said hello." Kate had never met a boy cuter than Marcy's son. For his seventh birthday, he insisted they all go to Super Splash Park, a small water park in neighboring Carbondale. He didn't care if any of his friends joined them, so long as "Aunt Kate" made it to his party.

"I'll tell him. Oh! Will you call Molly and let her know I can't make it?"

Kate breathed out a quick yes as she turned to keep up with Jake.

Marcy scoffed. "Are you running? Who answers the phone while they're running?"

Kate smiled. "I just turned into the town square! One of my favorite places!"

"Oh my God, Kate, please put down the phone and pay attention to what you're doing there. Some maniac is going to run you over."

"Yeah, sure. See you later." Kate anchored the phone back to her waist. Marcy was right. Marion's town square and clock tower had been established in practically prehistoric times, yet everyday people acted as if they didn't know when to stop or yield.

She would wait until she finished her run to call her sister. "She probably won't answer anyway," she mused. Molly had a notorious reputation for never picking up. She never checked her messages, either. If she noticed a missed call, she'd pick up and dial the person in the call log, complaining that checking voicemail was too time-consuming. Jake snorted a complaint at Kate's lagging. She picked her pace back up for the final leg of their morning routine.

~~~~~

Detective Alec Peterson brought his car to a halt at 2201 East Clark Street. The quaint home defied its age with a well-kept appearance, boasting a fresh coat of paint on the porch rails and shutters. The flower boxes under the windows brimmed with yellow flowers, matching the pots on the steps. Rose bushes created an inviting walkway, hedging the path around the house to the back yard. He pulled himself out of the car and leaned against the driver's side door as a hefty woman in uniform approached him. "Hello, sir. I'm Fran. I was the first to respond to the scene. It's nice to meet you." She held out her hand and smiled.

"I'm Detective Peterson," He replied. "Has the forensics team arrived?" He pushed past her extended hand without acknowledging it.

She dropped her hand awkwardly to her side. "Oh, the photographer is inside working the scene right now. A few guys are collecting possible evidence around the perimeter. Haven't turned up much. Found some shoe prints in the yard that don't match up with the victim. Frankly, sir, I think we have another one." She dropped her gaze to the concrete and shuffled a rock a few inches with her foot. "That would make three in our area over the past two weeks. Marion has never seen anything quite like it."

Alec spoke to her over his shoulder. "I think you should let us decide. Let's not jump to conclusions." Inwardly, he grimaced. He knew immediately that this new string of deaths closely resembled other cases he had seen. When he reached out to the local detective about working together to find connections, he was informed that the detective would soon retire. Hence Fran, an ambitious but green ally.

She nodded her head, appearing slightly embarrassed. "Of course. Did you already receive information from past victims?"

He nodded. "What's with all the ruckus coming from the backyard?" He walked to the edge of the sidewalk to see a smaller building in the backyard. It looked like a renovated pool house with an extra wing extending out to the side.

"The victim owned a small veterinary clinic. It's one of the reasons a foreign footprint doesn't mean much." She squinted, eying the building. "Anyway, the animals have been going crazy for hours. Neighbors say that's not like her to just leave 'em out there like that."

A lanky photographer meandered out of the house, peering in the sunlight at his camera screen. Alec nodded curtly. "He's done. Let's go."

The interior of the house boasted the same impeccable cleanliness as the outside with a quaint cottage motif. The shabby chic sofa and end tables contrasted the brightly colored walls. They walked through the first floor. The living room, kitchen, and guest bedroom were all clean. Not a speck of evidence to indicate a struggle.

"Did the clients for her clinic go around back or come through the house?" Alec asked, wondering if she kept it clean for people coming through.

"I'm not sure," Fran responded. "They pulled a list from her computer. We'll start making calls once we pull each file individually."

"Pull each file individually? If we have a full list with numbers, why would you need to do that?" She turned and gave him a look like he should know the reason. "What?"

"Sir, the records...they don't have...I mean," she paused. "The names of her clients are her actual patients."

Alec's eyes hardened. "You mean the contact information is listed under the pet names?" She nodded. He laughed to himself, "Hello, this is Agent Peterson calling. I have a few questions to ask Fluffy. Is she able to come to the phone?" Fran's sobering glance brought him back from his conversation with the imaginary cat. He cleared his throat, "I just don't understand animal lovers."

They filed up the staircase into the master bedroom situated in a finished attic. Three windows on each wall lit up the room. The aging hardwood floor creaked slightly as they approached the scene. A stout man from the forensics team handed him the coroner's report.

"Single gunshot wound to the head," he read. "Vic's prints on the gun. Gunshot residue on her hand." He looked up. "Picture's been knocked off the end table. She didn't fall anywhere close to there."

"Some suicide victims put pictures facedown to avoid feeling guilty," Fran commented. Her plastic glove slapped her wrist as she pulled it on before handling the edge of the frame. A photo of two smiling girls on a windy shore sat behind the broken glass. "It's broken, but she could have knocked it off herself. Maybe she had a fit of anger or a twinge of regret?"

Alec was staring at the tape on the floor. "Hm." He glanced back at the report. "Says here there was fresh bruising on the back of her hand. Maybe they can match that up with the frame." He turned back to the man working the scene. "May I keep this copy of the report?" The CSI didn't look up from his fingerprinting brush but nodded his head.

Detective Peterson led the way out to the clinic. He could hear all the animals howling in unison. Fran stopped on the path behind him about five feet from the door.

"Sorry," she said, rubbing her arm. "They're kind of freaking me out. Do you think they're all in cages?"

Alec hadn't considered that. Surely they were sectioned off somehow according to species. Still, some vets allowed one or two well-behaved favorites to roam the clinic. The thought of a mouthful of teeth clamped around his arm caused him to spin on his heels.

"You're right," he said, pulling a handgun from his holster. He stepped back, aiming at the door. "You open it, and I'll cover you."

5

The woman's small eyes widened. She opened her mouth to protest but then clamped it shut, chewing on her thoughts for a moment.

"Well?" he prodded. "Are you going to make me call another officer over here to help us deal with these fierce, domesticated furballs?"

She narrowed her eyes at him and stepped too close, uttering, "I hope you have to fight a gerbil off your jugular. I hear they're vicious." She inched forward, eyes locked on the door handle. Reaching out carefully, her fingertips touched the cold metal. A dog behind the door howled. She paused for a moment and then yanked the door open, quickly jumping sideways to allow Detective Peterson ample space for shooting.

Nothing happened. Fran opened one eye and looked at the detective. Mysteriously, the noise behind the door had instantly ceased. Every animal in the clinic was absolutely silent. Alec's gaze settled on a golden retriever in the middle of the clinic floor with its ears perked and head cocked to one side. Its tail began to swish on the tile floor. Before either of them could speak, it stood and slowly walked up to detective Peterson, placing its head against his thigh.

Alec lowered his gun. His hard gaze fixed on the dog. "Find the owners for these animals and get them back to their homes. This one might belong to our vic. I'll ask family members. I want a report on all evidence in the clinic by this afternoon," he said. He walked to the gate with his new friend in tow.

"Looks like this little girl found someone suitable to be her new master," Fran laughed.

"I hate animals." He turned and walked to his car, stopping the dog at the gate when he closed it behind him.

~~~~~

After multiple attempts, Alec put his phone back on the hook without leaving a message. "She didn't pick up," he turned to the chief. "I'll try her again in five minutes."

Chief Inspector Robert Miller pulled a hand out of his pocket and picked a piece of lint from his collar. "We got her cell number from the vic's phone," he placed a sticky note on the desk and turned for his office before Alec could respond.

Alec knew he didn't really want this lady to answer. He preferred that Miller pick someone else to make the call. He stared at the phone. "I should have stayed in bed," he mumbled.

~~~~~

After her first meeting of the day, Kate glanced at her watch. She called her sister before she left for work and got no answer. She didn't bother leaving a message. *Probably some poor puppy was hit this morning, and she's in surgery trying to get it stitched up,* she mused. Before going home, she tried one more time and finally left a message. "Molly! What's going on? Geez, I've been tryin' to call you all morning. Did you fall off the planet or what? Listen, just give me a call. I'm going to run home to let Jake out before I meet you. Love ya! Bye."

She walked in the door to find Jake waiting to plant slobbery dog kisses all over her face. "You're such a good boy." She snatched a Milk-Bone off the table and tossed it to him. He missed. He chased after the morsel, and she checked her home phone. Seven missed calls? She scrolled through. Five calls were from the same unfamiliar number. "Strange," she mumbled aloud. Maybe someone from the dating service had matched her up. Dating wasn't exactly her forte, and after some prodding from Marcy, she'd conceded to joining an online dating group. Upon taking the extensive perfect match test, asking for everything but her toothbrush color, she realized the slim possibility of any crazies getting into the system. She felt marginally better about putting her information out there for some stranger to see. Two weeks had passed, but she was too embarrassed to actually call and ask how long she would have to wait for her compatibility partner, or whatever they called it.

Jake barked her back from her thoughts. She looked at the patio doors where he stood, tail wagging. "I'm sorry, boy! Here ya go." She opened the door and let him romp in the backyard a few minutes before calling him back. He flopped on the floor in the sunlight and sighed his approval. Kate started for the door when her cell phone vibrated on the counter.

"Oh, I almost forgot." She scolded herself, "Kate, you'd lose your head if it weren't attached." She grabbed the phone. The screen displayed the same number that had called her home five times. She fumbled, hoping she hadn't let it ring too long, "Hello?"

"Hello, is this Katherine Gregory?" She didn't recognize the voice.

"Yes," she paused, "How may I help you?"

"This is Detective Alec Peterson. I work with the police department. Listen, I know this is sudden, but we need you to come down to the precinct..."

"Why?" Kate interrupted.

"I...Well..." he stumbled. "It would be best if you could come to the office as soon as you can."

Kate felt a knot forming in her stomach. "What is it? What's happened?"

"It's your sister, Molly..."

"Oh my God! Molly! Is she okay? Where is she now?" Kate hoped that Molly would grab the phone from this guy and interject her sweet voice. Just hearing that would keep her mind from going crazy with awful possibilities.

Compassion rang through Detective Peterson's voice. "I'm sorry, ma'am. We responded to a call from her neighbor reporting suspected gunshots. When we arrived on the scene, Molly was already gone."

"Wh—what?" Kate tried to swallow but couldn't. She felt her voice drop to a whisper. She tried to speak three times before she could manage to spit the words out. "It can't be her. Are you sure it's Molly?"

"When can you meet me?" he asked.

Kate jotted down the directions to the police department and hung up the phone. She leaned over the kitchen sink, feeling bile come up into the back of her throat. She grabbed a glass and filled it with water. *This can't be happening*, she thought. She sat the water on the counter without taking a drink.

~~~~~

Kate busted through the doors and almost right into the desk of an older woman seated in the front room. The secretary put her pen down started to talk, "May I ask who..."

"My name is Kate," she heard her voice ring loud through the empty room and cringed. She may need to tone it down a bit. She cleared her throat. "I'm here to see Agent Peterson."

"Katherine Gregory?" the secretary probed.

"Yeah."

"He'll be right out, dear. Please have a seat." She pointed to a row of chairs on the right wall and picked up the phone. Kate didn't want to sit but walked over to the row of chairs and stood.

Kate squinted against the stark white paint of the walls that compounded the fluorescent lights. The room felt as welcoming as a psychiatric ward. Burnt coffee lingered in the air. Pictures of the different officers and their ranks hung on the wall directly behind the chairs. In front of her, a black metal door with keypad access stuck out like a sore thumb. Other than the pictures, she had nothing to lay her eyes on. She cast about awkwardly for a magazine rack or a newspaper—anything to distract her while she waited. She just didn't want to think about her sister.

Molly. Just last night, they had joked and giggled on the phone. Kate didn't notice anything out of place. She knew her sister had struggled for two years with depression. The battle left a noticeable difference in her appearance and attitude. She'd lost too much weight, her hair thinned, her eyes lost their zeal for life. Things had changed, though. Molly began sessions with an excellent counselor. Over the past six months, Kate saw a drastic change in her sister's demeanor. Molls even started gaining the weight back. The counselor encouraged her to surround herself with loving friends and family. Since then, the two of them met for lunch twice weekly and spent at least one day out of each weekend together.

Kate closed her eyes. She could feel the knot creeping into her throat, and she swallowed hard. "Now's no time to cry, girl. Hold it together," she told herself. "Now's no time to cry..."

"Katherine?" Kate jerked herself to attention, wiping her eyes quickly. She hadn't even heard the big metal door swing open. A handsome man, a little taller than six feet, stood holding the door open behind him. He wore his brown hair tousled with some gel. Kate thought he looked a lot younger than she had imagined. His blue blazer matched his eyes perfectly and hung unbuttoned over a white collared shirt. His perfectly pressed khakis looked brand new.

"Kate," she corrected. She grabbed her purse and stood.

"I'm sorry, Kate. Would you please follow me?"

Chapter 2

Ashley flew into the alley as fast as possible, the size of her duffle bag slowing her down. She knew her time was limited. She had only allowed herself moments at her apartment to pack a few things and then split, realizing later that she forgot to feed her fish.

"Idiot," she chided herself, "the fish is the least of your worries."

She approached the red metal door at the end of the alley and knocked twice slowly, followed by three rapid beats. The door cracked, and a gaunt face greeted her.

"The gathering unites us," she spouted quickly between breaths.

The young man regarded her waywardly. "Knowing the phrase is a moot point, don't you think?"

"Are you going to let me in or not?" She could hear the fear in her own voice and tried to redeem herself. "C'mon, Wyatt, you know me. I'm starving. Let me in."

"You could tell me that you were the Queen of England incarnate. But I still wouldn't let you in. It's too late for you because we know what happened with your charge."

"How..."

He cut her off. "You're not stupid! We are everywhere, and where we are not watching...they..." He trailed off and looked around. "We never had this conversation; I'll do you the favor of 'forgetting' you came for a few minutes."

Tears filled her eyes. "Where am I supposed to go?"

"You know as well as I do that it doesn't matter where you go. They will find you. Three minutes." With that, he slammed the door in her face.

Ashley tried to suppress the fear rising from the pit of her stomach. She broke into a sprint from the alley. Wyatt was new to the organization, but he devoted himself completely to the cause. She knew that if he had any plans of staying with the project, he could

11

only risk three minutes. She aimlessly turned a few times, trying to figure out where she would stop running. Could she stop?

She heard the answer scurrying in the darkness behind her.

~~~~~

Marcy sat on the edge of the couch with her crying friend. When she got the call from a frenzied and panicked Kate, she immediately came to the house and made a pot of tea. For the past hour, Kate sat holding her cup, crying. Marcy knew that words weren't what her friend needed, so she let her presence be her support.

Kate sighed, "I don't know what to do."

Marcy handed Kate another tissue. "Let me contact your family. I'll take your address book and make some calls tonight." Kate didn't respond.

She'd never seen Kate like this. Kate had such a tendency to fight her way through tough situations that Marcy had never even seen her cry. She tried another approach. "You're going to get through this, but it's going to take a while. Maybe there's a support group for families who have lost loved ones this way."

Kate glanced at her through red eyes. "This way?"

Marcy gently placed a hand on Kate's shoulder. "I don't know what happened, Kate. But I trust that the authorities will figure it out. We'll let them come to a conclusion before we come to ours." She smiled, "I'm not assuming anything, especially not the worst."

"I want to hope that we can trust the police to sort it out." Kate's lips hardened into a line. "Detective Peterson doesn't know Molly, though. I should be doing something. Maybe I can go back through her house for something they missed. I'm sure they don't know what's what when going through a stranger's house, right? I can do that."

Marcy could practically feel the hysteria crawling into her friend. "These are not decisions that need to be made five minutes after you've received this kind of news."

"What if they think Molly really took her life? I feel like they weren't willing to listen to me when I said she'd gotten so much better."

Marcy nodded. "They work with families of victims all the time. Anyone in your position is going to become defensive. They probably give you time to grieve before really digging in. I don't really know how it works," Marcy sighed, feeling like she hadn't helped at all.

Kate placed her palms on her eyes. "What makes you think I got defensive?"

"Because you love Molly, and you know her best. Like you said, they don't know her like we do. They have to figure it out on their own. And even though they probably won't take your word for it, you know in your gut she didn't do this."

"I do know." Kate's expression changed from determined to deflated.

Marcy moved her hand to Kate's leg, knowing she'd helped deescalate the situation for now. "I know, too. Just give them time."

Kate sighed, "Maybe you're right. The detective just gave me a weird vibe. I don't think he's from around here. He's a little too..." she thought for a moment, "polished and crisp." She looked at Marcy, "He said we could go over a few more questions another time. Do you think you could be here when he does?"

Marcy nodded, "Of course. Do you want me to help contact family members?"

"Go ahead and take the address book. I've got to make some calls. They said I can't bury Molly until the investigation is finished. Since I don't know how long that's going to take, I want to put together a memorial service for her."

"Okay, what about Jake? Do you want me to take him off your hands for a few days? My little man loves to have him sleeping in his room, and I'd be glad to do it for you."

Kate glanced toward the patio door where Jake sat outside with his wet nose plastered to the glass. His ears perked when he saw her look his way. "No, thanks. I don't really want to be alone."

"Okay. I need to get going." Marcy walked to the kitchen and put their teacups in the dishwasher. She grabbed Kate's address book from the cubby hole under the cabinet and stuck it in her purse. She turned to face Kate. "I'll call you in the morning. Let me know if you need anything."

Kate looked at Marcy, eyes still brimming with tears. "I miss her. I just want to call her, and I can't." She looked down at her hands in her lap. "It's so hard to believe I can't call my sister."

Marcy walked back to Kate, laying a hand on her shoulder. "I know you miss her. We all will. I know you can't call her, but you can call me any time. Ok?" She smiled weakly.

Kate nodded, "I will. Thanks, Marcy."

~~~~~

As Marcy left, Kate sat in silence. She thought over Alec Peterson's words. He'd mentioned they didn't find a note. Kate knew there was no way Molly had committed suicide; the fact that they didn't find a note only convinced her further that Molly was somehow killed. Kate knew that her sister's sentimental side would pull through if she ever decided to do something brash. It just wasn't in Molly's nature to leave her family without saying goodbye.

Kate reached into her pocket and pulled out the blue post-it note Detective Peterson had given her. He told her that Helping Hands was an excellent support group for families who unexpectedly lost loved ones. She inwardly cringed. Sitting around with a group of people babbling about trauma did not appeal to her at all. Who wants to listen to other people cry? How could that help?

Marcy had also mentioned talking to others who knew what she was going through. Kate wrinkled her nose as if the post-it had an odor. This wouldn't lead her to what happened to Molly, so it did not deserve her time.

She crumpled the note and tossed it in the trash on her way to let Jake in.

~~~~~

A whisper of sound crossed the concrete room. Ashley held her breath, listening. The ensuing silence confirmed that her paranoia only fed her imagination. She let out a slow breath and opened her eyes. She shifted onto her side, trying to find a comfortable position on the rickety cot. The meals in shelters came free, but so did indigestion.

She had only been able to make it to the next town over in her day and a half of running. That didn't feel nearly far enough. The span of an entire continent couldn't put enough space between her and her fatal error. Just down the street, Southern Illinois University teemed with life and students full of aspirations. As a university town, Carbondale, IL offered endless possibilities for her mission. Most of her brothers and sisters either attended or pretended to attend the school. Young people in the transitional stages of their lives were particularly susceptible to their cause.

Simone, her mentor and guide, explained the detrimental consequences of revealing their secret group. At sixteen, Ashley ran away from home. She'd been on the streets nearly a year until the day she tried to snatch a Gucci bag from the wrong woman. She had long dark hair trailing down her back with blonde streaks framing her face. Her tall, slender figure made her look like a runway model. When Ashley seized her opportunity to grab at the purse she'd been eying, the woman retaliated. With one swift motion, Ashley was on her back, looking into two intensely intelligent green eyes.

"I have a business proposal for you," the woman smirked. "You, my dear deviant child, will work for me. If you agree to my terms, I will not report this little incident to the authorities. With this opportunity comes the chance for you to join a family with a common purpose and vision." The woman helped Ashley to her feet. "What do you say to my proposition?"

Ashley stood silently in front of her, weighing her options. She stole a few moments, pretending to dust herself off and straightening her jacket. She considered darting into an ally, surmising that the woman may use big words and fancy lingo, but she didn't have street smarts. Ashley knew the Chicago alleys like the back of her hand, and with a single sprint, could rid herself of this pesky problem without consequence. But something about the woman's eyes bore into Ashley's soul. She could feel herself taking a step back while coming closer to saying yes at the same time. Her challenger did not have a threatening appearance, but that had obviously been a miscalculation on Ashley's part. She didn't look athletic. She'd probably taken a self-defense class or two just to get by. Ashley concluded that she could definitely outrun her new adversary.

"I'm sorry, love, but you only have a moment more to decide if you'll take me as friend or foe." The woman dug through her purse, "You see, I have connections with everyone in this city, especially those in high places." She pulled out a cell phone. "I'll just call my sister's husband. You might know him. Mayor Donovan?"

Ashley hastily reached for the woman's phone only to be grabbed and pulled to the ground again, this time, face down. "Okay," she muttered through the concrete. "You've got a deal."

"Splendid." The woman she now knew as Simone had henceforth taken Ashley under her wing.

Another sound pulled Ashley back from her thoughts. What was it? Claws? It sounded very much like claws scraping lightly on the

15

bare floor. Her heartbeat quickened. With her eyes closed, she pictured the room full of people on cots, as it had been when she fell asleep. She could still remember the woman with the ugly yellow hat on the cot next to her. She knew that two girls lay with their mentally unstable mother on the cot to her other side. She pictured the man who talked to himself when he thought no one could hear him. She remembered the construction worker who lost his job six months ago. He cried himself to sleep.

Feeling more connected with her surroundings and reality, Ashley opened her eyes. She turned her head to look at the woman next to her but saw only darkness. This place really needed some night lights. What if someone got up to go to the bathroom? The cots stood so uncomfortably close that one accidental bump and the whole row would collapse like a series of mousetraps with the added frenzy of windmilling arms and dirty blankets.

She squinted her eyes, trying to focus. The claws scraped again. She sucked in another breath. *No! This can't be real. I have nothing to be afraid of.* Abruptly, she sat up, swinging her feet to the floor. She reached out for the bed next to hers to get her bearings. With her arm extended as far as it would go, she reached until her legs barely touched her own cot. Nothing but cold air greeted her fingertips.

She stood up and wrapped her arms around herself. She looked around the room, expecting to see lumps of bodies in the darkness. She waited for her eyes to adjust, hoping some light from outside might break through the windows. But even after a few moments, she still could not see anything. She listened for soft snoring, breathing, or the sound of people repositioning themselves restlessly. But the impossible silence told her she was alone.

Soft scratching echoed through the room again, louder this time. The darkness itself had become a physical presence. The air hung like a thick blanket and compressed around her. Breathing quickly, heart racing, she tried to make her eyes open wider so she could see something, anything.

Then it began. A language she couldn't understand. She stifled an audible sob. *Oh my God, I've gone crazy.* The voices grew in unison until she felt the rumble of their vibration in her extremities. The sounds of scratching intensified. Ashley knew *they* had found her.

She squeaked out a small cry when something brushed her leg. Should I fight? Will I have a chance? She remembered the knife in her pocket. She tried to reach for it before realizing that she couldn't move her arms. Filled with panic, her mind raced through options. She tried to make a run for it, but nothing happened. She might as well be made of stone.

Something whizzed by her ear, and she felt the air shift around her. Suddenly, the darkness filled with shapeless figures. Like shadows with no origins, they swirled through the room, moving in unnaturally jagged patterns. The voices stopped as the shadows collected into one ominous shape before her. She dared not blink. The thing looked like it took a deep breath and relaxed into a squatting position, putting what she thought to be the head at a level with her own eyes.

She wanted to scream. She wanted to run. Actually, she thought her heart might explode and put her out of her own misery. She simply stood there stupidly staring into the face of this thing.

"I have plans for her," a voice whispered. She furrowed her eyebrows. The shadow still spoke in an unfamiliar tongue, but somehow, she understood it.

"She is not the way to our end," another voice retorted.

"We should just eat her," one chimed.

The voices all rumbled together in what she interpreted as a laugh.

"We know where the angel is. Let us go to him and make a proposition ourselves."

"Silence!" The gravelly voice rang with finality. "We have our orders. You are welcome to desert Lucifer and join ranks with Tyrannus, as others have. Otherwise, we stick to the plan. No angel would work with us."

Suddenly, one shadow separated from the rest. Ashley could see it in her peripheral vision. She opened her mouth to scream too late, as it hit her like a ton of bricks.

~~~~~

The woman with the yellow hat heard a scuffle in the darkness. She turned over to see the young woman next to her wrestling with something under her blanket. Even in the dark, she instantly noticed two figures on the cot.

She grimaced. "Pretty girls ain't just for your pleasures, mister!" With that, she placed a foot squarely on the cot and folded it in on itself. The rustling stopped. The young woman slid out of the blanket and stood. Her dark, sweat-covered hair cascaded around her face.

Yellow Hat took a step back. The young woman's eyes seemed eerily dark.

"You okay, darlin'?" Yellow Hat stammered.

"Better than okay," the young woman replied, grabbing her green army jacket from the floor. She staggered unnaturally out of the shelter.

"Slut." Yellow Hat grabbed the blanket to reveal the young woman's lover, but there was no one there.

Chapter 3

Kate walked in her front door and softly closed it behind her. She rested her head on the door for a few moments, soaking in the silence. Jake came and sat next to her, tail swishing on the floor. She reached up and massaged the back of her neck. The memorial service took every bit of her energy, although it went well. She took a deep breath and realized she could smell something cooking.

She shuffled to the kitchen and opened the oven to reveal a casserole baking with ten minutes left on the timer. Kate picked up the note on the counter.

Thought you might be worn out after the service. This is Brendon's favorite, enchiladas. He insisted I make it to cheer you up. I'll take care of thank you notes for the flowers. Get some rest. Let me know if you need anything else!

Marcy & Brendon

She smiled and grabbed Jake's tennis ball from his basket. "Wanna play, boy? I gotta decompress."

Kate stepped out onto the back patio and into the evening sun. Jake darted to the edge of the yard before Kate even had a chance to throw the ball. She threw it the opposite way on purpose and laughed at him scrambling to change directions.

She did not realize how many people would attend the service. Molly had gone to SIU, so a lot of her old college classmates

20

came. Marion remained a small town, even though the university brought plenty of traffic to their neighboring city, Carbondale. She did not expect to see so many unfamiliar faces, and it caught her off guard. She expected to see Detective Peterson, but he didn't show up. She felt a little relieved that he didn't. She hoped he would come to understand her rising to Molly's defense.

She threw the ball again. Instead of having a traditional memorial service with a sermon and hymns, she opted to simply open the church to anyone who wanted to drop in. She and Marcy had worked on pictures they found of Molly. In one picture, Molly stood next to her animal clinic. Another showed her sitting on the beach, trying to avoid being photographed in her bikini. Kate's favorite picture, though, showed her and Molly grinning from ear to ear with their brand-new golden retriever puppies. Molly bought Jasmine, Jake's sister, from the same litter as Kate. Marcy had the pictures blown up and mounted at the front of the church where Kate stood with her extended family.

Jake touched his nose to her hand. "Sorry, boy." She tossed the ball a little further. She still didn't know what to do about Jasmine. Jake would probably like having her around, but Kate already struggled with his shedding. She could not imagine having two shedding dogs in the house. Any time Jake's tail wagged, plumes of hair swirled into the air, searching for a place to settle.

Kate couldn't leave Jasmine in the kennel much longer. Molly wouldn't want that. She contemplated giving the dog to Brendon on Saturday. It would make a great birthday present. The week flew by in such a frenzy of organizing and planning that she almost forgot the party altogether. Kate desperately needed a break. *I'll just make an appearance for an hour or so. I don't have to stay for the whole thing*, she thought. She pulled out her phone and texted Marcy to ask about Jasmine.

Stowing her phone back in her pocket, Kate looked around the yard and noticed Jake had wandered off. "Jake? Here, boy! C'mon!"

She listened for the jingling of his tags in response to her call. Nothing. She whistled and waited again. Nothing. "For crying out loud," she muttered, stomping off in the direction of the woods. He had probably found some foul-smelling carcass again. *As long as he doesn't roll on it,* she thought. She wrinkled her nose, remembering the last time he found something delicious to roll in.

21

About ten yards away, Jake backed slowly out of the woods. His hair stood straight up on his back, and Kate could see that he had his teeth bared. He snarled and let out an intimidating bark that stopped Kate cold. She side-stepped to see what Jake was looking at but saw nothing.

"Aww, boy, it's okay! There's nothing out there." She started to walk toward him, but he turned and growled a warning at her. She stopped again, watching him head back toward the woods. He obviously did not want her coming any closer to whatever he perceived as a threat. She squinted, checking the woods again. Kate saw nothing, but she could hear high-pitched bird cries and squirrels chattering. As a matter of fact, the woods sounded abnormally loud. Usually, when animals sensed a predator, they became unnaturally still. What would cause them all to carry on like this?

A rolling growl slipped out of Jake's clenched teeth again. He took another step back. She could feel the hair on her arms standing up. "Okay, boy, I'm freaked out. Let's go in." She turned just in time to see her back door slam shut.

~~~~~

Detective Peterson put the coroner's report on his desk. He sat down with his head in his hands and let out a long sigh. "I really wanted this to be suicide," he mumbled to himself. The bruising on the victim's hand supported foul play. Someone probably stood on her hand to keep her down for the kill. The angle of the bullet also suggested that Molly probably did not shoot the gun herself. The gunshot residue contradicted everything they had to support their murder theory.

A knock on the door brought him out of his thoughts. He looked up to see Fran peeking in through the window. He waved her in. "Sir, I just wanted to check in to see how the Gregory case is going."

"Come in," He cleared his throat, "Is there a particular reason you are showing interest in this case? They can assign a local detective to assist me." He heard another officer mention that in the wake of the other detective's retirement, they had been scrambling to keep up with the caseload.

"Well," she paused. "I'm sure you know I'm working on becoming a detective." She looked at him to see if he did.

"Nope."

22

"Oh." She looked down and thought for a moment. "Well, I am. I requested that the chief put me on this case for now. I just thought..."

Alec interrupted her, "I appreciate the help, but it would be better if they'd assigned someone more experienced."

Fran stared back at him without answering.

"Let me make myself clear," Alec stood to look her in the eye. "I don't need help doing my job. But these cases have piled up over the years, and I'm just one guy. Go ahead and toss some of these into the filing cabinet. I already went through them. We can decide what else to pull out that may be connected. If you're interested in this case, you can take a look at the files while you walk them to the cabinet. Maybe another set of eyes will help." His frustration about not having another detective on the case bubbled to the surface. This kind of situation led to cases falling through the cracks.

"I don't file. Our secretary can do that for you," Fran snapped. She walked out of his office and slammed his door shut.

He sat back down. The most recent string of suicides in local small towns particularly piqued his interest. He'd been working these cases for a couple years now, going wherever the cases led. Working outside of his own precinct was hard enough without having to deal with a glorified chaperone. He wondered if the chief would grant a temporary request in this situation for a detective from another precinct that he had already worked with. Then the person assisting would have background knowledge of his other cases. He could word the request in a way that supported any newly hired detectives joining the team once they filled the spot of their retiree.

He looked through the window of his conference room cage to see Fran murdering him with her eyes. *Maybe I was too hard on her,* he thought to himself. If he requested a different partner, he ran the risk of stepping on the chief's toes. He had never been to Marion before. Politics could have played a huge role in the chief's choice -- despite her lack of credentials.

His cell phone rang, and he pulled it out. "Peterson."

"Um, Alec?"

He looked again at the number, "Katherine?"

"Yes, it's Kate. Could you please come by my house for a moment? I feel so silly calling you, but I think someone is inside. I'm outside in the backyard and...Jake! I can't hear myself think! Hush!"

Alec could hear her dog going bonkers in the background. "I'll be right there." He clipped his phone to his belt and grabbed his keys.

23

He breezed through the icy cold atmosphere Fran had created around her desk. He reminded himself to give her a wide berth for a few days and maybe to bring her a cup of coffee when he came back. He chanced a glance in her direction. Her gaze could have burned holes through his very soul. An extra-large coffee, he decided, with lots of sugar.

"Where do you think you're going?" The chief stepped out of his office just as Peterson reluctantly turned around.

"Katherine Gregory just called me. She thinks someone is in her house. I'm gonna go check it out."

"Take Fran with you."

Fran stiffened. "Sir, I don't..."

"Come to my office when you return," the chief continued without acknowledging Fran's reluctance.

Fran grabbed her keys and said, "Fine."

"Thank you, Fran." The chief smiled before closing his office door and returning to his desk.

~~~~~

They pulled up to Katherine's house ten minutes later. Alec quickly opened his door and hopped out of the cop car. Having never joined Fran in the car before, he didn't know if she always drove like a crazy person or if her general anger toward him gave her a lead foot. He gathered his composure as he waited for her to heft herself out of the driver's side.

Each home on the street had matching mailboxes, beautiful azaleas, and green weed-free lawns. He knew Katherine Gregory worked in a low position on the totem pole and wondered how she could afford to live in this neighborhood. Maybe she rented. He looked down the street to see a woman pushing a red stroller. Across the street, an older man tended to his lawnmower while his wife swept grass clippings off the front porch. The sun only had a few minutes left, and the automatic streetlights hinted at the approaching dusk. A girl in an army jacket walked slowly past them. Her long dark hair shadowed her face. After she passed, Alec took a step toward her, prepared to ask her a few questions. Something in his gut said she didn't belong.

"Well? Are you going to stand out here or go check out the house?" Fran's question pulled him from his thoughts. Alec turned to see her standing with her hands on her broad hips.

"Go meet Katherine out back. I'll be there in a second. I want to ask that girl a few questions." He looked over his shoulder but didn't see anyone on the sidewalk. He stepped into the street and looked up and down to see if she'd turned around.

Fran studied him. "Detective?"

"What did you see?" He asked quickly.

She stared blankly at him.

He waved his arms, exasperated. "If you want to be a detective, you need to observe your surroundings! For someone who's working so hard to become one, I figured you probably looked up and down the street to see what's goin' on, right? So, what did you see?"

Fran visibly perked up. "Mr. Johnson, who just finished mowing, Dr. Sharon taking her son for a Friday evening walk," she looked toward the house, "and a dog going berserk in the back." Alec peered up and down the street again. "What?" she asked.

"Nothing." He walked around the house with Fran on his heels. Katherine stood in the backyard with her dog. The animal seemed spooked about something, pacing back and forth between his owner and the woods, barking every few steps.

"Detective!" Katherine waved. "Thank you for coming." She quickly explained that she saw the door close when she'd turned to go in. Jake walked up and placed his head on Alec's leg. Alec took a step to the side, attempting to avoid the animal. The dog laid at his feet and let out a huff.

"You did the right thing to call me, Katherine," Alec said, keeping an eye on the dog.

"Detective Peterson, I imagine we'll be speaking frequently as you investigate my sister's case. If you don't start calling me Kate, we're going to have issues. I feel like my Grams is calling me and I'm in trouble when you call me Katherine."

"He's not very personable," Fran said, peeking around the detective.

~~~~~

Detective Peterson went inside, leaving Fran with Kate. Fran gave Kate the once-over. Not a bad-looking woman, to be honest. Kate's

25

wavy sun-kissed hair hung just at her shoulders. She wore it sweeping across her face. She had a petite but athletic figure. She didn't carry herself like a fighter, but Fran could tell Kate had spunk. She seemed mildly shaken up about someone being in her home but hadn't lost her self-control like most people would. Maybe the dog gave her a sense of security. *Maybe*, Fran thought, *she didn't tell us the whole story*.

"All clear," Alec yelled from the back door. "Kate, come in and tell me if anything's missing."

Fran noticed that Kate didn't look all that surprised that Detective Peterson didn't find anyone in the house.

They walked inside, and Kate walked from room to room, checking her belongings. Her dog sat at the bottom of the steps when Kate went upstairs with Alec behind her. Kate had already gone through the kitchen, so Fran waited by the table.

"Yes, I'm sure nothing is missing," Kate answered Alec as they rounded back into the kitchen. "Oh no! Marcy's dish!" Kate rushed over to the stove. Fran detected a slight hint of smoke as the small woman heaved an over-baked casserole onto a potholder.

Fran looked at Alec, who remained detached. She couldn't read this man. He had a very stoic nature about him. He seemed to keep everyone at an arm's length. She didn't know if she could trust him, but at the same time, she felt he thought the same about her. He didn't make any kind of notes. Ever. She found that odd.

She noticed his face change to concern. "Kate? Are you okay?" he asked. Fran turned to see that Kate stood with her back to them, frozen at the stove. Even though Fran couldn't see her face, Kate's demeanor had changed.

Kate turned to face them and said, "Uh, everything's fine. Yeah. You guys can go."

Fran looked from Kate to Peterson. As usual, she couldn't tell what he was thinking. She looked back at Kate. "Miss Gregory, is there's something you're not telling us?"

Kate shook her head. "No, huh-uh. Nothing I can think of." She read the doubt in their faces and quickly added, "I'm just tired. You know, the memorial service took it right out of me. I think I need some rest, that's all."

"Okay," Alec responded. Fran shot him a confused look with her back to Kate. He ignored her. "You have my number if you need to contact me," he said with a pleasant grin. He turned and walked to the front door. "Fran, you stayin' to eat that burnt casserole, or are you coming with me?"

Fran opened her mouth to protest and then snapped it shut. She turned and looked at Kate again, who smiled reassuringly. *Am I the only normal person in this room?* She sighed and followed Peterson out of the house, turning the lock on the door handle before closing it behind her.

When they got back to the car, Fran asked, "Detective Peterson, why did we just leave? She was acting like something was up! We should have stayed and talked it out of her." She pulled a stray hair back into her tightly tucked bun.

"Because," he responded, "she was acting more than just a *little* suspicious." He turned to face her. "While we were upstairs, I told her I wanted to discuss some new developments in the case. She was very interested, naturally. Once we finished, I asked her if we could talk about it downstairs for a few minutes." He thought for a moment. "Whatever happened between upstairs and the kitchen stove rocked her enough to completely forget about discussing her dead sister and focused her thoughts on something else."

Fran wrinkled her brow. "Do you think we should stay out here for a while? Keep an eye on things?"

Alec shook his head. "No. She obviously doesn't want us to know about what's bothering her. If we sit out here, she'll see us and try to sneak around. That's why I acted like I believed nothing was wrong."

"Okay. So, what if she *doesn't* know we're watching," Fran wondered out loud, still fussing with her hair.

Alec smirked at her, "I think you're onto something. Let's get it approved by the chief."

~~~~~

In the house, Kate let out a breath and relaxed her shoulders. It took so long for her to hear their cruiser pull away that she thought they might realize something was wrong and come back in. She turned to look back at the partially crumpled blue post-it lying on the counter with the number for Helping Hands scribbled on it. She reflected to when she first found Marcy's note about the casserole. Could Marcy have left it laying there? No. And even in her exhausted state following the memorial service, she would have noticed. Her week seemed like such a blur, but she remembered throwing this

27

post-it away. Her hands began to shake. Who would break into her house to pull a meaningless piece of paper out of the garbage? *Looks like I'll be going to Helping Hands after all.*

Chapter 4

Kate walked into Carbondale Super Splash Park with Jasmine next to her. The kennel groomed Jasmine for free after hearing about what happened to her master. They only asked that Kate cover the expense for food and treats during the dog's stay. Though she seemed comfortable and well taken care of, Jasmine's tail hadn't stopped wagging since they left the kennel. Now, at the sight of all the kids splashing in the water, she let out an excited whimper.

"Kate! Over here!" Marcy waved Kate over from the deck under a shaded area. "How in the world did you convince the owner to let you in with Jasmine?" Marcy asked as Kate approached the table of presents.

"Oh, I actually know the owner of the park really well. He's a client of Browning. He always says that I do all the grunt work of the firm and if I ever need anything, just say the word. So, I pulled my strings." Kate smiled and cocked her head, "Where's the little guy?"

Marcy rolled her eyes. "With the big guy who's acting like a little guy." She pointed to one of the pools for Kate. Water cascaded off a mushroom and into the pool of screaming kids below. One bunch of kids seemed particularly rowdy. Kate could see that they all gathered around something under the water. Suddenly, a huge, muscular man shot up out of the water.

"ROOOOARRR!!!" The man screamed. He peeled two kids off his legs and tossed them into the water. He shook his head, and his sandy blond hair flopped over to one side. He waved at Kate and ran toward the side of the pool, wrestling kids the whole way.

Marcy sighed, "How did I meet such a handsome man? Would you take a look at those scrumptious muscles?" She eyed Kate. "Arthur said he could hook you up with one of his friends, ya know."

Kate could feel herself sincerely smiling for the first time all week. "First of all, don't talk to me about your husband like that. Awkward!" Kate laughed at Marcy flexing her arm, trying to make a bicep

29

appear. "Secondly, why is he trying to set me up with *anyone* when I have a friend like you signing me up for online dating services?"

"Oh yeah! I forgot about that. Any bites?"

"I don't think so. I mean, I haven't exactly had the time to set up a date this week. I'll check my email and let you know. But for the record, if I get set up with some freak, you're gonna pay."

"Hello, beautiful!" Arthur said, grabbing a towel from the beach bag. Marcy grinned, accepting a wet kiss. Kate thought they were an exceptionally cute couple. Marcy had a medium build and brown hair. The sun brought out her freckles. Her clothes hugged tightly on her round hips, but Arthur didn't care. He loved her with an obviously sincere passion.

They planned to celebrate their nine-year anniversary in October. Arthur already told Kate that he planned to take Marcy on a tour through Europe. He'd been saving for five years. It sounded unusual for a couples' trip, but Marcy's skin didn't do too well on the beach. He wanted to take her for their ninth anniversary because he said Marcy wouldn't be expecting anything until their tenth. He told Kate because they would be gone for two straight weeks, and he didn't think Brendon's grandmother could handle him for that long without any breaks. Kate had agreed to take Brendon off her hands a few nights. She nearly had to sign in her own blood that she wouldn't spill the beans to Marcy.

"What do we have here?" Arthur bent to pet Jasmine. "You're going to love your new home!" He grinned up at Kate. "You even tied her up in a pretty blue bow. I'm impressed."

Kate waved a hand. "Eh, the groomers did that. She's all powdered and pampered."

Brendon jumped out of the pool and did a hurried walk/run toward them. He eyed the lifeguard to make sure he wouldn't blow the whistle. He slowed when he got to Kate and the dog. Puzzled, he said, "Oh, from far away, this looked like Jake. Did you get a new dog, Aunt Kate?" He lifted his hand out to let Jasmine sniff it.

"Actually," Kate replied, "She's not my pet."

"Oh, it's a girl? Why does she have a blue bow? That's a boy color." He wrinkled his nose.

"She has a blue bow because she knows it's your favorite color, and she wants to impress you." Kate squatted down. "Do you like her?"

Jasmine licked his hand and wagged her tail when he giggled. "She's funny! So, she came for my birthday party?"

"Yeah, but there's a problem." Brendon looked at her questioningly. She sighed and shrugged. "Your mom and I can't figure out how she's going to fit on the gift table."

Brendon's eyes widened. He let his mouth drop open, looking from Arthur to Marcy, making sure they didn't have any last-minute disapprovals. They both nodded emphatically.

"OH MY GOSH!" Brendon jumped up and down, clapping his hands. "Does she already have a name?"

"Jasmine."

Brendon stopped jumping and stared at the dog. Kate realized he might not want to keep the name that Molly had given her. She hadn't thought about that. She felt a sinking sadness at the prospect of changing Jasmine's name. She tried to mask the pain by pretending to care about something going on at the hotdog stand. He didn't really understand everything happening with Molly, and she didn't want to make him feel bad if he wanted to name the dog something else.

"Honey?" Marcy said. "Are you okay?"

Brendon looked up at his mom with a huge grin and said, "Jasmine is perfect! I can call her Jazz for short!" He laughed at his own idea and turned back to Jasmine, "What do you think, Jazz?" She licked his face.

Kate smiled. "Jazz is a perfect nickname for her."

Brendon didn't want to tear himself away from his new companion, so they decided to have cake and open presents. He opened each present excitedly and posed with Jazz several times. They sang him "Happy Birthday," and after blowing out the candles, he asked, "Can Jazz have some cake too?"

"Actually," Kate said, "I think she's outstayed her welcome here. I'm going to drop her off at your house so she can rest before you get home, okay?" Marcy had already arranged for Kate to put Jasmine in the backyard on her way home.

"Okay," Brendon said, disappointed.

"What do you say to Aunt Kate for your gift?" Arthur reminded him.

"Thank you!" He threw his arms around her. "I love you! Bring Jake over to play soon!"

"I will. Happy birthday, little man."

Brendon went back to the pool with his friends. Marcy followed Arthur around with a trash bag, gathering plates and cups. "So,"

Arthur started, "has that detective told you anything new about the case?"

Marcy shot him a look.

"What?" He asked.

"It's okay," Kate interjected. "I can't pretend like nothing is happening, and I don't expect you guys to do that either." Marcy relaxed a little bit, and Arthur threw away the last of the plastic forks. Kate continued, "I'm actually supposed to meet him this afternoon. He said the coroner's report was interesting."

"Interesting?" Marcy asked.

"He didn't elaborate. He just said he wanted to talk with me in person, so I told him I'd be home around four. I kind of need to get going if I want to make it back in time." She glanced at her watch.

Marcy sat the bag on the ground. "Do you still want me to come with you? I can leave now, and Arthur can deal with getting the kids back to their houses."

"Thanks a lot," Arthur said sarcastically.

"No." Kate grabbed the end of Jasmine's leash. "I'm going to meet with him alone. He doesn't give me warm fuzzies, but I think he's a good detective. I'm not as worked up about talking with him now." Kate had no idea why she didn't have any reservations about meeting with the detective alone. But she welcomed the change of heart if it meant Marcy could stay at Brendon's party.

Marcy eyed her. "Okay, well, just call me if you need me to come over. There should be a few more casseroles in the freezer for you to warm up. I'm going grocery shopping on Monday. You need anything?"

"Nah, but thanks. I'll call you and let you know how the meeting goes with Detective Peterson."

~~~~~

Simone steamed, walking back and forth in her apartment. "No! I don't know where she is! If I knew, we wouldn't be having this conversation!"

The voice on the other line billowed. "You have no idea what she's done!"

"Oh, I know." She lifted her hand to press her forefinger and thumb on her temples.

"Do you realize that her trainee, Molly, actually waited for Ashley's gun to fire first?"

Simone stopped pacing. "Ashley's gun had blanks in it. She followed her mentor training. Her charge unexpectedly deviated from the plan."

"That's not the point! Your novice mentor got hasty. She assured you that her trainee trusted her completely when obviously she didn't. Trust in the mentor is essential to our cause. Now, that leaves me with two possible conclusions. Either the girl really thought she had convinced her 'friend' to join the gathering, or..." the voice trailed off.

Simone spoke through gritted teeth, "Or what?"

"She has been a student of yours for quite some time, yes? Perhaps she grew tired of the mission and sought a way out. We would never expel her from the cause without good reason. She only convinced you that she had this soul in our clutches because you have gone soft, my dear."

Simone seethed. "I have not gone soft. I emphasize to all mentors that the consequences of their mistakes would be worse than death. They all fear what would happen to their own pathetic, insignificant lives should they slip up. She is not foolish enough to betray me outright. I blame this whole incident on simple human miscalculation, a mistake she will pay dearly for."

"Well then, am I to assume that you lack the ability to suitably train our mentors? If she properly understood how to read the assigned soul, she would never have made the mistake in the first place. Maybe I gave you too much credit, calling you soft. Perhaps you're just incompetent. Do I need to send someone to teach you more effective measures?"

Simone could hear the grin in his gravelly voice. She cringed at the thought of the last accomplice he sent to straighten her out. She could still feel the burning of the jagged and hideous scar he left stretching from the back of her hip to the front of her chest. She sat down to keep her knees from quivering. She steadied her voice, concealing her fear. "That will not be necessary."

"Catch the girl, or I assure you, it will be."

~~~~~

"Where's Fran?" Kate asked, opening the door for the detective.

"We got a call that she had to follow up on," he smiled easily, "but she said to tell you hey." He wore a baby blue button-down polo on with light brown khakis. He pulled out the manila folder he had tucked under his arm and laid it on the coffee table.

"Oh." Kate shrugged and walked over to the couch. "Well, what are the new developments?"

Alec looked to the door where her dog sat outside, nose plastered to the glass. "Thank you for putting him outside. I'm not really an animal person."

"No problem."

Alec noticed that she had an easy way about her. She didn't seem nervous or upset. Her almond eyes were warm and comforting. She had the sides of her hair swept back in clips, revealing sun-kissed cheeks. "How are you doing?" He asked.

She looked surprised that he asked. "Okay..." she glanced at him as if to assess whether he was really listening. He sat down, focusing on her, giving her the go-ahead. "Well, I mean, it's not easy. Molly and I were really close, even for sisters. We did almost everything together.

"My parents divorced when we were in middle school. They both wanted to pursue careers that would require traveling. Mom suggested that each of them take one of us, but Molly and I wanted to stay in the same school district, and we wanted to stay together. So, my grandmother took care of us from then on out. We saw our parents a few times a year, and we got presents in the mail, but we obviously weren't close with them. I don't think they would ever admit it, but they weren't exactly made for kids.

"Since then, Molly and I were just inseparable. Grams still lives close, so she made it to the memorial service. I suppose, all in all, I'm doing okay. I'm not going to lie and say it's easy, though. I'm hoping you have some news that will make it easier." She nervously played with the edge of her sleeve.

Alec pressed his lips into a hard line and let out a slow breath. "Well, I think I do."

"Go ahead," Kate prodded, looking hopeful.

He tilted his head toward the file, indicating that he wanted her to take a look at it. She opened it up and perused the documents. He gave her a couple of minutes to soak it all in before he started.

"Evidence does not support suicide in your sister's case. The bullet wound to her head came at an angle that would be difficult for her to accomplish herself. The bruise she sustained on her hand is from a shoe, a women's size seven, we believe.

"We do, however, have a bit of evidence we're having trouble with. She had gunshot residue on her hand. She obviously shot the other weapon. We know it only fired once, though, because only one bullet was missing. And the bullets in that gun were blanks." He shook his head. "I can't explain why she would have a gun with no usable ammo.

Unfortunately, we don't have any suspects yet. The castings of shoeprints outside her home don't match with the size and style of the shoe that we believe caused bruising on her hand." He stopped and looked at Kate.

She stared at the documents in the folder, tears pooling on her lower eyelashes. "I knew it wasn't suicide," she whispered. "But I also don't understand the blanks. I didn't even know Molly owned a gun at all."

"Kate," Alec began, "I have some questions for you. Are you up to that?"

She nodded.

"Good. Do you know any customers from the clinic that may have been angry with your sister?"

She shook her head. "No. Everyone loved Molly. Of course, she had to break bad news sometimes, but she never mentioned anyone holding her personally responsible for a pet's illness."

"So, what about her circle of friends? Do you know who she was hanging out with? Did she have a boyfriend?"

"Well," she thought for a moment. "Yeah, Molly dated a few guys, but nothing serious. She was kind of picky. I don't know many of her friends. I mean, we were close, but she had a lot of friends from SIU that I didn't know. I attended John A. Logan and got my two-year degree, so we didn't share the same college experience." She paused again before continuing. "I want to say that most of the time she went out, it was with a group of friends. She never really singled anyone out that she liked to hang out with."

Alec shifted in his seat. "I have another question," he started.

"Sure." Kate put the file back on the coffee table and stood up. "Do you want anything to drink?" He shook his head. She walked to the kitchen and grabbed a glass.

"What can you tell me about The Gathering of Souls?" he asked.

She turned from the sink to face him, her expression puzzled. "The what?"

"The Gathering of Souls. Did Molly ever mention it?"

"I'm sorry, I have no idea what you're talking about." Kate came back to the couch with her water.

"We sent Molly's computer to the lab for one of our techies to work on. She had a few emails from a friend that mentioned 'The Gathering.' The tech cross-referenced it with a few sites and found that Molly was *possibly* a member of a website called The Gathering of Souls. It is very..." he stumbled, searching for the right word, "...exclusive. The website will neither confirm nor deny her membership."

Kate furrowed her brow. "What is it for?"

Alec hesitated to answer. Kate stared at him, letting him know she expected one. "From what I understand, it's an internet site that helps members find ways to commit suicide. The members all share similar struggles in life. They can find others who relate to what they're going through and share ideas about how to end it all. They refer to it as 'cutting in line,' 'boarding the train,' or 'getting a ticket.' The point is that their language is cryptic.

"There was a lawsuit against the site over a year ago. A family pressed charges, saying their daughter would never have killed herself if it weren't for the site's influence on her life. They argued that for the site to be fair, they should have links to counselors, support groups, and other alternatives to suicide. The site's one-sidedness sparked a huge debate in the media, as you can imagine.

"The court ruling was that the site itself could not be held responsible for the deaths of members because the members' blogs were clearly independent thoughts. The site neither endorses nor supports any specific opinion; it simply allows members to freely speak their minds."

Kate fidgeted. "But Molly hasn't talked about anything like that since college."

He nodded, "I remembered that you mentioned her brief battle with depression. Unfortunately, the site believes heavily in protecting its members and will not release any information without a warrant. So, any data like join dates, blogs between members, and meeting places are all kept confidential. That makes my job sticky because I don't know when Molly actually joined the group. Some of the personal emails that she exchanged outside of the site have been slightly helpful, but we're still working on getting a name for the person she was in contact with.

"Also," he continued slowly, "Molly isn't the first suspicious death linked to the group. Unfortunately, we don't have enough to go on to implicate the site. Just like the victims could have shared pizza at the same restaurant or gotten their hair cut at the same salon, it could be coincidental. There are plenty of such cases with random connections. At least, that's what the site would argue. Our evidence is only circumstantial at this point."

"What do you mean when you say "suspicious death"?" Kate asked.

"Not all members actually end up taking their lives. But from the outside looking in, it seems that not many leave the site easily, either," Alec said, pulling out his phone. He tapped it a few times as if searching for something.

Kate blurted before he'd finished his search, "Are these people all being killed like my sister? Do their lives just mean nothing? Molly was amazing, Detective Peterson. She was smart and funny and my," her breath caught in her throat as she continued, "best friend. She means everything to me. She's all I've got." She caught herself and corrected, "She was all I had."

Alec put his phone down and folded his hands. "I know this is difficult to hear. Please know we're doing everything we can to catch the person who did this."

Kate nodded and sniffled a bit.

He picked up his phone again. "She's the fifth case of a murder made to look like a suicide in the span of two months." He held his phone out for her to look at. "Do you recognize any of these people by face or by name?" He scrolled down.

Kate shook her head at each one, slowly deflating.

"It's okay, Kate," he said. "Maybe something will come to you later. Even if it's just a tiny detail that seems meaningless, please call me."

Kate nodded and searched the face of the last victim on his phone. "It's a relief to know it wasn't suicide. I feel like part of the burden has been lifted." She looked at Detective Peterson. "Now I know it's not my fault that she isn't here anymore, but somehow I don't feel better." Her eyes filled with tears. "Molly looked into someone else's eyes while they took her life from her. It was a life she fought for, and they stole it from her."

She looked again at the girl on his phone. "And it wasn't the first time this person did this." She shook her head. "This is a lot to digest."

"I know, and I completely understand that you're going to need some time to let this settle." He stood. "If you think of anything that will be helpful, give me a call. I'll keep in touch as the case develops." He picked up the file and walked to the door.

Kate jumped up hastily, wiping her tears on her hands and then her hands on her jeans. She walked with him to the door and hesitated about whether she had anything to add to their conversation. She bit the inside of her lip. "Well," she said, "thank you for coming and telling me more about the case. I appreciate it more than you can know."

Chapter 5

Helping Hands occupied a small office space behind an outdoor shopping center about twenty minutes from where Kate worked. She hadn't gone back officially yet, and her boss told her to take as much time as she needed. She never missed work, and therefore had plenty of paid time off stocked up. She originally planned to use that time for a honeymoon and maternity leave, but Mr. Right decided that he wanted to pursue a career as a full-time musician. Always the practical thinker, she suggested that he pursue his dreams while developing a career so they could support a family. Apparently, musicians don't have families. Three years of her life went down the drain when he moved out.

She hadn't seen him since. She smiled at the inward satisfaction she got from never hearing him on the radio, either. Molly told her from the beginning that the musician was a mistake, but Kate could not get past her infatuation. Most women would agree that a guitar adds a certain degree of hotness to a guy.

She also found his spontaneity incredibly attractive. She had grown too accustomed to making plans. He taught her that planning ahead, while sensible, did not mean that she had to stick to it. His ability to desert plans at the drop of a hat in order to chase a more interesting course threw her for a loop. At first, she struggled to adapt to his whimsical personality, but after a few months, she fell in love with the idea that tomorrow might bring something unexpected. She craved adventure, and he delivered.

Molly, usually the one telling Kate to let go and chill out, talked with her several times about cutting back on her new relationship. She warned that the extreme personality difference would only lead to future trouble. Kate dismissed her persistent sister for a year or so before Molly gave up. That was right around the time that Molly began acting strangely. Kate did not catch on because she had completely enveloped herself in her own world. By not listening to

Molly, she had isolated herself with her new love and missed the shift in Molly's behavior.

In Molly's sophomore year at SIU, she began failing all her classes. By the time Kate noticed Molly's depression, the Molly she knew and loved seemed impossible to bring back. Kate did all that she could to encourage her sister, but she continued to drown in her dark world. She kept saying things like, "Kate, you won't be able to understand how I got here. I can't tell you. You will think I'm crazy." Encased in a prison of negative thoughts, Molly stopped talking to Kate altogether. Kate didn't know how to combat something she couldn't see, but she knew she needed to find someone to help Molly.

She asked her then-fiancé to help her find Molly a counselor. He agreed that Molly needed help but could not seem to set aside the time to focus on the issue with Kate. She desperately began the search herself. After a few phone calls, she found a counselor willing to sit down and talk with Molly once a week.

Although Molly resisted at first, she finally agreed to meet with the counselor and started her long climb out of the pit she had dug herself into. Kate couldn't believe that she had let Molly go so far into her depression without noticing, and she felt responsible. Since they grew up with such a close relationship, she never thought it would be possible for them to grow apart. She inwardly blamed herself for letting Molly slip away while she selfishly pursued a lifestyle and relationship that she knew would ultimately have to end.

When the counselor suggested that she and Molly work on their relationship by meeting weekly, Kate dove in head-first. They got together for lunch every week, and Kate watched her sister slowly change back into the woman she remembered. Even after Molly stopped going to counseling, they continued their weekly lunches. Until a couple of weeks ago, they never missed.

Kate walked into a surprisingly huge lobby with a chandelier hanging over the security desk. Momentarily, she thought she'd walked into the wrong place. Detective Peterson had explained that Helping Hands offered free service to community members who lost loved ones, but he didn't mention how they raised money for their organization. The outside of the building presented a plain, run-of-the-mill feel, but upon entry, she was greeted with rich carpets, warm lighting, vaulted ceilings, and a security desk made of marble. It took Kate a moment to wrap her mind around the stark contrast.

The woman behind the desk explained how to get to room 207. Several large conference rooms took up the entire first floor that Kate assumed the public could rent out. That could bring in a substantial amount of money, but she couldn't imagine that they got a lot of business in such a small town. Marion hardly had the demographic for such elegance. The town grew every year, though. Perhaps Marion's plans for development would interest the kind of people who needed conference centers.

The complex construction pattern drew her eye as she passed each ornately decorated room. Half-pillars, molded to the walls, surrounded the seating area. In the center of each room, an elaborate bouquet brought out the color of the deep red, purple, and navy-blue carpets.

The meetings for support groups actually took place in the less-spacious, minimally decorated rooms on the second floor. *This is more like I expected,* Kate thought to herself, walking into the room where eight people already stood around talking in small groups. A stout man stepped aside from a group and approached her with a wide grin. He wore jeans and a loose-fitting button-up Hawaiian shirt to cover up his bulging belly. His ruddy reddish hair sparsely covered his head, and he had vibrant, warm eyes.

"Kate, I presume?" he said.

She nodded, afraid to do more than listen.

"Great! You're a little bit early, but we already have some refreshments on the table over there," he pointed to the table and continued to give a brief history on Helping Hands and each person in the group, but Kate's attention lingered on someone.

The man at the refreshment table looked somehow familiar, although she knew they had never met. His unruly white hair pointed at all angles from his head. A light layer of scruff covered his thin face, and although his clothes appeared clean, he made no effort to match. His striped black shirt hung over light blue plaid shorts, and a pair of brown work boots weighed down his stringy legs. Kate realized she didn't know him, but she couldn't shake the recognition in her mind. He didn't fit the profile of someone who would come to her office. She wondered if maybe she'd seen him at the park on one of her runs.

"...in our humble office. That's what happens when death rates spike. It's not something we like to see in a small town like ours, but we're happy to be able to help so many people."

Kate snapped her attention back to the group leader. "I'm sorry. I believe I missed your name."

"Oh, yes, yes. It's Joe," he replied. To her relief, he didn't seem to notice that she'd tuned him out for a second.

He clapped his hands as two more people walked in. "Okay, everyone's here! Let's get started."

Everyone slowly stopped their conversations and meandered toward the circle of chairs in the middle of the room. Kate noted that it felt very much like alcoholics anonymous and started to get nervous. Did he expect her to open up to all these people? How did these meetings work? She regrettably realized Joe probably explained everything to her while she studied the man at the refreshment table.

Her stomach knotted itself up, and she began to feel anxious. *Somebody* wanted her here. Her curiosity piqued; she decided to come, but her concern about the note and who had moved it outweighed her practical thinking. She probably should have put a story together to share or thought about what she wanted to say. The knot in her stomach moved up into her throat. What if they expected her to talk about Molly? She didn't think she could do that with strangers, even if they had the same experience.

Joe smiled as everyone sat down. "Well, we'll get this meeting started, eh? As you may have noticed, we have a new visitor." He waved his hand toward Kate. "We'd like to welcome you to our group, Kate. Please ask any questions you like, or you can simply observe how a meeting usually goes. We'll go around the group and introduce ourselves. Pat, why don't you start us?"

A woman in her fifties stood. "Hi, I'm Pat Goldstein. I've been a member of this group for a little over a year now. I joined after my sweet Raymond died in a car accident. My new hobby is making and selling candles. Uh, is that all I have to say?" Joe nodded his approval, and she sat down.

A young man in his late twenties started. "Hey, I'm Kyle Walters. My roommate took his own life. I have been a member for six months, and my new hobby is basketball. I play for the hell of it in a church league," he began to sit and quickly added, "but I don't really go to church. They're just the only league if I don't want to drive to the campus for rec leagues in Carbondale."

The man from the refreshment table stood next. "Finneus Koche. Everyone calls me Fin. I don't have a new hobby, although everyone in the group relentlessly encourages me to take one up," he rolled his eyes as Pat clapped. "I've been a part of this group for a while." He then seated himself without ceremony.

"I'm Blanch," started the next woman, probably in her late forties. She had a country accent and a slightly overweight figure. "Fin can deny that he has any hobbies, but I think we all know the truth." She pointed to the pile of cookies on his lap. "I'd just like to know where he keeps all the food he packs away!" The group laughed, and she looked at Kate with eyes like her grandmother's. "My hobby's bakin', which fits in perfectly with his hobby of eatin'." She sat down.

Joe chimed in, "Blanch has been with us for three years, which is nearly since the beginning. Her father took his own life shortly after her mother had an unfortunate run-in with someone on the wrong side of the law. She didn't make it."

"Hooligans," Blanch added.

As the next few people introduced themselves, Kate realized where she'd seen Fin. At her sister's funeral, she saw him in the hallway near the restroom. He never stepped in to see Molly, so Kate dismissed him. Yes, that was most definitely the face. Could that be a coincidence? Could he have broken into her house? She watched him wet a finger with his tongue and dab it over each crumb on his shirt and concluded that he wasn't dangerous. He glanced up at her, and she quickly changed her gaze to the last people introducing themselves. She could feel him studying her, but she pretended not to notice.

The last introduction, a couple in their late thirties, continued, "And so we haven't found a hobby that we both enjoy, but we have our separate ones." The woman looked up at her husband. "Mr. Campbell likes to work on old cars, and I enjoy scrapbooking."

"Well, Kate," Joe turned to her. "As you may have noticed, we encourage each member to take up a new hobby or establish a goal to work toward outside of the pain and stress of their loss. Taking on a new project when you're ready can help you recover. Can you think of anything that you might enjoy that you'd like to share?"

Kate thought for a moment. She rolled through the hobbies other people had mentioned, but none of those sounded remarkable. She never favored artsy activities, and she certainly didn't want to tinker on cars. "Well," she started, "I really enjoy running. Maybe I could train for some races or something."

Kyle visibly perked up. "The basketball league lets women play, too. Maybe I could ask if they could fit you in on a team or somethin'."

Kate shrugged in a non-committal way. "I guess I'll just have to think about it." She didn't want to hurt his feelings, but she knew she didn't want to join any league with Kyle. She could tell by the way he looked at her he thought she was attractive. She also didn't want to use anything associated with the church as her new hobby. She envisioned pastors with hair-sprayed stage hair, people talking out both sides of their mouths, casserole bake-offs, and haughty stares of judgment. Nothing about the religious scene appealed to her.

Joe gently added, "No pressure, Kate. It's just something to think about."

Kate looked around the group. Everyone's eyes displayed an understanding warmness, except for two people. Blanch, who looked like she was trying to display something similar to sympathy, had something else brooding below the surface. Kate couldn't put her finger on it, but she didn't like it. Finneus portrayed an indifferent demeanor. He seemed too interested in his cookie to care about anything else. Kate knew his eyes, though – they sparkled with intelligence, which explained why he avoided eye contact if he didn't want anyone to know what went on inside his head.

Kate had a knack for reading people. Her first impressions and assumptions seldom steered her wrong. She enjoyed having such a talent since it came in handy when she went on dates, met new friends, and dealt with clients. On the downside, sometimes she ran into people who she couldn't read. It made her uneasy not knowing what kind of person she was talking to.

Her gut told her that Blanch fit into the small category of unreadables. Fin, on the other hand, she labeled as plain crazy.

As the meeting continued with people telling how their weeks had gone, she resigned herself to simply watch. The Campbells had experienced a rough spot in their week, so the group session mostly centered on them and their arguments. Their 18-year-old son had taken his own life, and they blamed each other. Everyone listened and offered advice and support.

At the end of the session, they all discussed the possibility of having a group outing. A few people went over possible dates and activities, while others took their cue that the meeting was adjourned.

Erica Darnell

Mrs. Campbell asked Kate a few questions about where she worked before turning to give her input on the location of the outing.

Kate stood, intent on speaking with Fin to ask him about Molly's funeral. But she couldn't find him anywhere in the room. She hadn't even seen him get up. She went to the snack table to get a drink and stall. He might have gone to the bathroom or something. She slowly sipped through a cup of Hawaiian Punch. He didn't come back. Disappointed, she turned for the door and nearly ran right into Kyle.

"Woah, there!" He caught her arms to keep her from stumbling. "You oughta watch where you're going."

"Yeah, I guess so," she replied, quickly retracting her arms.

Her obvious discomfort with him touching her didn't faze him. "So, do you think you'll keep coming to our meetings?" He smiled at her.

"Well, uh, I think I might. It depends on my work schedule. It was nice to meet everyone, though." She kept her tone relaxed and polite, carefully side-stepping around him.

"It's just nice to have somebody my age around," he said, stepping along with her. "Honestly, it's kind of hard for me to relate to everyone. I mean, I try, but it would be nice to have someone like you here."

Was he hitting on her at a support group for mourning people? Should she feel offended or flattered? She admitted to herself that she liked the attention. He had a striking build and a handsome face. He smiled down at her with his gorgeous brown eyes, but she just couldn't accept the fact that he had the balls to hit on her in a situation like this. If he wanted to take advantage of her in a vulnerable spot, he had another thing coming.

At the same time, she couldn't presume to know his intentions, so she gave him the benefit of the doubt and replied, "Yeah, I see what you mean. Well, I'm beat, and I have to get home to let out my dog. I guess I'll see you around." Thank you, Jake, for a completely valid excuse.

Kate hurriedly walked around him so he wouldn't have the chance to respond. With her hand on the door, she heard Blanch call from across the room, "Oh, Kate, dear?"

So close, Kate thought as she turned and replied, "Yeah?"

"You have a great week, hon. I've added you to our email list, so you'll get updates. I'll send you a contact sheet with our phone numbers, too, in case you need anything." Blanch smiled warmly.

Kate began to feel like joining the group wasn't really a choice. She fumbled for some sort of control. "Uh, okay, thanks. Maybe I'll send you my phone number sometime so you can add it." She still hadn't made up her mind about Helping Hands, and she sure as hell wasn't going to let someone make it up for her.

Blanch giggled. "Oh, sweetie, don't you worry about that. Detective Peterson already gave us your number! Such a nice man."

Kyle, standing between her and Blanch, flashed a huge smile.

Kate tried to hide the oh-my-God-I'm-going-to-kill-him look on her face by waving and turning to leave. She fumed all the way to the car about the presumptuous Detective Alec Peterson.

"He's going to get it," she seethed.

~~~~~

A voice spoke into the darkness, "Where is the angel now?" violent hacking and ragged breathing followed the question.

The meek voice of a young woman answered. "He follows her, Lord."

"She has joined the group, then?"

"She will in time."

"Show her the way, but do not harm her."

Ashley's shape hunkered forward. "She may not follow without appropriate measures. Surely you don't expect her to escape our little encounter without a scratch."

"Do not presume to tell me what to do! Have you forgotten your place, Enhydris? Your reputation precedes you. One scratch is never enough."

The young woman took a step back, surprise on her face. Voices rose together, "How do you know which of us speaks? Can you afford to rid yourself of everyone who occupies the girl?"

A massive form moved in the darkness. The girl's sneer turned to terror as a clawed hand reached out and grabbed her neck. His hot breath came inches from her face, his fangs visible. His eyes sent Ashley's small frame into panicked tremors.

"And what's more…" the girl's voice wheezed shakily through her constricted throat, "you insult us by forcing us to occupy such a weak being! Even now, she trembles at the sight of you."

"Her quivering soul should remind you of your place! Or need I remind you?" Smoke manifested from the corners of the small room and gathered into a cloud before the girl's face. It slowly trickled through her mouth and into her throat. The girl did not cough, but sounds of violent hacking rose from within her. Her eyes shifted out of focus, and her body writhed and thrashed about like an expressionless puppet before relaxing, dangling limply from the dark creature's fist.

Suddenly, her eyes snapped into awareness. Ashley looked into the eyes of the huge being as it stood, holding her feet barely above the ground. Voices inside her head wailed for their master to cease his oppression. He smiled down at her.

She whimpered. "Please," a tear trailed down her cheek. "Please let me go."

The voices screamed in agony.

The creature raised his head and cackled with amusement. "There are so many things worse than eliminating all of you. I can trap you in this insignificant being until the end of her days. Instead of feeding off her emotions, you will be forced to feel them. Do not make the same mistake as Tyrannus. He thinks he fools me simply because I allow him to believe it. He does not know I am aware of his wanderings. I plan to make an example out of his ignorance by delivering the worst fate of all. Only the One can deliver such a hideous demise. You know of Whom I speak?"

With that, he let her fall into a heap on the ground. The girl looked up, darkness in her eyes again. "It will be done."

"Do not disappoint me."

Chapter 6

Brodey Hill folded a page in his schoolbook and stretched his arms above his head. He looked out across the lake waters at the groups of students. A couple of guys played guitars, attracting a crowd of young ladies who sat around, putting in requests. Two guys and a girl played Frisbee. Two sweethearts sat on a picnic blanket; they needed a room. Everyone seemed so carefree out in the fresh air.

Brodey looked down at his book. His scholastic achievements ensured him a sensational career in the world, but comparing himself to the people around him, he felt very unsuccessful. No one invited him to parties because his social skills were subpar. He never got asked to play any sports because he had two left feet. His face, not completely hopeless, won a few girls' attention, but they never made it past the first date. His awkwardness trumped any of his outward attractiveness.

Naturally, he'd tried everything he could to fit in. Like a bad puzzle piece, he never clicked anywhere. It felt like all the pieces around him came from a completely different box. Finally, in his high school years, he found his niche in the science club. Everyone in the club gushed over his natural problem-solving skills. His parents, mostly happy he'd found something that he enjoyed, encouraged him to involve himself in their competitions. He felt like he'd finally found a place to fit in.

Unfortunately for him, he'd picked the wrong club to join. Although he finally felt like he could be himself, his peers went from ignoring him to relentlessly teasing him. He went from sitting alone at lunch to having random people come up to him and feign interest in his scientific achievements, only to turn it around later to use as ammunition. He stopped trusting people and withdrew into himself. Why put any efforts to fit into the social scene if all such efforts only brought about further rejection? It turned into a simple equation for him, and the answer was obvious.

While his classmates looked forward to the college experience, he looked at it as a simple steppingstone into his career. He hadn't decided what he wanted to do with his life, but he liked science, so he decided to get through a few science classes in different focuses of study before declaring a specific major.

He requested a room alone. His coed dorm had several single rooms available. Although he shared the bathroom with his neighbor, he never ran into whoever lived there. He actually thought that no one lived in the room because the door remained closed, and he never heard a peep from it. Only his belongings occupied the cabinet space below the double sink. He never saw anyone coming or going, either. He suspected that the room's occupant unexpectedly dropped out.

His screwed-up family didn't give a damn what he did with his life, as long as he got out. His mother died when he was young. He could remember her, but only faint glimpses. Mostly, he remembered what people said about his mother, Elaine. Everyone spoke very highly of her, and he mentally grasped onto each trait, each characteristic mentioned that made her so special. He created an image and memories through the stories he'd heard of her, and he'd done it so efficiently that he couldn't remember which memories were his and which memories came from stories he'd heard. In a way, he felt nostalgic without really knowing what he felt nostalgic for.

His father remarried a woman half his age who only cared about herself. Brodey didn't understand how he could settle for someone so shallow after having someone as wonderful as Elaine. Nevertheless, he tried to make the best out of the situation. She didn't like his social awkwardness. She wanted him to talk, smile pleasantly, ooh and ahh over whatever she said, but most of the time, he just looked at her. He didn't purposely act rude. Brodey tried to cultivate a relationship with her, but she had already made up her mind about him.

His father rarely spoke to him. He didn't go out of his way to hurt Brodey, but he never helped either. Sometimes he would catch his father studying him curiously. He wondered if he reminded his dad of Elaine, and therefore, he avoided talking with his own son because of the pain of old scars. Maybe the old man just harbored bitterness because Brodey didn't fit the son model. Who wants a son that can't throw a football a respectable distance? He rolled his eyes at the social constraints put on gender.

He stood from his bench and threw his bag over his shoulder, chancing a glance behind him at the sorority girls setting up a giant barrel of water for something. Probably some sort of fundraiser. He saw Thea, a girl he'd met in calculus class during the spring semester.

Her eyes caught his. Her blonde hair with big curls lay in a lazy ponytail on her back. She wore a pair of cutoff sweats and a t-shirt with a heather gray zip-up hoodie. Her smile lit up his world. Brodey froze. Icy tendrils pumped from his heart and filled his veins. *Turn around and go to the dorm, you idiot!* She waved at him. He couldn't bring himself to wave back.

Earlier in the year, he'd helped her with her calculus homework. He remembered how she'd chanced upon him at one of the campus restaurants and boldly sat across from him, asking how he was doing in class.

"Uh, fine," he'd stuttered.

"Well, I'm getting a B, and I really want to bring it up to an A. I don't know why I can't seem to focus." She rolled her eyes and flipped her hair over her shoulder. "I feel like I study all the time!"

He gave her a look. *Okay, it's nice of you to stop and say hi to the nerd, but you've done your good deed now, time to leave.* She didn't follow.

She reached out and plucked a French fry from his plate "Mind if I have one?"

He made a shocked noise.

She looked a little hurt and said, "Oh, sorry. I guess I'm being kind of rude. Should I put it back?"

"No," he said, scowling. "You've already got your germs all over it."

She leaned back and laughed. Then she looked at his indignant face and laughed again, popping the fry in her mouth. "Well," she said between chuckles, "I need to get going, but do you think you could help me out with my homework sometime? It takes me an eternity to get it right, and I think I might be making it more complicated than I need to. Maybe you can show me some shortcuts or something?"

"Short cuts in *calculus*? I think the class description is: A class making you do everything the long way, and if you find a shorter way, you will be flogged."

She laughed at him. He felt like it was genuine. "Well, maybe you can help me sometime. I'll be in Morris Friday afternoon studying for a test if you want to drop by." She winked at him and left.

Against his better judgment, he went to Morris Library that Friday afternoon. Thea sat alone, diligently reading a book by the windows, and waved him over. After a few moments of helping her with her homework, he couldn't convince her that she really didn't need him. She seemed to already know all the answers. He felt useless to her, but the longer they sat and talked, the more he realized she tactfully steered the topic of conversation to anything but calculus. He found himself enjoying her personality. She made conversation flow naturally with her easy-going manner.

He began to feel like he'd known her for years. After a couple hours of chatting, one of her sorority friends walked up, eyeing Brodey. "Thea?"

"Oh, hey," Thea smiled.

"Where's Mike?" the girl said.

Thea frowned up at her, "Why should I care where he is? He's probably off with some tramp."

"I thought you were getting back together," the girl said, studying Brodey in a way that made him feel like a cockroach. He uneasily picked up a pen and pretended not to pay attention.

"He can think what he wants. We broke up two months ago. I've made it clear that I'm not interested." Thea closed the book in front of her, adding a thud of finality to her statement.

"Maybe we can talk about this somewhere *else*." The girl tilted her head toward Brodey.

Thea shot her friend a glance that Brodey couldn't quite interpret before looking at him. "Do you mind if we pick this up some other time?"

He shook his head yes as she slid him a folded-up piece of paper with her number on it. Her friend's eyes widened as Thea stood and said, "Call me."

With that, the other girl grabbed Thea's wrist, muttered something under her breath, and dragged her off. Thea didn't look back, but her friend gave him one final departing sneer over her shoulder.

Brodey cringed at the thought of how awful and insignificant the girl made him feel. Even now, his guts knotted at the memory. At least, if he avoided friendship, nobody seemed to notice him, but as soon as the attention turned to him, bad things happened.

A little voice probed at his mind, *But aren't the good things worth the bad?*

Brodey looked up. While he was thinking about his first encounter with Thea, she'd started walking toward him. *AH! She's walking over here, you numb nut!* He wanted to scream and run. He wanted to tell her to leave him alone. Instead, stranded on his island of fear, he stood motionless. Thea slowed down to a jog and stopped in front of him.

"Whew," she said, panting. "I need to work out! I thought you were gonna run off on me, Brodey." She smiled her huge, beautiful smile, pulling her hair back behind her ear. "Why didn't you call me back? I called and left messages on your phone over a month ago."

He planned on hedging the question, but her intense gaze told him she intended to find out exactly why he hadn't called her. She waited for him to answer, her brown eyes prodding.

He licked his lips, "Well, I've been busy. That's all."

"Are you busy now?" she asked.

He searched for a way to say yes, to suddenly fill his agenda with a to-do list. "Um, I have to go back to my room and grab some stuff for my lab, and..."

"Oh, when does the lab start?"

He looked at his watch. "Three, so I guess I'll catch you later."

He turned to go, and she reached out to grab his wrist, yanking him back. She bent it, craning her neck to see his watch. "Brodey, it's only 1:30. Why don't you come help us put our dunking booth together?" She wagged her thumb over her shoulder. "Some of these girls claim this thing is structurally sound, but I wouldn't get on it for any amount of money."

He pulled his arm out of her grasp, narrowing his eyes at her. Then he bent to the side, peering at her friends. "I don't think I'll get along with your crowd," he stated, rubbing his wrist. Contrary to what she said, he didn't think she needed to work out.

"C'mon, you're weird, but not *that* weird." She rolled her eyes and walked away, obviously expecting him to follow.

"It's a bunch of girls. I'd rather not." He felt as though the words poured thoughtlessly out of his mouth. He sounded like a sissy! Suddenly feeling hot, he took a step back.

She turned and studied him with her head cocked to the side. "Okay," she said.

He breathed a sigh of relief, relaxing his tense shoulders. He turned to walk to his dorm, feeling rather accomplished for effectively dodging this bullet. He jumped when he heard her yell back to her friends, "Sorry, guys, I'm gonna bail. I'll be back later, okay?"

A few of the girls groaned, someone called her a flake, and most everyone else kept working on the horrible-looking booth.

She turned and ran a few quick steps to catch up with him, speaking without missing a beat, "So. I've got a 93 in calc. Feelin' pretty good about it. I'm hoping the final doesn't kill me."

He quickened his pace, hoping she'd give up and turn around. She knew he'd been avoiding her, but she wouldn't go away. What if she really liked him? He shook the thought from his head.

He sighed, "You're giving me a headache."

"What? Why?" She played with the rubber band on her wrist.

"Because I just — I'm not a people person. You are obviously comfortable in social settings while I'm not. I don't understand why you're hanging around with a weirdo." He surprised himself with his bluntness. She brought out his honest side, apparently.

She laughed. "You're right."

He stopped walking and looked at her. "About what?"

"You *are* weird." She smiled. "But I think you're interesting." She held his gaze, waiting for him to challenge her answer. He didn't.

"Oh," he said, sounding rather pathetic. She hadn't offended him by calling him weird. He really liked that she'd spoken truthfully. Not only did she think him odd, but she liked it. Interesting.

He decided to let down his icy front, and he talked with her on the way back to the dorm. She asked how he liked dorm life, if he had a part-time job, and where he liked to eat. To his surprise, she followed him up to his room and walked in uninvited. He couldn't think of any one word to describe her, except maybe charismatic.

She plopped down on his bed. "You like Disturbed?"

He looked up at her holding his iPod that he'd left lying there. "Yeah."

"I have two of their songs. I really like them, but like any group with that kind of uniqueness, their songs run together after a while."

"Uniqueness? Playing hard rock with killer guitar solos and angry screaming is hardly unique. Now, if you want to hear unique, I've got a great band for you to listen to." He swiped the iPod from her hand and plugged it into his stereo. A moment later, folky-sounding music rolled out of the speakers.

She sat up straight, "You like Nickel Creek?"

"Yeah! They're so relaxing. No matter what's on my mind, I can turn it on, and by the end of the song, I just feel like a weight has been lifted off of me, ya know?"

She was smiling, but her smile faded. "Oh," she said, looking over his shoulder, "I thought you said you didn't have a roommate."

He turned and jumped a little when he saw a thin-faced boy standing in the doorway to the bathroom. Brodey tried not to let his voice show his surprise, "Uh, can I help you?"

The guy looked around the room and then at the girl on the bed with an expression that said he didn't think she belonged there. "Yeah," he said. "Sorry, the door was open, and I heard voices. I'm just moving into the adjoining room."

"Oh, I'm Brodey." Brodey kept a friendly tone but stayed put.

"Don't worry," the boy said, "I'm not a people person, so you won't see much of me. I'm just moving over from another dorm."

"Ok. Well, I use the cabinet under the right sink. You can have the left."

"Sure." The boy wove his hands together, looking from Thea to Brodey.

"Oh, uh, this is Thea," Brodey said. She waved her hand, but the friendly smile had been pressed into a thin line of concern.

"Right." The boy grinned sharply. Brodey shifted his weight, uncomfortable standing in his new roommate's probing gaze.

Thea stood and walked to stand next to Brodey, intertwining her fingers with his. Shocked, his mouth opened a bit, and he barely stifled a surprised squeak. His heart skipped a beat. Despite keeping his voice under control, he felt his face flush.

She spoke almost too quietly to hear, "I think I'm going to go make sure the girls didn't hurt themselves."

Brodey struggled to say anything without stuttering. She still had her hand in his, and she was looking up at him with her gorgeous brown eyes. "Uh," he stammered. *I can't believe I'm doing this.* "Do you want to grab something to eat after my lab?"

For a moment, she beamed. "Do you like pizza?"

The lump in his throat felt like it might suffocate him, so he just nodded.

"Meet me at Pagliai's around seven?"

He nodded again, and she gave his hand a quick squeeze. She crossed her arms tightly over her chest and hugged the opposite wall on her way out, eyes on the visitor in his doorway.

At least he'd get some great pizza out of the deal. Pag's was a college-town favorite. Better yet, he could watch the kitchen staff make pizza through the glass half wall to avoid eye-contact with Thea. *Or I could just back out last minute.* He imagined her walking into Pagliai's and looking around the room full of tiny blue lamps, dejectedly. *Nah, I can't do that. It's beat-up.*

"Well, that was...awkward. I guess I'll see you around," his new roommate turned on his heels and unceremoniously strode back toward his room.

Brodey half mumbled, "I didn't catch your name."

"Wyatt," he shouted over his shoulder, closing the door behind him.

Chapter 7

The phone woke Kate from her troubled sleep. Her heart hammered in her chest. She threw off her sweat-soaked sheets. Her hand drifted to her head as she attempted to organize her thoughts. She'd had the same nightmare for days on end.

The phone rang again. She nabbed it from the nightstand, sighing. "Hello?"

It was her boss, explaining that he needed her to type up a few documents for him. She jotted down some notes. Glancing at the clock, she promised to finish by noon.

She'd been working from home for two weeks. She actually preferred to go into the office but dealing with Molly's house occupied a good bit of her time. She had to meet people there nearly every day to get it ready to sell. Carpet cleaners, painters, woodworkers, landscapers, cleaners; the list went on and on.

She went to the bathroom sink and splashed water on her face. Placing her hands on the cold edge of the sink, she allowed it to bear her weight, hoping to make her heart lighter. Pulling the hand towel from its bar, she buried her face in it. She breathed in the fresh smell of the cloth, attempting to ground herself. Nightmares plagued every night. Hot tears stung her eyes before the towel absorbed them. For some reason, having something on her face gave her permission to cry. She missed Molly fiercely.

Mourning was a funny thing. She'd never wanted people around her so badly while at the same time yearning to be left alone. She couldn't help crying herself to sleep in the quiet darkness of her bedroom each night.

She bit her lip, trying to quell the tears. The dream played in her mind again. Every night, she knew what to expect, each one more vivid than the last. She shivered at the thought of the creatures -- then took a shaky breath. *I'm ok.*

Picking up her toothbrush, she turned her thoughts to Detective Peterson. He would probably call her today. He tried to check in a couple times a week. He had another case in a neighboring town, so she didn't see him much. He'd already linked that case to Molly's. He told her the thing that originally turned him on to doubt some of these 'suicides' was the fact that they didn't statistically make sense. He explained that women tended to do things that left less of a mess. Even in planning their own death, their thoughts dwelled on the possible untidiness they would cause with a gun or slitting their wrists. Often, women would take their lives using the overdose method. Men, however, chose much more brazen ways to take their lives.

He had explained that he noticed the trend change a little over a year ago while looking into a few cases in Chicago and decided to further investigate. After a few months, he'd made some random ties to the website called The Gathering of Souls. He still didn't have enough to go on to force them to give him more information than what they would voluntarily surrender, and their red tape only enticed him further.

Most of the cases he checked into actually *were* suicides. He'd only had a handful that turned out like Molly's, which left such cases in the coincidence category. How could he prove wrongdoing or foul play by one particular entity when other avenues of explanation made so much more sense? He had nothing to go on but a hunch. Suicide rates in the area had risen exponentially compared to the rest of the country, but again, that fell in the circumstantial evidence category.

After chatting with him a few times, she began to understand his serious personality a little better. His stoic, all-business nature came from the sacrifice of any life outside of detective work. His guarded demeanor came from years of practice protecting himself from the job. The moment it became personal, he would lose his objectivity. It must be a difficult line to walk - to care enough to find answers, but not enough to expose raw emotions.

But somehow, Kate felt he guarded more than just his emotions. Of course, she'd surmised all of this on her own. Maybe he didn't guard himself at all. Perhaps that was just his personality. She just couldn't shake the feeling of a quivering force, like a dam with too much pressure behind it. Under the surface, he had more brewing than he let on.

Her phone rang again. She checked the screen. Kyle. She let out an exasperated breath. She'd attended several Helping Hands meetings. They provided a nice break in each week. Even though the people were great, she didn't feel any kind of connection with them. They'd all experienced a similar loss, yet she still felt like a lone tree in the middle of an infinitely empty field. She'd effectively hedged Kyle's advances so far.

Kate couldn't explain what was so wrong with accepting his invite. She found Kyle attractive. She admitted to herself that she feared getting back into the dating game. Nobody liked playing a game they couldn't win.

Kate looked at herself in the mirror. "Be strong." Then she put the phone to her ear, "Hello?"

"Kate! Oh my gosh, ha, I didn't think you'd answer. But, uh, you did." There was a small pause before he realized he hadn't said his name. "Oh, yeah, it's Kyle." He let out another nervous laugh.

The corners of her mouth turned up. She made him nervous? He'd never given her that kind of vibe. Maybe he wasn't as macho as she thought. Or, she thought, amused, maybe she'd turned him down enough to put him in his place. He had the face of a guy who wasn't used to being turned down. She grinned again, finally speaking. "Hi, Kyle. What's up?"

"Well, I don't know if you've noticed, but the weather's been so nice outside. It just got me thinkin', I mean, maybe we could go for a run together. I know you like runnin' and such. So, I thought I'd ask ya to go on a...run. Ha! How many times did I just say run?"

She laughed softly. "Um, a few. I didn't know you liked to run."

"I don't, but you do. And so far, you don't like movies, concerts, or baseball games. So, I thought I'd take a chance with something you *do* like."

She began thinking of reasons she couldn't go. Her voice caught in her throat before the "no" came out. Her life needed a little excitement. She hadn't bonded with anyone else in the group, so maybe she just needed to take a risk. Hanging out with Kyle for a bit couldn't be any worse than showing up to a restaurant for another blind date set up by Marcy or a systematic match from the dating site. She had finally closed the account. At least with Kyle, she knew what to expect.

"I'll go on one condition," she said.

"Yeah? What's that?" He asked, sounding wary.

"My dog, Jake, gets to come along," she replied.

"Great! That's totally doable. He's not gonna, like, gnaw off my leg, is he?"

"No!" she laughed. "I can't do it this morning, but maybe we can go after I meet the realtor this afternoon. Will that work?"

She heard him rustling through some papers. "Yes. I can make it work. Where do you want to meet?"

They decided to meet at Molly's house since Kate had to meet the realtor. She gave him directions and hung up. She gave herself a final once-over before turning to leave the bathroom. Jake sat in the doorway, examining her with curious eyes.

"What?" She shrugged. "I can't be single forever! Besides, you'll be a good buffer."

~~~~~

Alec Peterson paced back and forth behind a redhead as her fingers swept across the keyboard to her computer. A pencil held her bun in place, but she still blew one stray hair from her eye without missing a beat.

"How long does this usually take?" he asked, looking at his watch for the 3rd time in the span of a few minutes.

She didn't answer. Her unblinking eyes stared; her mouth made tiny movements as she typed.

Alec rubbed both of his eyes and pulled his hands down his face. "Just forget it." He crossed the room and put his hand on the door.

"I'm in," the girl reached for her large gas station coke and took a satisfied sip. "This was the weirdest interview ever, by the way," she stretched.

"What can you find for me?" Alec whispered without turning from the door.

"Anything," she grinned. "The Gathering of Souls is your oyster. But it'll cost you."

He walked back to her computer. "I'll bring a folder with the information I need by morning. I'll be paying cash." He handed her a wad of money and said, "Hire help if you need it."

"Just shoot me an email with the file. I can get started sooner." She raised her feet to the edge of her desk, giving him a sly look.

He grinned, "C'mon, Kelsey. This one's off the books. I'm not *that* stupid."

~~~~~

After finishing up her work, Kate threw on her running shorts and a long-sleeved shirt before going on a quick walk with Jake. She didn't want him getting too excited about meeting the new realtor. She thought taking a walk would ease some of the tension for both of them.

Once they'd finished their "calming" walk, she grabbed a few toys for Jake and headed to Molly's.

She pulled up behind a car she didn't recognize in front of Molly's. She glanced around the yard for Jed, the realtor. The plates were from the Chicago area. She didn't remember him mentioning a recent move.

Shrugging it off, she hopped out of the car and walked around to the passenger side to let Jake out. He didn't budge.

"It's okay, boy, c'mon." Kate tried to encourage him.

To her bewilderment, he sat in the car, holding his ground. She noticed the hair on his back standing up. He bared his teeth slightly. Instinctively, she turned around to make sure nothing snuck up on her. Apart from the realtor's car, she didn't see anything out of the ordinary. She'd been a little edgy lately. He probably just sensed her nervousness.

"Have it your way," she conceded. She rolled down the window and closed the door.

He let out a low growl.

"Get over it," she shouted over her shoulder.

She'd left the door locked, so Jed probably went around to the backyard to get a feel for the property. She rounded the house and nearly tripped herself coming to a quick halt. A tall, lean woman stood in the center of the backyard, holding a clipboard. She wore a tailored, gray business suit with a pop of pink in her blouse. Her long hair had strips of white in the front around her face. She'd been scribbling something onto the pad of paper and hadn't noticed Kate.

"Excuse me," Kate called.

The well-dressed woman's head snapped up. She momentarily looked ready to defend herself. Her feline gaze softened when she saw Kate. "Oh, hello!" she called. "You must be Katherine Gregory." She crossed the short distance between them with an easy gait, despite her sky-scraper heels. "I was just taking some notes and writing a brief description of the home. I didn't see you come around." With the shoes, the woman seemed to tower over Kate's small build. She reached out a manicured hand, shaking Kate's.

62

Kate reached up, nervously tucking her hair behind her ears. "Uh, yeah, I noticed. Who are you?"

The woman's eyebrows drew together over sparkling green eyes. "Jed didn't tell you? I'm your new realtor, Everly." Kate glanced briefly toward the front yard when she heard Jake's barks from the car. He carried on like he'd spotted a critter.

"Hm. No, I don't remember him saying anything." She probed her memory. Sleep deprivation and stress made her feel a little out of sorts. She hadn't gone and forgotten a whole conversation, had she?

"Water under the bridge, dear," Everly said, waving her jewelry-covered fingers. Her bracelets clanked against each other. "We'll just start fresh." Without missing a beat, she turned and strode toward the back door. Kate realized that Everly intended to lead the way, so she unfroze her feet and dumbly followed.

"Now, I've made plenty of notes about the yard and the clinic. Are you planning on selling them together?" Everly asked.

Kate couldn't shake her uneasy feeling, and Jake's barking wasn't helping. She tried to sound pleasant, nonetheless. "Didn't Jed give you any notes? We've already discussed all of this over the phone."

The woman flipped through her clipboard, quickly perusing the documents attached. "Oh, dear," she lamented. "I guess he didn't." Her broad smile didn't quite touch her eyes. "No worries, darling, he just had something pop up at the last minute. It's nothing we can't cover while you give me a tour of this quaint little abode, right?"

Jake continued with his howling from the car.

Kate hesitated. This woman had a predatory quality under her polished exterior. She briefly entertained the idea of telling her that she'd just wait until Jed could make it out. That seemed like a reasonable request, considering that he'd already established a rapport with her. She reasoned, though, that she really didn't want to draw this out any longer than she needed to.

She inwardly scoffed at herself. *It's not like this woman is dangerous! What's the matter with you, Kate? You've got to let go of these jitters. She's just selling the house. It's not like you have to be best buddies.* Besides, she had no reason to feel any allegiance to Jed since she'd technically never met him.

"Right," Kate replied, turning to unlock the door.

Everly grinned like a cat about to pounce on a cornered mouse, "I knew we'd get along splendidly."

Kate gave Everly a tour of the home, answering all her questions about additions and improvements made over the years. It was an older home, and Molly took advantage of it by using shabby-chic décor. Each room felt like a warm cottage with distressed furniture but bright popping colors to keep it from appearing drab. Molly had updated many of the light fixtures but kept the style relative to the rest of the home. Even the doorknobs had a naturally dark and worn appearance that lent itself to the cottage theme.

Kate took her through the bathrooms, pointing out the new tile floors and raised faucets. Everly scribbled everything down on her notepad, interjecting the occasional "uh-huh," and "very nice."

In Molly's room, Kate said very little, uncomfortable knowing that Molly took her last breaths in it. She stood to the side as Everly walked around checking the windows and closet. "The windows have also been replaced in the last couple of years it seems," She pointed out.

Kate nodded. "Some of the wood around the windows is also new. The old ones let water in on occasion."

At the end of the tour, Everly told Kate she would email her with an approximate asking price after comparing Molly's house to other homes in the neighborhood.

"That's fine. I didn't expect you to give me one today, anyway," Kate admitted. She opened the front door for the woman.

Everly reached into her Coach bag and plucked out a pair of oversized Gucci sunglasses as she stepped out into the sunny afternoon air. "Oh," she said, clearly a new thought striking her. "I did mean to say I'm so sorry about your sister. It's a terrible thing, suicide. Let me know if you need anything."

Kate dropped her keys and fumbled to pick them up. Trying to hide her hot face, she simply replied, "It wasn't suicide."

"Of course it wasn't, dear." Everly let a coy smile escape her lips. "No one ever wants to believe people are capable of such thoughtless acts."

Kate fought the urge to scratch the woman's eyes out. She let go of her attempts to be polite, snapping, "It has nothing to do with my inability to *accept* it. The detective on the case has already proven it." Her knuckles whitened, clutched around her keys.

"Oh! I'm so sorry I offended you. I merely meant that..." she seemed to recoil when she noticed Kate's expression. "Well, never mind what I meant. I'm so glad you have an excellent detective working on the case. What did you say his name was?" She cocked her head.

"Peterson," Kate spat.

"Peterson," Everly drew out the name. "Can't say that I've met him. Good luck, anyway. Be on the lookout for my email!" She strutted to her little sports car, eying Jake the whole way.

He had his nose plastered to the windshield; teeth bared. His hair still stood straight up. Everly pulled a few houses down to another home with a sign in the yard and turned off her car. It looked like she planned on waiting for someone to arrive before getting out.

Kate looked back at her car and jumped when she noticed Kyle had already arrived. He waved at her through the windshield.

She walked over to his cracked passenger window. "Hey," she muttered. "How long have you been sitting here?"

He pushed his sunglasses to the top of his head. "Long enough to realize that your realtor's a bitch, and your dog is scarier than you let on." He gave her an understanding look. "Want me to beat her up?"

Kate felt herself smile through the burning in her face. She glanced down the block at the predator's car and narrowed her eyes. "I'd rather do it myself."

He grimaced at the harshness in her voice. "Do you want to skip the run, then?"

"On the contrary," she responded. "I think a run is precisely what I need."

"Well, I'm not getting out of the car without a taser. Your dog's been going nuts since I got here."

Kate glanced up at Jake, who had his head out the window with his ears perked. He licked his lips, ready to get out of the car. "Well, he seems fine now. Why don't you come meet him?"

~~~~~

Simone watched Kate talk the young man into coming to the passenger window of her car. Kate giggled at him when he flinched as the filthy animal licked his hand.

She hoped her new "customer" wouldn't try to call Jed up and ask him about Everly. Jed certainly wouldn't be returning any of her calls if she did. Simone smirked to herself. He didn't buy her back story and asked too many questions. She couldn't afford that, so she took care of him.

She sighed, relieved the whole exchange was over. For a brief moment, it seemed like Kate didn't believe her. Simone waited patiently, biting the inside of her mouth. She certainly didn't want to get her hands dirty if she didn't have to. Nobody wants to mess up a face like Katherine Gregory's, anyhow. She probably could have avoided making the poor girl upset in the end, but she couldn't help herself. She needed information, and she got what she needed.

She watched Kate and the young man head in the opposite direction at a slow jog. She pulled her cell phone out of her Coach bag and dialed a familiar number. When she heard an answer, she said, "Yeah, it's Simone. Tell them that Alec Peterson is in Marion."

After a brief pause, she said, "No. I haven't found Ashley yet. You'll be the first to know."

Chapter 8

Kate grew tired of the Helping Hands meetings, but because of the unexplained note on her counter, she showed up nearly every week. For the most part, she enjoyed everyone in the group. She didn't like Blanch very much, but she could get along with her just fine. Of the ten members, only seven showed up religiously. A few outliers would come and go, but for the most part, the same crowd gathered every week. Kate couldn't imagine how anyone could fall out of the group with Blanch leading the no-show calls. Kate missed one meeting due to work and got a call first thing the next morning asking if she would be coming to the next meeting.

Kyle sat next to her at every meeting; she felt like he was more serious about her than she was about him. He had let on several times that he wanted to take the next step in their relationship, but Kate evaded his not-so-subtle hints.

In one awkward moment, she had shown up to watch part of one of his basketball games. At the end, he ran up to her, thanking her for coming. He leaned, intending to kiss her on the cheek, but she pulled her head to the side, leading him into a hug instead.

He also offered several times to host movie nights at his house. She politely declined, citing a myriad of reasons. The most important reason she kept to herself, though. Kyle in a dark room meant trouble. She inwardly shrank at the thought that she might be sending mixed signals, but she enjoyed his company and wanted to keep it at that.

Pat Goldstein started talking about a garage sale she had begun organizing. She nervously tugged at the short hair on her neck, explaining, "It's so much more difficult to do things like that without Raymond around."

Kate took the opportunity to get a little more involved. "Pat, you know you can ask for help if your family can't step in. I usually have the weekends free and would be happy to put price stickers on things," she offered.

Pat looked shocked that she had said anything. The only person that spoke less than Kate was Fin. Pat shook her head, "Thank you, sweetie, but you don't need to do anything like that. Besides, most of the things I struggle with are heavy."

Kyle interjected, "Well, I can help too. When are you having the garage sale?"

Not knowing Kyle well enough, Kate wondered if he would offer to do something like that if she wasn't there. She hated dating people she had only recently met. Every relationship that started with interest or immediate attraction led to disappointment. Both people in the relationship would display what they thought the other person wanted to see, only delaying an inevitable break up when the truth came out.

Pat looked from Kate to Kyle and then back again. Kate gave her a reassuring smile. Satisfied that they wouldn't change their minds, Pat said, "Well, I was thinking of doing it next weekend," she stuttered.

"Kyle and I will come over Friday evening to help you get everything ready," Kate said. "I can come back on Saturday morning to sit with you, too." She turned to Kyle. "You probably don't want to come early on a weekend morning, right?" She thought if she gave him an out, he would take it.

Kyle winced. "How early are we talking about on Saturday morning?"

"Usually, the crack of dawn with all the old ladies who treat garage sales like a sport," Kate said, smiling.

Pat nodded her head in confirmation. "Thank you so much. I'll make coffee for everyone that morning." She wrote herself a note in her planner.

Kyle's shoulders slumped a little. "It's going to have to be some damn strong coffee," he muttered. A few people snickered.

"Well, Kate," Joe said, "since you have the floor, why don't you tell us how you've been doing?"

Ugh. This is why I don't talk, she thought. Instead of diverting the attention like she usually did, she conceded. She briefly explained how getting Molly's house market-ready was a bigger job than she had anticipated. She also told them she met with the realtor but left out how awful the woman treated her at the end of their walk-through.

"I'm not sure what to do with the furniture and her belongings. I'm considering either offering them with the house or taking most of the bigger pieces to second-hand stores and donating the rest."

"I told her she should rent it out," Kyle chimed in. "Who wouldn't like renting a fully furnished home?"

"Or you could consider making it a bed and breakfast," Pat added. She seemed to want to return the favor of Kate helping her with the garage sale.

Kate shrugged one shoulder. "I haven't made any decisions, really. I guess I'm kind of playing it by ear. It's on the market now. If I don't sell it, I'm open to other opportunities."

It felt better to let all of that out, so Kate took a chance wondering if she would regret it. "Also," she continued, picking at her nails, "I've been having nightmares." She hoped others had experienced the same thing, and she needed to know it was normal. She swallowed hard, waiting for their response.

Fin nearly dropped his chocolate-covered rice crispy treat on his lap. His eyes searched her for an uncomfortable amount of time. Kate moved her gaze to a few others in the room, pleading with her eyes that they give her a place to land.

"It's nothing, really," she said, dismissively waving a hand.

Fin sat his plate on the floor and picked up his punch. Swishing it around in his cup, he asked, "What kind of nightmares?" He kept his eyes on the cup.

Everyone in the room looked at him and then at Kate, the surprise at this new interaction painted on their faces. The normally supportive and chatty group had been shocked into silence. Kate picked at the corner of her notebook. Should she tell them what haunted her dreams? No way. They would think she'd dropped off the deep end. She didn't want to answer Fin's question, anyway. What gave him the right to suddenly care about something more than himself?

"The disturbing kind," she answered, shooting him a look that said she had disclosed all she cared to.

He kept his head down but slowly turned his gray eyes on her. She met his gaze and tried to keep her stomach from coming up into her throat. *Really,* she scolded herself, *why bring up the dreams?*

She didn't like his probing stare, but she mustered as much confidence as she could and held it. He always looked slightly deranged, wild hair framing his unreadable face. She never did ask why she saw him at Molly's funeral, and in her embarrassment, she took the opportunity to land a blow. "Why would someone who funeral hops care about dreams. It's hardly as strange as your past time."

He dropped his eyes to his unfinished punch, his eyebrows furrowed. He sat silently for a moment more before saying, "Nobody made you bring it up." He reached for his snack and shoved the rest of it into his mouth. Kate felt her cheeks heat, and she untucked her hair from behind her ears to try to hide it.

Blanch spoke sharply, "I think Finneus just wanted to make sure you're okay." She shot him a sideways glance before looking back at Kate. "Having nightmares can leave ya on edge, hon."

Kate sighed, thankful the uncomfortable exchange was over.

Blanch continued. "Don't worry, though. The nightmares are probably just your way of dealing with what happened. With time, they'll pass on their own."

Joe grunted in agreement.

"Yeah," Kate said. She tried to think of something to say to change the subject.

Luckily, Pat chimed in about the garage sale again, and Kate didn't have to change the subject. After fifteen minutes of group discussion, they called it quits.

Kyle waited for Kate to finish chatting at the door. "Want me to walk you to your car?" He asked.

"Sure," she replied, thankful to have someone next to her. She sank into the familiar friendship and let it cleanse her guilt over her stab at Fin.

"Don't let Fin bother you. He's just kind of weird, ya know? A lot of us wonder why he even comes. We've all had our theories. Mine was that he's homeless and depends on the group for food." He smiled sideways at her. "I've heard Blanch tell people that she's been to his house, though, so I guess that tosses my theory out the window."

Kate wondered why Blanch would go to Fin's house in the first place. They certainly weren't buddies. She imagined what she would do if Blanch showed up at her house and quickly scrubbed the awkward thought from her mind. Although she stuck with her commitment to their weekly meetings, it felt like she hadn't learned anything from observing interactions between group members. Kate thought again about their uncanny ability to appear innocent as they basically forced her to join the group. She lightened her own mood thinking, *maybe they're all aliens*. She tucked her theory into the back pocket of her mind, wondering for the hundredth time why she was here.

Most of what she knew about the members of Helping Hands came from her time hanging out with Kyle. She took every opportunity she could to purge information from him when it came up. She had to be careful about how she asked her questions, though. He tended to shut down when he caught on to her digging. Whether he did it evasively or not, she didn't know.

She took a chance and joked, "What'd he do? Miss a group?"

Kyle laughed and shook his head. "Nah, he just said something that upset another girl during one of the meetings. Blanch had a few words with him about being careful what he says to people in such fragile positions."

"What did he say?"

Kyle opened his mouth to answer but stopped. "Well, I don't remember, actually. You know how he is, though." He shrugged it off.

No, I don't know how he is, Kate thought. *He seldom speaks, and he's kinda freaky.*

As they got to the front door in the lobby, Kate reached into her jeans pocket for her phone. "Oh, crap! I left my phone upstairs." She patted her other pockets to make sure she hadn't put it somewhere else.

Kyle stopped, "Okay. I'll wait for you here."

"That's okay. I feel bad dragging your night on. I'll just go grab it. I think Joe and Blanch are still upstairs. I'll be fine."

"You sure?"

"Yeah. I'll see you Friday at Pat's," she smiled reassuringly and headed back to the room.

"I'll email you directions," Kyle shouted before leaving.

The click of the door closing behind him echoed around her. Before he left, Kate hadn't noticed the janitor had already turned off all the hallway lights. The darkness felt more ominous without someone else. It almost had a presence of its own. She tried to tame her imagination as she made her way back to the stairs. What was she, nine?

The expansive rooms on each side intimidated her. Vast, empty, echoing space stared her down through each doorway. She felt like something could come out from one of them and stalk her down the remainder of the hallway and stole a quick glance, just to make sure.

Luckily, the stairwell had a light on at all times. She focused on the shard of light shining out from underneath the door, quickening her pace a bit. She looked over her shoulder again before opening it. She took the stairs two at a time and swung the big metal door open. Light still poured out of room 207. Thankful for the beacon amidst shadows, she made her way down the hallway.

She heard Joe and Blanch talking and slowed down. She didn't want to scare them by bursting through the door like a scared animal. She curiously peeked around the frame. Joe's back was to her; he gestured wildly, describing something to Blanch. She stood facing him with her arms folded. By the woman's rigidity, Kate deduced that the topic wasn't the garage sale. The woman that Kate knew -- carefully controlled Blanch that only displayed deliberately chosen emotions -- did not stand in front of Joe. She gripped her own folded, plump arms with such ferocity that her fingers stood out stark white against her plum-colored blouse. She held her mouth in a grimace as if loosening her lips could lead to demise.

Kate wanted to turn around and leave. This conversation felt very private. She thought she might need to make a noise to let them know they weren't alone. *Then again, I could just listen in to see what has Blanch's panties in a wad.* Joe continued rambling. Kate couldn't hear from where she stood, but if she took a few more steps, she thought she might be able to pick up a few words before they detected her. *Then again, Blanch and I aren't exactly friends. Maybe I should attend a few more meetings and buddy up to her before I make any waves. Best to just make a noisy entrance and pretend I saw nothing.*

Before Kate could make her loud entrance, Blanch leaned around Joe's shoulder.

"Well, dear, we weren't expecting anyone back until next week," her smile did not touch her eyes. Her instant demeanor change stopped Joe midsentence. He did not turn around.

Kate froze, knowing she probably looked guilty. "Sorry. I just forgot my phone." She crossed the room quickly. Happy for a reason to keep her eyes on the floor, she searched the area around her chair. "Did anyone pick it up?" She asked without making eye contact.

Blanch responded without pause, "No."

"Oh," Kate said. She tried to backtrack to the last time she saw it. She fumbled through her thoughts, struggling to focus under Blanch's scrutinizing stare.

"Maybe I left it in the car." Although she knew she had the phone with her when she came in, she was ready to leave this prickly silence between the three of them.

"Maybe you did." Blanch waved to the door dismissively.

Such a control freak! What if I'm not ready to leave? What if I want to check the snack table? Kate tried to keep her tone cordial, "I'm just going to check a few more places before I jet, okay?"

Joe kept his back to Kate and still had not acknowledged her in any way. Blanch's eyes shifted to him for a moment and then back at Kate. She looked at her watch, "We were actually just leaving, dear. You wouldn't want to keep us out late, would you? I know you don't want to be any trouble."

Kate's stubbornness got the best of her. "It'll just take a second," she replied, stepping around the two of them to cross the room.

Joe's arm darted out and snatched her wrist. "Actually, I think Kyle picked it up. He was sitting next to you, wasn't he? Maybe you should ask him."

Kate stared at his hand on her wrist and then locked her eyes on him. She didn't like being touched, and she let it show in her tone. "I doubt that's what happened, considering Kyle walked me to the front door. I was standing right next to him when I realized I didn't have my phone. If he had it, I would say he missed his chance to tell me." She instantly regretted being so curt with him.

Joe licked his lips nervously. "M-maybe he didn't realize he picked up *your* phone. I'll send an email out to the group letting them know that you lost it, just in case."

Blanch nodded in agreement behind him.

Kate wanted to throw her arms in the air and ask them what was so secretive. She wanted to grab them by the shoulders and shake them until answers popped out of their bobbling heads. Instead, she said, "That's fine. Have a nice night. See you next week."

She marched down the hallway, thinking about Joe's unusual conduct. She would give anything to have her phone in her hand so she could call Marcy and explain what happened.

It would be better if she could just call Molly. She knew Molly would respond with, "Like aliens!" It would be all the validation Kate needed to call in a team of whoever dealt with freaky events. Maybe the real-life X-files unit could come and take care of this before it got to the whole city.

...or maybe they were mafia. Drug cartel?

73

She puffed out a sigh, letting her heel strikes echo down the remainder of the first floor. It was meant to cleanse her anger. She tried to blow out every bit of her lung capacity. Just as her lungs completely emptied, she heard a clank in the darkness behind her. She sucked in a quick breath and stopped cold in her steps.

She thought about turning around with a quick glance just to put herself at ease. It was probably Blanch and Joe coming out of the stairwell behind her. She listened for steps but heard nothing. She wanted to turn and look, but she knew the dreams she had each night played tricks on her imagination throughout the day. She blew out the air and quickly took the five remaining strides to the front door, ignoring the urge to turn and face whatever stalked the darkness.

She may have convinced her mind, but her body hadn't caught up from the initial fright. She fumbled with her keys before she unlocked her car. The hair on the back of her neck stood straight up. With her hand on the door handle, she finally gave up trying to ignore the darkness and turned around despite herself.

A man stood inches from her.

A squeak escaped her lungs, followed by an angry growl of recognition. "God, Fin! You scared me to death! Do you mind?" She put her hand over her heart, trying to settle down. She put the other hand on the car to steady herself.

He didn't respond immediately, looking a little surprised that he had scared her so badly. Obviously, his intentions weren't to give her a heart attack. Kate took little solace from his reaction.

She held out a hand, inviting him to speak. "Well? Other than scaring an innocent woman out of her mind, would you like to explain what you're doing out here?"

He slowly reached into his pocket, giving Kate pause. Pulling out her cell phone, he held it out for her. His movements mimicked that of someone approaching a scared animal. "I just noticed you left this in there. So, I picked it up for you."

She frowned. "You left before me."

Still holding the cell phone in the space between them, he took a step forward. "Do you want your phone back or not?"

She reached up and snatched it from him. "I'd say thanks, but considering the fact that you stole it, that response doesn't seem fitting." She scowled at him. She probably shouldn't be so rude, but the night's events made it felt warranted. If he hadn't taken her phone, she could have avoided the awkward encounter with Joe and Blanch.

He leaned in so close that she could feel herself backing into the car. She wanted to spit out some smart remark about personal space or boundary recognition, but she could only stare into his eyes.

Finally satisfied that he had her full attention, he said, "Trust no one, got it?"

She nodded her head yes. His intense gaze held her for a few moments. She had questions for him, but one stood out more than the rest. It burned in her mind every time she saw him. "What were you doing at my sister's funeral?"

He shrugged. "I go to a lot of funerals." He turned and walked to his bike. With one foot on the ground and the other ready to pedal off, he shouted over his shoulder, "My number is in your contacts if you need anything."

Chapter 9

After the garage sale on Saturday, Kate met Marcy at Waltz, a local pizza dive, for lunch. Marcy ordered a small salad, and Kate ordered her usual double-decker supreme pizza. She generally tried to eat healthily but reasoned, as a runner, she needed extra calories, and she wanted a bit of food therapy after the week she had. She ordered some cheese sticks on the side.

Marcy wrinkled her nose, "I hope you're not planning to ask me to help you eat those. I swear, Kate, one of these days, you're going to drop dead from a heart attack. You really oughta eat healthier."

"Life's short," Kate replied. "And besides, I could use some love handles."

"You can have some of mine," Marcy said, sipping her diet drink. "Okay," she slid her drink to the side and propped her folded hands upon the table between them. "What's the juicy stuff going on you mentioned over the phone?"

"Well," Kate started but then paused. She hadn't really thought of how much she wanted to share with her best friend. She hadn't told Marcy about the nightmares, the incident with Finneus Koche, or the conversation she'd stumbled upon between Blanch and Joe. Although she did not want to admit it, Fin's warning rang in her head the rest of the week. Who exactly did he mean not to trust? She decided to start easy. "Kyle and I have been having a lot of fun together."

Instead of getting the excited schoolgirl look Kate expected, Marcy sighed. "C'mon, Kate! You know that's not going anywhere. Why are you filling the air with low-grade news when you know I want the juicy stuff? Arthur is only going to watch the little guy for a couple of hours, ya know. Then," her hands flitted out to the sides, "he's off to the golf course."

"Excuse me?" Kate leaned in on one elbow. "What do you mean by 'it's not going anywhere'? I like Kyle just fine." Even after she'd said it, she knew it didn't sound the least bit believable. Marcy knew her better than she knew herself sometimes.

"First of all, I haven't met him. Secondly, the only conversations you tell me about are when you're trying to drag information out about that group you guys go to. I still don't understand your fascination with those people. I mean, you never really talk about how it's helping you through your grieving process, ya know? Why do you still go?"

Kate hadn't told Marcy about the note that made its way back to the counter on the day someone broke into her house and didn't plan to. She dodged the group question, opting for the lesser of two evils. "Kyle is really nice. I mean," she tried to think about what she liked about him. "He brought me coffee this morning at the garage sale. He's very thoughtful." Never mind that he said he brought it because Pat's coffee was watery, and he grabbed her one as an afterthought.

Marcy let her hands flop onto the table like dead fish. "Coffee? That's all you got?"

Kate knew the relationship would not go anywhere, and she came to a stark realization that she'd maybe been using Kyle; adding him to her pile of problems wasn't on the agenda. She honestly knew all along, but Marcy brought the idea to the forefront of her mind. Embarrassed, Kate snapped, "Why can't you just let me be happy seeing this guy for a while? Huh?" She dropped her eyes to the table. She always lashed out when she felt embarrassed or hurt. She did not have a way with words when she got upset, and Marcy knew it.

Marcy's eyebrows shot up. "Well, now that we know *that* isn't going anywhere..."

"I'm sorry, I didn't..."

Marcy raised her hands back to their rightful place for conversation. "Okay, okay. Apology accepted. Sheesh. Now can we talk juicy?" She grinned mischievously, tapping her fingers on the table.

"Okay, let me think of a good place to start."

The waitress brought the cheese sticks to the table. Before Kate could grab one, Marcy had half of one in her mouth. Kate shot her a look.

"What?" She gave Kate her best innocent look. "I'm just having one. Okay, so why don't you start with, um, Detective Peterson?"

"Oh." Kate had not even thought about talking about Alec Peterson. He fell low on the list of strange happenings for the week. He was, however, on the list. His absence bothered her. She had grown fond of him and his checking in on her. "Well, I haven't heard from him in a while. He said he was going to call me after he looked into another case. I even called and left messages for him."

"Weird," Marcy drew out the word while gnawing on a second cheese stick. "Did you leave him a message on his cell or at the precinct?"

"Both, kinda. I left a message on his cell, and then I talked to Fran at the precinct. She said she expected him back any day. I don't know. Maybe the other case was more complicated than he thought?"

"Maybe. Did Fran say she'd talked with him?"

"I don't know. I didn't ask." Kate regretted not digging more. Marcy had a way of asking questions in just the right way to get the answers she wanted. Often, in retrospect, Kate would think of all the things she could have said that would have made a conversation more productive.

A voice came from behind Kate. "Katherine? Hello, darling!" Kate turned to see the most unwelcome face she could have possibly anticipated. Everly wore a pastel pink jogging suit and had her streaky hair pulled into a ponytail. *As if she's ever worked out a day in her life,* Kate thought. She looked out of place in a small dive like Waltz, even dressed down.

"Hello, Everly. How are you?" Kate strained to keep her tone polite as she spoke through a forced smile. She had been avoiding the realtor's calls, childishly hoping that eventually, a different person would be assigned to Molly's house. Kate remembered her manners and held up her hand to introduce Marcy, but before she could, Everly interrupted.

"And Marcy! How lovely it is to see you again!"

"Hey," Marcy beamed. She held up the basket of cheese sticks. "Would you like to join us?"

Kate looked at Marcy, shocked that she seemed so acquainted with Everly. She looked back and forth between the two, feeling very much like someone should explain how the hell they knew each other. Neither one jumped at the opportunity, so Kate put her obvious question into words.

Kate shifted in her seat before speaking. "I didn't realize you two knew each other," she slid her gaze from Everly to Marcy. Her lack of a poker face wasn't lost on Marcy.

Marcy drew her eyebrows together. "Really, Kate? I thought..."

Everly jumped in. "Well, Marcy's name was on the emergency contacts for showing the house. I knew she had a spare key, too. I stopped by to visit her so I could put a face with the name. I hope I didn't step on anyone's toes. When you didn't return my calls, I

78

figured you must be out of town." Her apology seemed nice enough, but Everly's eyes reminded Kate of a snake in the grass, waiting to strike.

Kate tried to reign in her feelings. While she made no excuse for Everly's behavior during their first meeting, the woman's rudeness did not mean she couldn't sell a house. Everly's comments sent Kate in a tailspin that detoured her from the purpose of their interaction in the first place -- selling Molly's house. Kate had enough problems without allowing this one to linger. The sooner she worked with Everly, the sooner she would be out of the picture.

"I just didn't know. That's all." Kate felt her cheeks flush. Although she had good reasons for ghosting Everly, Marcy didn't know about any of that. That lifted the label of betrayal off their secret meeting.

Marcy could read Kate like a book and chimed in. "Well, you probably wouldn't want to join us after all. Our order should be out any minute."

"No problem!" Everly waved her hand, and her bracelets jingled. "I just wanted to say hello to you ladies. I hope you have a great weekend!"

Kate rolled her eyes when she realized the woman had high heels on with her workout clothes. What a fashion freak. She tried to imagine Everly on a treadmill, taking short staccato steps in her glamorous stilettos. The image made her smile to herself. Kate really didn't make any effort or know anything about fashion. She prided herself in being rather plain. Most days, she stuck to athletic shorts and a tank top. It directly reflected her true self, anyway. Who wants to look at someone adorned with the latest accessories and colors like that's all they have to offer? Of course, hating to dress up had its downsides, too. First impressions were important, and Marcy told her that if she didn't present herself more appropriately, people would begin to assume she didn't care about herself, which inevitably led to the this-is-why-you're-single discussion.

"Well, that was weird," Marcy said, pulling Kate from her thoughts.

"Yeah," Kate replied. "I'm sorry, I'm just...weird these days. I feel like I need to be watching my back, you know? It might be making me a little paranoid. I feel so stupid."

Marcy moved the cheese sticks out of the way for their pizza. "Well, Kate, I don't really think it is fair for you to feel stupid about being paranoid. First, someone killed your sister. Then, before you've even had a chance to grieve, someone breaks into your house! I can't say I understand what you're going through, but I think your reaction is merited."

"I guess." Kate had lost her desire to chat. The weight of her emotional exhaustion hung on her shoulders. What Marcy said rang true. She had been through a lot the past several weeks. Now she had to think about breaking things off with Kyle too.

Marcy kept talking, "You know, Everly said you are really lucky nobody stole anything. She said if you have to file a police report, it can hurt your odds of selling later."

Kate snapped out of her pity party. Her mind rolled quickly through her horrible interaction with the realtor. She cocked her head to the side, certain she'd never told Everly about the break-in. But if Marcy brought it up in conversation, that would explain it. She decided to prod a bit.

"Why was Everly talking about the break-in?"

Marcy didn't seem to notice that Kate's self-admitted paranoia had kicked back in. "Well," she turned her eyes to the ceiling. "Let me think. We were talking about Molly, and she mentioned how sad the whole situation was. I agreed and mentioned that Detective Peterson had come out to talk with you a while back about Molly's case.

"Then she said you were lucky it was your house that got broken into and not Molly's. It seems like Everly is quite fond of Molly's house. I guess she is a realtor, and that's her job. But she really carried on about how quaint it is."

Kate felt her skin crawl. Why was that weasel of a woman snooping in her life? She did not need that information to sell the house. Her story behind contacting Marcy sounded legitimate. If Everly reached out to Marcy to leverage information unrelated to selling Molly's house, Kate needed to know why.

"I'm glad she likes the house," Kate said, sprinkling parmesan cheese on her pizza. "I am ready to have that sold and behind me.

"Marcy, can you do me a favor?"

Marcy held a thumbs up out as she stuffed her mouth with pizza.

"Be careful around Everly. I don't like her very much. To be honest, I have been avoiding her. So just don't talk to her about me or Molly's case.

Marcy swallowed, "I really don't know where you are coming from on this, but I will be careful about what I say." She smiled at Kate and added, "Now can we get to the juicy stuff?"

~~~~~

Brodey plopped down on his bed. His last class of the day dragged on forever. He laid back with his hands behind his head and cleared his thoughts. Later, he would sit down and type his notes out. He typically did that right after class partially to help him remember the lecture and partially because his handwriting looked like chicken scratch. He found that if he waited too long, even he had a hard time deciphering his own hurried scribbling.

A knock came through the bathroom door. Brodey let out a sigh. Wyatt turned out to be a pretty nice guy. He had a lot of the same societal views that Brodey had. The more they talked, the more Brodey felt like he had finally met someone who understood exactly how he felt. That being said, Wyatt had a lot of hatred brewing about the world and all the people who made life tough for him. Although Brodey understood, he had moved on to a measured indifference about how people treated him. He had become accustomed to it or maybe desensitized. Wyatt still spoke from a place of hurt and anguish that someone must have the desire to work their way out of. Their weighty conversations about life typically rolled downhill quickly.

Not only that, but Thea had been coming around more often. Everything about her brightened his days. He loved the way she smiled at him, the way she teased him, and the way that she didn't feel the need to hide the fact that they dated. At first, Brodey figured she might want to hang out in private or just at night when no one could really see them walking around campus. She surprised him by meeting him outside and walking to class with him daily. He really enjoyed her company. Although Thea had a pretty face, her intelligence won him over. She didn't boast about it or shove it down anyone's throat. She didn't have anything to prove. He loved that she was comfortable in her own skin.

Brody shouted toward the door, "Come in!"

Wyatt sauntered through and said, "God, today just sucks, doesn't it?"

Brody propped himself up on his elbows. "I guess so." He'd learned early on not to argue with Wyatt's dark perspective on the world. Brodey understood how he felt, after all.

81

Wyatt lifted his finger to his forehead and pulled an imaginary trigger behind it. "If I have to listen to these people in my class one more day, I might just put myself out of my misery. They sit there and hold these philosophical discussions like they are so open-minded. Then, right after class, look at me like I'm crazy when I suggest we study together. Oh no!" he waved his black fingernails flamboyantly through the air, "Not the kid who isn't a jock! He might be gay or worse." He sat on the edge of Brodey's bed.

"What's worse than gay?" Brodey joked.

Wyatt squinted in his direction, "Hilarious, bro. How do you know I'm not?"

Brody shrugged a shoulder, "I don't. You hungry?" He reached into his bag for his wallet.

"I guess so," Wyatt replied morosely.

"Well, let's go get something to eat. I'll call Thea."

Wyatt visibly cringed. "Why does she need to come? Actually, let's just order some Chinese and eat here. We can get a movie or something."

Brodey tried not to let his friend offend him. "I haven't seen her all day and she leaves town this weekend, so I wanted to spend as much time with her as I could. You don't have to come if you don't want to."

"No, man, that's cool. I don't know why you spend so much time with her, anyway. She's way out of your league. How do you think you are going to make that work? Do you *really* believe she is into you?" Wyatt leaned on his knees and picked at the holes in his jeans that matched his chipping nail polish.

"I really don't think she's that good of an actress. She seems to really enjoy hanging out. I am telling you, I tried to push her away, and she kept coming back. I thought the same thing you do. At first, I just thought she wanted to buddy up so I would tutor her, but she is smart. She has a better GPA than I do. There really is nothing in it for her except...me."

Brodey texted Thea to let her know he was on his way to pick her up at the dorm while Wyatt continued his drudge report. "Well, whatever, man. I'm going to meet some friends online. I found a pretty cool forum. All the people on there just...get it. You heard of The Gathering of Souls?"

Brodey put his phone in his pocket. "Nope."

"Well, it is all these people who have had the same experiences. They're just done with the world. They're sick of how they're treated, and they're ready to take control of their lives. It's inspirational, really. My friend turned me onto them. You should check it out sometime."

"Sure," Brodey said. He knew an online whine-fest didn't sound like his current cup of tea, but he could always tell Wyatt that he checked it out later. "Well, I'm out. Call me if you change your mind."

Brodey quickly covered the distance to Thea's dorm. He smiled when he thought about her face lighting up at the sight of him. When she'd spotted him at Pag's the week before, her grin made him feel like the luckiest person in the room. He rounded the corner into the main entry, and the pep in his step fizzled out. Thea stood with her back to the entrance talking to some guy. He had on a black undershirt and jeans. He had a thin layer of scruff over his face, and his hair stood perfectly gelled.

Brodey thought the guy might be her ex-boyfriend, Mike. By the way Thea was acting, that seemed the most probable scenario. He knew their breakup didn't go so well, and Mike had a problem with the distance Thea tried to keep between them. Even her friends tried to convince her that they belonged together. They didn't seem to mind that meant she would have to leave Brodey out in the cold. Some of her friends were nice enough, but most of them were brats. While Thea did not condone their actions, she also did not tell them what to do. For the most part, those cliques had plenty of people in them who were not really friends, but just part of the same group and, therefore, by happenstance, acquaintances.

"Oh, hey, Bro." He hadn't heard Megan approaching from behind. He did not particularly care for her, and the feeling was mutual. "What are you doing standing out here all by your lonesome?"

"My name is Brodey," he sighed. She often used her pet name for him as a jab.

"Haven't you heard? Thea and Mike are getting back together." She tilted her head toward them. "Seems Mike has a lot that she's been missing, you know?"

Brodey rolled his eyes. If she thought she could scare him off with some petty gossip, she had another thing coming to her. "Whatever, Megan. Can you just go tell her I'm out here waiting for her? I don't want to get into anything with Mike."

She laughed. "Why? Maybe because you'd lose?"

He stood his ground. "Never mind. I'll just go in and get her myself."

Before he could turn around, Megan gasped. "Well," she drew the word out, "that is going to be pretty hard to do, I think."

Wyatt turned around to see Mike and Thea kissing. He had one hand on the small of her back and the other on the back of her head. Brodey's stomach dropped to his feet. He turned away and felt his cheeks burn. Under Megan's heavy gaze, he took a couple of breaths to try to calm himself. He let each one out slower than the last. Even with his effort to control his emotions, he felt hot tears roll down his face.

Megan giggled. "You had to know it wouldn't last all that long, Bro." She put extra emphasis on her pet name for him. "Looks like you just don't have what it takes to make her happy."

Brodey looked at the pavement. "Don't tell her I saw this. I don't want her to know." With that, he walked back to his dorm.

His mind reeling, he kept his eyes on the ground to avoid eye contact with anyone else as he briskly walked back to the dorm. He reached up and wiped the tears away so Wyatt would not know he had been crying. *God. I am so stupid!* He thought. *She could at least have the decency to tell me she didn't want to see me anymore. She didn't have to go all slutty behind my back. Just TELL me! 'Brodey, you suck, I don't like you. Turns out dorks were just a phase for me.'*

He stormed into his room and then through the bathroom into Wyatt's room without knocking. Wyatt looked up from his computer with half a mouthful of chips.

"You were right," Brodey said. "Today does suck."

"Perfect timing," Wyatt said through his mouthful of food.

Chapter 10

Kate took the rest of the weekend and the following week in stride. She ran with Jake, hedged Kyle's calls, and she even skipped a Helping Hands meeting. She already had a message from Blanch that she promptly deleted without skipping a beat. She felt like she needed time off from her problems. It seemed to work, too. She felt lighter somehow, like a weight had been lifted from her heart. The nightmares still haunted her some nights, but not all of them. It really seemed like they stemmed from her stress.

Although avoiding Kyle didn't really solve the problem, Kate hated conflict. She felt like avoidance was the best tactic. He left a few messages and texted, but after a few days, he seemingly gave up.

Fran called, letting Kate know that Detective Peterson expected to come back to town shortly, and asked her to arrange a meeting between them. She couldn't explain it, but Kate felt a sinking feeling that he hadn't contacted her himself. She had come to enjoy his calls and felt a little more at ease with him. She worked out a meeting time with Fran and put it on her calendar with a smiley face. She hoped for good news about developments in the case.

She opened her front door, and her heart skipped a beat at the sight of Molly's car. Like a ray of sunshine, the bright yellow Volkswagen Beetle cheered up the curb. It took a moment for her to remember that Molly wouldn't be popping out of the driver's side door. Kate sighed at the usual ache that accompanied thinking of her sister. She also chided herself for leaving the car there to fool her each time she stepped out of the house. Selling it would be bittersweet. She welcomed the reprieve from a constant reminder of her loss, but another part of Molly would wither away. She hopped into her car and tried to shake off her grey mood on her way to a nearby store to grab a new ball for Jake.

She noticed that, although he always loved the woods in her backyard, he wouldn't venture into them lately. She thought he may have seen a snake or something that freaked him out, or perhaps another dog had come through the woods and marked its territory. She tried to ease his mind by going deep into the woods and calling for him, but he wouldn't budge past a certain point of the yard. So, she did what any reasonable owner would do. She threw his favorite ball back there. Her brilliant plan backfired when she realized he wouldn't chase it, but he knew it was lost in the briars. He paced the yard all week, brown eyes probing the shadows, pondering how to get it without stepping across his imaginary line of safety. That part didn't bother her as much as his incessant whining every time he looked out the back door.

She took her time walking through the pet store, stopping to look at the puppies and kittens. Like most days, it was a small thing that reminded her of Molly. Her Grams must have told Molly a thousand times that they couldn't have pets in the house, but Molly insisted on coming to the pet store "just to look." Grams fell for the ploy a couple of times before catching on to her sister. Molly couldn't help but push harder for a pet, depending heavily on big-eyed puppies in her lap to convince Grams, too. But she never did.

Kate browsed the pet toys and picked up one that had a hole in it to stuff treats. Naturally, she had tried to find the old toy herself and dejectedly left the woods with nothing to show for it but a couple of ticks and burrs on her socks. The treat-filled toy would be a good option. He would never approve of anything but his original precious ball, but maybe with the treats...

"Kate!" Kyle's voice filled the aisle.

Oh my God, why? Kate thought. With her shoulders nearly touching her earlobes, she turned to see him speedily approaching her before she had a chance to dart off.

"Wow! Where ya been? I almost stopped by your house last night, but I didn't want you to feel like I was being pushy."

"Yeah, uh," *Why can't I just be a good liar?* "This week has been so crazy, and I just, uh, haven't checked my messages."

Kyle stared at her for an uncomfortable amount of time. "Did I do something to offend you? Are you okay, Kate?"

She dismissively waved a hand. "Yeah, yeah, I'm fine. I just really need a break from everything right now." She saw that he needed a better response than that, and she knew he deserved it. "It's just that...well, I don't think I really need anything new right now. I need time to just grieve and get my life back to normal."

Kyle whispered, "Are you really breaking up with me in the pet aisle? I mean, really, Kate. We get along so well, and I'm crazy about you. You know I would give you a break if that's what you need."

She played with the edge of the price tag on the toy. "Kyle, we were never officially together. You are great. You just aren't exactly what I need right now. This was never anything serious, and I don't think we can even classify it as a breakup."

"What do you need right now?" He asked.

"I..." she stammered, "can we just talk about this another time?" She walked briskly past him and toward the checkout lane.

"No," he replied, following her. "Look, let's go grab some lunch. I'd really like to hear what you're thinking, and I feel like you're being a little brash."

"I already ate," she said, paying the cashier.

Kyle followed her into the parking lot. "Kate, please, just talk to me."

She gathered that he wasn't going to give up easily, so she tried to finish the conversation with no hope for him to hold onto. "Kyle, I don't want to talk about it. I know what I want in life, and it isn't you. I just filled the space around Molly's death with you, and I feel really bad about it. But that doesn't mean I need to continue feeding my mistake. I'm sorry, but I just want to be friends." The truth sounded awful. His eyes darted away from her as the sting of her words hit him. It pained her, but she knew leaving him a sliver of hope would do him no good.

Dejected, he stood to the side of her car. She could have rolled down the window to see if he had anything to add, but she really didn't want to drag it out. She hurriedly backed out.

A loud thump reverberated from behind, and she slammed on her breaks. Had she hit something? She looked up at Kyle, who stood in her empty parking space. His eyes were as wide as dinner plates. She slammed her car into park and jumped out as quickly as she could. Panic mounted when she rounded the back of her car. A girl laid under her bumper, moaning. She struggled to get up, wincing.

"Oh my God!" Kate yelled. "I'm so sorry! Are you okay? Is there any blood? Here, let me help you." She leaned down and extended her hand. The girl sat silently with wild eyes shadowed by dark hair that fell like curtains around her face. Her palm traveled down the length of her leg, probing for an injury.

Kate thought twice about her hasty offer to help the girl up. "Never mind, just don't move. Your leg looks broken, and you are probably in shock. You don't have to talk. I am going to call 911."

She grabbed her phone from her pocket and turned to Kyle. "I didn't see her. I just backed out without looking. God, I am so stupid." She felt queasy.

Kyle's pale face spoke volumes, but he still muttered, "I didn't see her either. It's like she just...appeared. Was she there the whole time?"

Exasperated, Kate sighed, "Okay, whatever. Just talk to her until I can get an ambulance here." She began dialing with her shaky fingers.

"No!" the girl uttered, barely audible.

Kate turned just as the girl worked herself halfway into a standing position and snatched the phone. She ended the call and tossed it to the side. It clattered noisily across the pavement. "No police." Her words came out contorted.

Kate and Kyle exchanged glances. Kate couldn't help but notice the color had left Kyle's lips, and he regarded the helpless victim with caution. He had his body turned in preparation to flee the scene at any minute. Kate decided to try to reason with the girl, as Kyle clearly did not have the right state of mind to do so.

She turned back to the stranger and took in her rugged appearance. Her army jacket looked like hand-me-down tissue paper, and her hair stuck to itself in different spots on her head. Kate tried to keep her panic from bubbling into her voice and took a timid step forward, "Honey, you are obviously hurt. You may even have a serious concussion. We need to get you to a hospital. I can take you there without calling the police. Would you like that?"

She looked from Kate to Kyle and back again. "I think I'll be okay." She gradually put weight on the leg that appeared to be broken. The bone and gristle ground together audibly.

Kate's stomach turned at the sound. "Oh, no, honey, you aren't okay. What is your name?" She hoped to use conversation as a distraction long enough to stop her from trying to walk on her injury. Clearly, she had no idea of the extent of the damage.

"Ashley," she responded. She still had her weight on the injured leg, and she took a step away, which produced more crackling noises in her pant leg. Surprisingly, her face remained steady. Her expression revealed no hint of pain.

Kate could feel heat traveling up her neck and into her face. She swallowed hard. "Okay, Ashley. I am going to ask my friend here to go into the store and tell them what happened. That will give us a couple of minutes to get you into the car and on the way to the hospital. We don't have to notify the police. I can just drop you off at the doors. Deal?" She knew the staff in the hospital would most likely file a police report anyway, but she hoped Ashley wouldn't think that far ahead. Kate nodded her head at Kyle, who hastily welcomed the opportunity to leave and moved instantly toward the store.

She saw him reach the door out of the corner of her eye and turned her attention back toward Ashley, who stood with her head cocked to the side, observing her. Ashley's piercing gaze gave Kate pause. She suddenly realized that asking Kyle to leave may have been a mistake. The girl's dark eyes reflected moving shadows not present around them. *No, that's impossible,* Kate thought, *stop letting this situation freak you out.*

She took a cleansing breath and resolved herself once more to attempt to coax the girl into the car. Before she opened her mouth to speak, Ashley closed the distance between the two of them with cat-like grace. She stopped close enough for Kate to feel her breath in her ear and said, "Well, then take me to the hospital, *child.*" Her voice rang with confidence and clarity leaving behind no trace of fear despite the accident that should have left her leg useless. A sideways smirk danced on her lips while her shadowy eyes waited for Kate's response.

Child? Kate felt her breath coming shakily out of her mouth. She tried to control the next breath, but she trembled anyway. She caught herself looking toward the store, hoping that Kyle would exit at any moment. She could not see beyond the glare of the sun on the doors, and she felt her heart sink when she realized he must not be watching. Desperation mounted inside her. She chanced a glance back in Ashley's direction only to find that she had noiselessly moved to the passenger side of the car. Kate's feet were glued to the concrete, her arms felt like noodles, and she most certainly had a new idea about where to send this estranged person for help. Everything inside her screamed for her to just run to the store, but she couldn't. This incident was her fault, and she needed to get the young lady, no matter how insane, to help.

Kate went to the passenger side door to open it. Ashley removed her army coat and handed it over before dropping her tiny body into the seat without the slightest regard for her injury. It seemed she could feel nothing at all. Kate closed the door, and on the way to the driver's side, she tossed the jacket into the back seat. She slid behind the steering wheel and cranked the engine, glancing longingly once more toward the store in hopes of catching a glimpse of Kyle coming out with more help. Nothing.

"Well," she started as she put the car in reverse, "Looks like it's just you and…" a squeak popped out of Kate's mouth when she saw the empty seat next to her. "Holy mother…of…what the hell?!" She craned her neck to check every window, but she didn't see Ashley at all. She hadn't even heard her close the door behind her! She popped out of the car like a canned snake, checking in every direction. Just in case, she walked slowly around to the passenger side to make sure Ashley hadn't tried to get out and fallen due to her wound. After confirming that she hadn't lost her mind with one final scan of the parking lot, Kate accepted an impossible truth.

The girl had disappeared.

~~~~~

"What do you mean she just disappeared?" the cop asked Kate for what felt like the millionth time.

Kate looked down at her feet for answers she didn't have. This looked crazy, it sounded insane, and nobody regarded her story as having even an ounce of truth to it. Kyle had called 911 in the store, which she couldn't fault him for; however, she didn't know how to explain what happened. Every detail she recited scribbled through a pen with extreme scrutiny until she got to the disappearing part. She couldn't blame the officer; she had a hard time believing the facts herself.

She sighed, "I'm sorry. I don't know what else to tell you. That's exactly what happened. She was there, and I glanced away for a moment, and then," Kate lifted her arms to show him the empty seat, "poof. She's gone."

The cop stared at her dubiously for a moment, opened his mouth to ask another question, but then changed his mind. He popped his notebook with his pen and put them both in his pocket.

A young man walked up behind him and said, "Sir, we have the video you asked for. Come on into the store, and we will play it back for you."

Part of Kate wanted to rejoice, but the young man's demeanor conveyed disappointment.

"What is it?" the older cop asked. "Can you see them on the surveillance tape, or can't you?"

"It's strange, sir. I would rather you just take a look for yourself."

"Come with me," the cop said to Kate. "Let's see if we can make heads or tails of this situation, shall we?" He looked at her with pity. She didn't know whether to be happy that his grilling session had ended or upset that he clearly thought she belonged in a straitjacket. He probably wanted to watch her reaction when the video somehow proved she'd lost her marbles. Other than that, she could not imagine why he would want her to see it.

They made their way back into the store's tiny security room. Kate tried to stuff herself into the side so she wouldn't have to stand up against anyone else. The younger officer pulled the video up on the small monitor. He pressed play and stepped back for the other two to see. The grainy picture showed a wide view of the parking lot. She could see herself and Kyle walking up to her car. She felt the angst of that conversation all over again. Even on the grainy video, anyone could see what was happening between her and Kyle. Embarrassed for yet another thing happening in her life, she silently watched the end of their quarrel and held onto the hope that they would understand the story once they saw it for themselves.

Just as the video showed Kate shutting her car door, everything on the screen fuzzed. The younger cop said, "This interruption to the feed happens for a solid 10 minutes." He fast-forwarded and hit pause when the picture showed Kate standing outside her car.

Kate thought her head might explode. The universe hadn't done her any favors today, and her entire week of blissfulness just unraveled right before her eyes. How could the video possibly stop at the exact moment she needed to show them? She felt hollow inside and knew now that she could not prove her story. It was her word against the laws of nature. Kyle hadn't seen the girl disappear from her car, and he had downplayed how frightened he was when he relayed his story to the police. She looked up at the officer's face and tried to discern what he thought about the whole string of events.

He turned to her and said, "So, you forgot to mention you broke up with your boyfriend right before this occurred."

"I, uh, didn't think that mattered," she stammered.

"Of course it matters," his big husky voice filled the room. "I do believe you are having the worst day ever." He raised his eyebrows at her, "And this video is a rather unfortunate dead end." His tone took a softer turn.

She just stared back, unsure how to reply.

He smiled tightly and nodded to himself. "We will send out a description to local clinics and hospitals. If she was hurt as badly as you described, she's gonna turn up. Until then," he turned to her, "just be careful."

Chapter 11

Ashley approached awkwardly on her crunching, broken leg. Kate tried to back away but felt the cold metal of the car behind her. There was nowhere left to go. Black, piercing eyes dug into Kate's soul. Shadows passed like clouds through the darkness behind Ashley. Kate looked up, noticing only now that the moon shined brightly on them. A nagging feeling told her it should not be night in this memory. On the fringes of her mind, a thought tried to creep in, but she could not grasp it.

"I know who you are," Ashley whispered, breaking the silence. She stood so close that Kate could feel her breath again, cold as the creepy gleam in her eyes. Kate squeezed her eyes shut tightly.

"This is wrong," Kate mumbled. She opened her eyes, hoping to have changed her surroundings, but it hadn't. Her shaky legs sent tremors through her body. She could just run away. She felt confident that Ashley wouldn't catch her, but a terrifying thought crept into her mind like a burrowing insect. Ashley did not need to run after her because Ashley had an otherworldly essence. She had, after all, disappeared into thin air.

Ashley appeared amused. She snarled her lip into a devious smile. "I have something for you," she said, reaching into her pocket.

Kate closed her eyes again, shouting, "I don't want anything! I don't want anything from you. Just go away." Her sweaty fists shook at her sides. She mustered every ounce of inner strength to stop this. Finally, she grasped the concept her mind had been trying to feed her. "This is a dream," she said aloud. She felt the relief sweep over her.

She opened her eyes, fully expecting to see her perfectly safe bedroom, but Ashley still stood in front of her. Kate felt something cold in her hand, and against her instinct to keep her gaze on Ashley, she risked a glance down. A cylinder-shaped object had

94

somehow appeared in her clenched fist. She held it up to observe. Ornate swirls of dark and light metal wove down the core of the cylinder. It looked like a baton she had seen used in relay races, but its length barely exceeded the palm of her hand from wrist to fingertip. The metals appeared so opposite in nature that she did not know how they could both occupy the same space. Each end had a cone-shaped metal cap. One end boasted the light metal, and the other end was constructed with the darker metal.

An ominous shape in her peripheral vision brought her back from her thoughts. She tried to look but saw nothing. She could feel things slinking around them in the darkness like ghosts. She looked back at Ashley, who had somehow moved further from her. The shadows seemed to be growing more and more active. Although ominous, they seemingly presented no immediate threat. She finally stopped her attempts to catch a full glimpse of the ghostly figures and opted to address the mystery of the metal object instead.

Kate raised it in her clenched fist toward Ashley. "What is this?" She yelled. Only now that she had to raise her voice did she realize the wind between them had picked up. Ashley's long dark hair whipped violently around her pale face.

She smiled eerily back at Kate, "I have another gift for you." She made no effort to amplify her voice like Kate had to. The lanky girl lifted her arms to the sky and laughed.

"Stop! Just stop it!" Kate tried to scream, but the whirlwind of shadows stole her voice.

Kate woke from her fitful sleep. She sat up with sweat-soaked hair sticking to her face in wet streaks. Her nightmares had new ammunition. For months, she battled memories of Molly and disturbing visions of her, but those nightmares seemed normal. Kate reasoned that anyone mourning sudden loss would dream about the same thing. But this dream wove its way into her core.

She felt herself nodding back off and quickly threw her covers off to get up for the day. She already dreamed the same thing three times, so it stood to reason that she would only fall back into the horror of reliving a reunion with Ashley.

She picked up her phone and decided that 4:00 am could not have come soon enough. Jake raised his head from the floor but did not

95

bother to stand. Kate put her head in her hands and said aloud, "Lots of coffee today, buddy. Lots of coffee."

She staggered down the stairs, still trying to shake the fog of sleep from her head. Her mounting fear felt like seeds falling from a bag with a hole in the bottom. With each passing moment, more seeds escaped the bag, but she couldn't replenish them fast enough. The hole kept growing larger and larger. Letting the sobs rack her body, she cried for the answers she didn't have. She cried for Molly. She allowed her fear to bubble up through her cracks of doubt.

Clamoring to control her life only caused her to lose control completely. She tried to assure herself that her paranoia had no foundation, but everything pointed her back here. No one could be trusted. Desperate and isolated, her sobs filled the empty house. The answers she sobbed for did not echo back. What did she expect? Discovering her path back to sanity might take a while. Jake leaned into her leg and looked up at her with his sweet, comforting eyes. She let her other hand graze the top of his head a few times before making her way into the kitchen.

"Well, boy," she said, shuffling to the couch with her coffee, "maybe we can play with your new ball." She glanced around the living room for her shopping bag but must have left it in her car. After everything with the police, she had returned and hastily made her way into the safety and stability of her home. She had hoped the familiar setting of her living room would help anchor her back to something that felt real and completely forgot that she had a reason for going to the store. She had no desire to go out into the darkness of early morning to find his ball, but needing the therapeutic redundancy of throwing something over and over drove her to the door.

Upon seeing the quiet night shroud, she felt childish for fearing the gloom. Her bare feet clapped the ground as she covered the distance quickly while trying to pretend she was not fazed by her nightmares. She attempted to walk at a regular pace in order to partially convince herself that she had nothing to fear. The beep of her car unlocking intruded on the stillness. When she opened the door, the dome light revealed an unwelcome surprise.

The green army jacket laid wadded in the back seat. Kate's breath caught in her throat. She stood rigidly, afraid to stick her head into the car. She immediately thought of calling the police but then reconsidered because of the time. How could she explain her failure to mention the evidence in her back seat? Furthermore, wouldn't they want to know why she discovered her 'accidental omission' of evidence at four in the morning? She reached in with two fingers and gently peeled the jacket from the seat. She would just grab the toy and call the police at a more reasonable hour. A jacket was hardly a reason to wake people up if they could handle it later. But what if they viewed her actions as suspicious? Could they think she purposely concealed the fact that Ashley threw it into the back seat? She checked the street behind her, second-guessing her decision to wait.

Her mind cranked through her options, but before she could choose one, something fell from the pocket of the coat and clanked onto the floor. Relieved, Kate assumed she had rustled the toy free. She leaned in and blindly felt around on the floorboard for it. Her fingers brushed the surface of...*something*. She passed back over and grabbed the object. A cylindrical, metal object chilled her hand. Bringing it closer to her face, her body turned to ice. In her hand, she held the object from her dream.

~~~~~

Kelsey's fingers pounded the letters on her keyboard more frantically. For weeks, she'd been sneaking in the back door of The Gathering's site with a hacking code she'd designed herself. Her fiery red hair wrapped around a pencil she'd hastily stashed on her head.

The door across the room opened, and Detective Alec Peterson walked in, pinching the bridge of his nose. He sighed, "Tell me you've got something, Kels."

"More than something." She popped her head up from behind her screens. "We're about to intercept a kill."

Alec visibly perked up, new life filling his bones. "Tell me you're serious."

"It's this kid who's been active this week in particular. I think you should pay him a visit. He's going for it. If we're quick, we can stop him."

"This is a bad idea," a boy said from the other side of the room with a new computer set up.

Alec shot a look at Kelsey. "Who is that?"

"I needed help," was all Kelsey would offer.

~~~~~

97

The early dawn reached across the lawn in front of Brodey's dorm. He smiled at the thought that dawn symbolizes new beginnings. Although he felt certainty in his head, his heart ached with his new decision to take control of his future. He wondered how long it would be until someone found his body. Probably immediately since people would hear the gunshot.

Wyatt truly understood how Brodey felt. He had spent weeks explaining his membership to The Gathering and how everyone there understood people like them. Brodey became a regular blogger on the site, receiving hundreds of responses daily. He read in-depth and heartfelt stories about other members who got their ticket to board the train. They took control of their own lives, and he admired them for it. Not all of them executed their plans in the same way. Some had elaborate designs that had multifaceted steps to their final moments. Others did it with haste, simply swallowing the nearest bottle of pills they had. Most, however, did it with a mentor or friend.

Wyatt had become a guide and mentor. He taught Brodey how to write in a fashion that attracted readers and won them over to their cause. He put Brodey at ease about his choices leading up to this very morning. Because of that, Brodey felt ready and at peace. His goodbye letter had already received enormous praise from his peers. He felt pride for the inspiration he would bring to their lives. His knowledge that fellow members would celebrate the step he took to display his bravery gave him resolve.

The bathroom door quietly clicked as Wyatt came into the room. He reverently laid his backpack on the bed next to Brodey and pulled two guns from the center pouch. He looked at Brodey, waiting for him to nod his consent that he was ready.

Wyatt took a deep breath. "Are you ready to be a hero?"

Brodey studied the gun in his hand. He nodded and steeled himself for the task at hand.

"On the count of three," Wyatt said. "We go together."

Brodey lifted the cold metal to his temple and closed his eyes. He had never felt so sure of anything.

"One, two...."

A loud *CLANG* interrupted the silence, and Brodey dropped his gun. For a moment, he thought Wyatt had fired his gun early. He turned to look at Wyatt, who had his gun pointed toward the door to Brodey's room. Brodey followed his gaze to a rather unpleasant sight.

A girl, disheveled and scraggly, stood in the doorway. Sweat broke over her brow, and her long dark hair shadowed most of her face. She stood awkwardly, seeking support from the door frame with both arms. Clearly, one of her legs was severely injured.

"Hello, Wyatt," Ashley purred. "You're going to wish you had let me in when I came to you in the alley." Her body quivered under her as she depended on some unseen force to keep moving. She let out a low, unearthly growl. "This body won't last much longer, and we have much to discuss."

~~~~~

Kate sipped her third coffee of the morning. She sat perched on the edge of her couch, studying the object she had found in her car. Her cell phone lay next to her leg. She picked it up and sat it back down several times just trying to decide what to do. She picked it up again, scrolling to Alec Peterson's number. Perhaps he would shed some light on how she could explain to the police what happened. That would require him to answer, though. To her knowledge, he had not yet resurfaced from investigating other deaths that bore resemblance to Molly's. Giving it to the police also meant that she would not know the purpose of the object. Although it was hard to admit to herself, she did not want to relinquish it until she understood why a demented stranger wanted her to have it.

A small rumble pulled her attention from her phone back to the table. Did the object just...*move*? She slowly reached up and rolled it back. She left her index finger on it for a moment before snatching it from the table. Best just to hold it so her mind could not play tricks on her.

The doorbell rang, and Kate froze. She hadn't called anyone. She expected no guests. What if Ashley had found her? She looked back to the object, wondering if it could have some kind of tracking ability. How could she know what it was for? She instantly felt foolish for bringing it into her home.

She walked swiftly to the door and grabbed the handle. At the last moment, she realized she still held the object and hastily tucked her hand behind her back.

She peeked out the door, and in the early morning light, she could see unruly hair, a wrinkly t-shirt, and loosely laced boots that barely dangled on the legs of their owner.

"Kate!"

"Fin? What are you doing here? How—how do you know where I live? What..."

"No time to explain," the words tumbled out of his mouth like water bursting from a dam. He pressed his thin frame through the crack in her door. Startled at his entry, she backed away from him, still holding her hand behind her back. He gently closed the door and locked the deadbolt, then turned and held out his hands, "This is going to sound crazy, but..." His gaze fell on her arm behind her.

"Kate," he cautiously whispered. "What do you have behind your back?" Without shifting his gaze from her, he tried to inconspicuously search for the door handle behind his back. Under his breath, he whispered something about being too late.

"I — none of your business," she stammered. "What the Hell are you doing in my house? Who just shows up unannounced like this?" She swallowed hard. "Why did you lock the door behind you?" She didn't want him to know that she felt threatened, but how could he not know? Who barged into homes, locking doors behind them?

Abandoning hope of finding the door handle, Fin held up both hands. "I'm an unarmed old man. I am not here to hurt you. Understand?"

Kate eyed him up and down but kept her hand behind her back. Why did it seem that *he* felt unsafe? "No," she replied.

He sighed, appearing exasperated. "We don't have time for this, I have to talk to you, and you are probably going to think I'm crazy..."

She cut him off, saying, "Oh, I think you're crazy. And frankly, I have enough crazy going on in my life right now." She took a step back. "And I think you should leave." Her voice sounded shakier than she wanted it to, but she tried to sound as firm as possible. Jake, who had been sitting behind her complacently, stood at the sound of fear in her voice. He glanced up at her and then at Fin, who he had apparently decided presented no threat. He let out a small whimper.

Instead of turning to leave like she expected him to, he took two steps toward her and shouted urgently, "What do you have behind your back?"

~~~~~

Wyatt stood from the bed, keeping his gun aimed toward the girl in the doorway.

100

The girl tilted her head toward Brodey, "Well, don't you want to know why he hasn't shot me yet? All mentors follow protocol, don't they?" She shifted her questioning gaze to Wyatt.

He did not respond but curled his lips into a line. For a few moments, no one spoke. Finally, Wyatt said, "Brodey, pick up your gun and shoot her."

Before Brodey could move, a guttural laugh echoed from the girl's direction. Terror drove Brodey's pulse so quickly that he could hear it in his eardrums. Judging by Wyatt's demeanor, Brodey could easily deduce that they were not friends.

"Why don't you just shoot me?" She cackled, pointing her gun to Wyatt. When she removed her hand from the door, her stance seemed to become unstable, but her confidence did not waiver. One of her legs made a popping noise.

"You know why," he replied through clenched teeth.

"I know," she drawled. "Does he?" She indicated Brodey with her gaze.

Brodey looked back and forth between the two of them, still too stunned to respond.

"It's full of blanks, you incompetent ape," she said, rolling her eyes.

He looked back at Wyatt, eyebrows furrowed. "What?"

Wyatt's brow glistened. Ignoring Brodey's question, he addressed the girl. "Well, at least I didn't botch my mentorship on my own. You had to murder a woman to collect her soul when she should have willingly taken her own life. And now, here you are, interrupting my mentorship to make sure I am not successful. Still reeling from your recent failure, aren't you?" He shrugged one shoulder, setting his useless gun to the side. "Not that it matters. I can see our masters are doing quite well with torturing you in what remains of your pathetic existence."

The girl unnaturally walked over to Wyatt and grabbed him by his shirt collar. She pulled him close enough to whisper but kept her gaze on Brodey. Her eyes shimmered into darkness, and her hair slowly picked up a bit as if she stood in a light breeze. She lightly kissed Wyatt's cheek and said, "You are mistaken. We are much older than your masters, and they will pay the same price you now pay. You aren't collecting souls -- you're stealing them from the king by intercepting them unnaturally." She licked the edges of her teeth. "He's not happy about it."

She turned with Wyatt so that Brodey could see his face, pale and horrified. His eyes registered an understanding that worse than death awaited him.

Brodey reached for his gun, but on his way to the floor, something more powerful than gravity slammed his body down onto the tile. It felt like a car parked on him, pinning him down. He tried to lift his arm unsuccessfully. He could only watch as the girl grabbed Wyatt by the throat and drained the life from his body. His complexion turned grey, and his eyes lost their light. Slowly, they shifted out of focus. When she took her hand from his throat, Wyatt fell to the ground like a rag doll. Over her palm, a ball of light hovered. It stole all other light from the room, and Brodey's eyes burned. He tried to close them but could not.

"Careful," she said in a low whisper. "If you look at a soul's pure light for too long, it can blind you."

The girl closed her eyes and threw her head back. Darkness appeared in her hands, first accompanying and then enveloping the light. The dark sphere remained suspended in the air for a brief moment before it disappeared, releasing the girl's body with a jolt. She fell limply across Wyatt's lifeless body. Finally able to move, Brodey scrambled over to them. Just as he feared, Wyatt was dead. The now frail-looking girl let out a long breath. Brodey pushed her body away from him with his feet. She made a desperate sound, turning her face toward him. Her eyes filled with tears that ran down her ashen face.

"Please, help me," she hoarsely whispered.

Still afraid she might hurt him, Brodey moved slowly for his phone in his pocket. She passively watched through glassy, but human, eyes. He dialed 911.

~~~~~

Fin backed squarely into the door with wide eyes. His face had gone pale. Kate opened her mouth to ask him what was happening, but nothing came out. The room had become a vacuum. Jake leapt away from her, snarling. She looked at Fin with questioning eyes, fearful to speak, lest her voice betray her again with silence. He simply stared behind her, muttering inaudibly, eyes wide.

The object in her hand grew warm, and a ringing filled the air. A gray light shone from behind her. She yanked her hand around to release or throw it, but she could not let go. The metals began to individually illuminate. Darkness and light emanated in swirls from her hand. She tried again in vain to drop it. She opened her mouth, but the vacuum stole her scream from the air as if the scream never existed. For a moment, she thought she must still be in bed dreaming. That certainly explained Fin's odd visit and the enigmatic object from her car. She frantically tried to wake herself.

One of the dark swirls of metal shifted its appearance, mimicking the light metal. A shock wave moved through the room in the form of dark shadows, knocking over pictures and lifting the curtains. Her ears popped. Kate finally released the object from her hand and backed into the corner like a frightened animal as it rolled to a stop between her and Fin.

Fin took inventory of his arms, legs, abdomen, and finally, his head. He turned in a circle and then patted himself down once more. A look of relief washed over his face. He then looked from the floor to her several times. "Where did you get that, Kate?" He asked with biting words.

She shook her head, still unwilling to trust her voice. Her tousled hair bounced across her shoulders. She leaned against the wall and released the breath she had been holding in. She had finally come to terms with the fact that this was not a dream at all.

Fin ran his hand through his wild hair and paced back and forth a few times. He chose his next words carefully, searching for a question she would answer. "How long have you had it?"

Tears filled Kate's eyes. She replied, "I don't understand what is happening." She lifted her hands to her face, blocking the room from view.

His voice rose. "Don't *play* with me, Kate. I want to know the truth. Can you be honest with me?"

Her hands dropped, but she nodded fiercely. She had to trust *someone*. Might as well trust the only person who would believe what just happened because he also witnessed it.

"Who knows about this? Who have you told?" He began.

"No one."

"How long have you had it?"

"Not long."

"Who have you used it on?"

She puzzled for a moment. "I don't understand the question."

He spoke harsher. "Who have you used it on? How many people have you killed?" He pointed accusingly to the object as if that would clarify.

She put both hands up in front of her. "I haven't killed anyone! What are you talking about?"

Chapter 12

Brodey sat outside the dorm, his head buried in his hands. When the officers arrived, he had no concept of how long he'd been sitting there, listening to the girl cry. They tried to ask him questions, but he just stared into their faces; the only response he could muster was the same thing he'd repeated to the 911 operator. "She killed him. She just took the life right out of his body. He's gone."

The paramedics tended to the girl, who frantically shouted, "He was a horrible person! He was going to kill that boy. He was going to kill him! They stopped the murder. Please, they'll come for me again! They're coming for me again! Don't let them inside me!"

As two gurneys rolled out the front door, one zipped in a body bag, the other flanked by paramedics, an officer standing nearby picked up his cellphone. He paced back and forth, explaining the situation to the other person on the line. Brodey overheard him say, "The young man who dialed 911 did not just find the bodies. We believe he may be a witness."

A moment passed as he listened to the response. "No, sir, not yet. We will do that soon. He seems to be in shock." The officer lifted his hat from his head, wiping sweat from his forehead. "There's something else," he said, his tone hushed. "Is Peterson back in town yet?" He turned, pacing away, and Brodey couldn't hear much more of the conversation.

A hand on his shoulder tore him from his thoughts. He looked up into Thea's eyes. A female officer stood with her. "Brodey," she said, her eyes filled with compassion. She sat down next to him. Brodey turned his gaze back to his lap, pitying himself. He had a girlfriend who had cheated on him and a best friend who tried to dupe him into killing himself. Some life.

But I am alive, a voice spoke in his head.

"I've been calling and leaving messages for weeks," Thea said. "Did you get any of them? I texted, too."

Brodey didn't respond. He'd deleted everything after the first week. While she didn't deny that Mike kissed her, she adamantly denied that she kissed back. Most of her messages pleaded that he call her and let her explain. Wyatt, the new voice in Brodey's life, argued that she had already deceived him, and he did not need to open himself up to anything else she had to say.

And Brodey believed him. Everything Wyatt sold him he bought because of the heartbreak Thea had caused. Joining The Gathering, taking his own life, and convincing others to take theirs; he did it all from a place of pain and anger. Now he doubted himself, and he doubted Wyatt's motives. Why had he lied?

The other officer slid his phone back into his pocket and turned. He looked mildly alarmed at Thea's presence and motioned the female officer over. He heard her say that Brodey's family hadn't responded to any calls, but Thea said that she knew him well. "We need him to tell us what happened," she whispered. "We can't do that if he doesn't snap out of it. You know as well as I do that a stranger in an interrogation room won't be nearly as successful as a close friend when it comes to bringing him back from the edge."

Brodey, sullen and still pitying himself, wondered what edge she thought he needed pulling back from. He felt very grounded and sane, which made explaining what he had just witnessed nearly impossible. He knew the moment he gave a statement he would sound quite the opposite of sane. He replayed what happened in his head, trying to think about how he could tell the story as honestly as possible without sounding like he had lost his marbles. Could he omit enough to keep himself from ending up in a mental institution, but not so much that they would notice pieces were missing?

Thea broke his concentration. She spoke urgently, obviously trying to beat the officers before they finished their side conversation. "Brodey, please, let me tell you what happened with Mike. Don't you at least owe me that? If you don't believe me, I'll leave."

He took one look at her sweet blue eyes and robotically nodded. What did he have to lose?

"My friends told Mike that you and I were together. He got this notion in his head that he could make me understand that he could make me happier. We were arguing in the lobby, and I think he finally understood that I wouldn't budge on the matter. So, with one last-ditch effort, he kissed me. I pushed him away immediately and..."

"Don't pull some damsel in distress story on me," Brodey responded, disgusted with her. "Let me guess, you slapped him in the face? How dare he put his muscular arms around you! That monster!" His voice dripped with sarcasm.

"Of course not!" She whispered hastily. "I punched him in the face," she sat up a little straighter, looking proud of herself. "Broke his nose, too."

Brodey looked back up at her, unable to hide a smile. He loved her spunk, and it didn't surprise him that she'd left a mark on him if he really did push himself on her. Why didn't he just stop and listen before? The path to anger and resentment was just easier.

She let her hand rest on his as the officers approached, having finished their debate. Before either of them spoke, Brodey asked, "Do I have come with you?"

"If you're more comfortable here, that's fine. We may call you in as the investigation unfolds, but you're not a suspect. We would just like to hear your account of what happened."

Brodey's cheeks heated. He couldn't explain the two guns without going into detail about his suicide plan. He didn't want Thea to know how far he'd let himself go down the rabbit hole. But if he'd allowed her to defend herself from the beginning, he wouldn't be in this mess. "I was having a hard time, emotionally," he said, leaning back against the bench. "I thought Wyatt was my friend, but I honestly didn't know him very well at all. He moved in recently. I think he took advantage of my situation."

He gave Thea an apologetic look before continuing. "I shouldn't have let him steer me like he did. I thought I'd lost Thea. It made my life seem so worthless and hopeless. Wyatt was already really depressed and talking about suicide, so I joined him. We were going to kill ourselves together." He sighed, staring at the concrete.

The male officer leaned in, "Are you still having thoughts of harming yourself, son?"

Brodey shook his head emphatically, "No."

The officers exchanged glances, trying to decide if he still posed a risk to himself or others.

Brodey thought if they heard the whole story, they might understand why he'd changed his mind. "That's when the girl showed up," he added, hoping to pique their interest.

Once he felt certain he had their attention, he continued. "She knew Wyatt's name. She seemed to hate him. She told me that he lied to me and that his gun had blanks in it."

Now came the tricky part. "I think she might have been on something. She wasn't making a lot of sense, talking about masters and stuff. She was outrageously strong. Like I said, she had to be on something because she overpowered Wyatt and strangled him to death." He stuck as close to the truth as possible without mentioning the light, invisible forces, or calculating black eyes. He hoped forensics would corroborate what he said.

"Brodey," Thea said, her shoulders sank into a disappointed slouch.

"I'm sorry." He muttered, unable to meet her gaze. "It was really selfish, I know."

"His gun did have blanks in it," the female officer confirmed. "What about the girl's injuries?"

"She was already hurt when she found us," Brodey answered. "I think her leg was broken or something."

"Was Wyatt sick?" The other officer asked, flipping back through his notepad.

Brodey shrugged. "I don't know. If he was, he didn't tell me. Like I said, I thought we were friends, but he was trying to get me to kill myself."

"Why would he want you to do that?"

"Well," Brodey stopped for a moment, thinking. "Maybe you're right. He was sick. I can't speak to any physical illness, but now I'm sure he was sick in the head."

~~~~~

Kate could hear the teacup chattering against the saucer as she tried to hand it to Fin. She couldn't comprehend his relaxed demeanor after all they'd witnessed together. Once he decided she wasn't a threat, he simply asked for hot tea and some food. Kate didn't have much in either category, but some digging revealed an old box of chamomile tea in her pantry.

She sat next to him, staring off into the distance. He studied the tag on the teabag. She didn't even know how to form a question about what she had just experienced. Instead, she sat on the edge of the couch, hands perched on her knees, waiting for Fin to speak. Jake had his nose on Fin's leg, waiting for any morsels that may have accompanied the tea.

Fin dipped his tea bag up and down in the water. With one eye, he studied the item that they'd left lying in the middle of the room. It hadn't moved, but Kate had to resist the urge to open the door and kick it out into the street.

Without moving her gaze, she asked, "What is it?"

Fin took a sip of tea and grimaced at the taste. She felt his eyes on her before he tried to discretely spit the tea back into the cup. He cleared his throat, setting the dissatisfactory tea on the end table. Jake perked his ears, realized he had begged for nothing, and laid down with a thump.

"I think it is a *kenasai*," Fin said matter-of-factly.

Kate had been waiting long enough. "You have seen it before?"

"Not that particular one, no."

Her eyes widened. "There are more objects? I mean, kenasai things? This isn't the only one?"

His eyebrows furrowed. "I don't know. Before tonight I would have said no."

Unwilling to let him off the hook, Kate pressed, "Well, the other one that you saw, did it..." she didn't know how to describe what happened, so she put her hands out in front of her waving them in a small circular motion.

"I didn't say I saw one. I have seen renderings of them. I have never been in the same room," he waved his hands in front of him, copying her motion, "for obvious reasons. Where did you get this?"

"My car," she answered simply. "Who showed you pictures of a kenasai? What does it do besides scare the shit out of people?"

He raised his eyebrows. "Your car?"

"It's a long story. Just tell me how you even know what this is."

"It's a long story," he repeated after her. "It would seem we both have some explaining to do. Shall we pick up the kenasai and pass it back and forth to signify whose turn it is to speak? You know, like cheerleaders and their spirit stick?"

"How can you joke at a time like this? Do you have any idea how terrified I am? I can't even begin to explain to you what the past few weeks have been like for me, and you're going to joke about something supernatural that just happened! *Real* things in my life have been difficult, Fin! *Real things.* I don't even know how to categorize this! Furthermore, I felt guilty about a jacket in my possession that I should probably tell the police about. Now I don't even think I can call them because they'll send me to the looney bin."

He smirked. "I guess I'll go first, then."

Kate huffed and folded her arms against her chest. She finally turned to look at him.

He folded his hands in his lap. "I have been going to Helping Hands for quite some time now. But I only keep going because I'm hoping I can gather information about deaths in the community. Police don't really like to work with people like me." He ran his hand up and down his torso to indicate he meant his appearance.

"So, you have been *using* a support group to glean information from people who are hurting?"

"Before you pass your judgment, Kate, I'd like to know why you go to the group. I know it isn't for that stud muffin you've been dragging along."

She pressed her lips into a line. She didn't appreciate someone she didn't know passing judgement on her, either. Marcy could speak liberally only because of their long-standing friendship. Who did he think he was?

"We broke it off," she said, snipping off the end of her statement

"You don't have to answer my question about why you go, but it may help us both in the long run. Just mull that over.

"There has been a rise in suicides in our community. Not only that but there has also been a rise in cases that are initially suspected as foul play but are later written off as suicide. The suicides also do not conform to their normal statistical parameters. For instance, most women tend to choose methods that are going to be easier on their families. They do things like take a bottle of pills because, in their mind, the family who finds them would be far less devastated than if they did something messier.

"I want to know why. What would cause a rise in cases as well as deviation from the norm?"

Kate thought out loud, "Are you saying it is the government? Like, some sort of conspiracy theory?"

Fin gave her a sideways glance. "Really? You think the *government* is responsible for that?" He tilted his head toward the kenasai. "No, Kate. It's far more sinister than that.

"You said just a few moments ago that it was supernatural. Yet you're guessing the government because you're trying to fool yourself into believing the least of evil choices. Often, when humans are faced with something we're afraid of, we try to rationalize it or categorize it in a simple box we can understand. The truth is, though, the supernatural realm cannot fit into a box."

Kate raised an eyebrow, "So, you think it's ghosts?"

"Ghosts?" Fin shook his head, looking frustrated. "Kate, open your mind a little more. What do you think a ghost is?"

She leaned back into the couch cushion. "It's a spirit from this world that does not move into the next world. You know, like loved ones."

"Have you always believed in ghosts?" He asked.

Kate pondered for a moment. "I wouldn't say I believe in them. But I have never had any kind of experience that I would say is other-worldly. So, while I don't actively believe, I guess the best way I could describe myself is that I'm not opposed to the idea."

"It's not ghosts."

Kate suspected that, while Fin was keeping his face straight, she was exasperating him. She wanted to conjure up anything that would fit into the puzzle except that which she fervently hoped couldn't be real.

"My dreams," she murmured out loud.

Fin nodded.

"How do you know about them?" She asked.

"I had them too. Horrible and terrifying dreams. Demonic dreams." His haunted eyes searched her face for affirmation.

She nodded.

"Demonic experiences are not as uncommon as you think," Fin said, his throat sounding tight. "And once that world is revealed, you realize they're everywhere. We think of demons as terrifying in nature, but the truth is, if they presented themselves in that form, humans would never come to accept and love them. They choose more inviting forms like ghostly apparitions of those we love. They have a remarkable ability to disguise themselves into things that seem innocent. Otherwise, who would ever want to go down that path?

"Deception is their best-utilized tool. They promise something beautiful but deliver plague, illness, and death. For years, they've been among us humans, wreaking havoc while we blindly follow.

111

There are no limits to who they can turn because we love the easy path."

Fin looked at her, his eyes sincere, "I'm sorry, Kate. But it seems like Molly's death opened this door for you. I want to tell you that this will be easy — that you can fight this battle and move on with your life. But I really don't think that's possible. You cannot deny the truth once you've seen it."

Kate wanted to argue with him. She wanted to throw her arm toward the door and tell him to get out of her house. She wanted to run out the back door and disappear into the woods. Instead, she sighed. Jake's head popped up on the other end of the coffee table. With a grunt, he stood and walked over to her, laying his head on her lap.

"So why do they need the kenasai?" she asked.

"Are you sure you don't have any biscuits or cookies?" Fin glanced woefully in the direction of the kitchen.

"Well, if you answer my question about the kenasai, I can probably find you a date paste ball or some quinoa granola."

Fin gave her a humorless look. "That better be a joke."

Kate shrugged. "I try to keep healthy options at home, but I can also eat a mean pizza." She walked to the kitchen and grabbed a bag of almonds and raisins, bringing them back to the table.

Fin grimaced. "I'll pass on that feast, thanks. As far as the kenasai's use, I'm not completely certain, but I think they are used to collect souls. Human souls are a hot commodity in the spiritual realms, I suppose. Until tonight, I had assumed that the kenasai had to be in the same room during death to collect a soul. Seeing as both of our souls are completely intact, I've been proven wrong."

"So, what just happened in my living room was someone's soul being trapped in some sort of spiritual object? That's insane."

Fin caved and opened the bag Kate had given to him. He popped an almond in his mouth and frowned, reading the bag. "These don't even have salt on them. Disgusting."

"Fin! You can't just collect souls in metal cylinders. That's impossible."

He looked up at her with a twinkle in his eye. "It's impossible? Where does the soul go when it leaves our bodies?"

"Well, when we die, we — uh," Kate stammered. She shook her head. Her hair, still tousled, fell from behind her ear and onto her face. "We just die. Or maybe we are reincarnated into animals or trees. Nobody really knows or can prove what happens after death."

"I guess you'll have to humor me, then." Fin leaned back into the couch. "While I cannot tell you exactly where souls go while we wait for the final spiritual battle that the Bible talks about, I *can* tell you that we do indeed have souls, and I'm fairly sure you just saw one right here in your living room.

"Not only that, but this is not the first time for demonic forces to attempt to steal souls from their intended destinations. As far back as human history records, tragic events can be linked to spiritual influence. There are even theories that Hitler, for example, enabled millions of souls to be harvested for other-worldly purposes. Another theory implicates demonic forces in the bubonic plague. There has long been a spiritual battle over humankind and our destinies. That is what I believe is happening with some of the unexplained deaths around here."

"You must realize that sounds ridiculous," Kate snorted. "Why do demons need human souls? And you're telling me that people who are meant for Heaven can be stolen and whisked away to a place they are not destined for? That's just one more reason for me not to believe in Heaven or Hell."

"I said that could happen, but I didn't say it was the end of the story. I believe that it can be stopped, and that's why I called it a battle. I have to believe that eventually, good will win. But if those who believe in the power of God do not step up to fight for him, who else is there? What if you could save your sister's soul for eternity?"

Kate knew she would do anything for Molly. If she had to unravel her whole world, she would. If it meant changing everything she founded her belief system on, she would. If it meant going to stupid Helping Hands meetings without knowing why, she would.

She bit her lip and tried to blink away the tears gathering in her eyes. "I haven't been going to the group for that stud muffin. You are right," she confessed. "Even my best friend doesn't know why I go. I guess I haven't even known for sure myself. I was told to go."

Fin nodded, "By the police. They often refer people to Helping Hands."

She shook her head, "No. I mean, yes, initially the police referred me to the group and gave me Joe's contact information. But I didn't want to go because I didn't know how to mourn something that I don't understand. Molly didn't commit suicide. I know the group isn't only for families who've experienced suicide, but without even knowing what I was supposed to be mourning, I didn't want to talk about it. So, I threw away the note with Joe's number. But something wanted me to go."

"Something? Like a feeling in your gut?" Fin asked.

"No. Something else. Something I can't explain. The note just appeared again on my stove."

"Do you think someone put it there?"

"I thought there might have been someone in my house, but I didn't ever actually see a person. I had Detective Peterson come over to look around for me before I went back in, and the note was back on my stove. Nothing else had been touched."

Fin thought for a moment. "What did Detective Peterson think about the note's reappearance?"

Kate glanced away. "I didn't tell him." She paused, expecting Fin to tell her how ridiculous she was for not sharing critical information with the detective.

"Is Peterson the one who referred you to Helping Hands?" Fin asked.

Kate nodded.

And he was in the house before you went back in?" he asked.

She nodded again but slower, trying to remember. "Yeah, he walked through the house first while I waited outside. Do you think he may have moved the note from the trash?"

Fin shook his head. "I don't know. I guess the question is, do *you* think he would?"

Kate pondered it for a moment. "No. He seems very professional. Even if he saw that I threw away the note, I don't think he would have messed with it. But who would break into my house just for the note?"

Fin shrugged. "So," he leaned back into the couch, running his fingers through his crazy hair, "you haven't explained how you found the kenasai."

Kate sighed, placing her hands flat on her thighs. "Well, I guess if you believe in demons, you won't think I'm crazy." She managed a small smile.

Chapter 13

Detective Peterson rubbed his eyes, weary from travel. The beeping of Ashley's heartrate monitor filled the empty room with echoes of life. A nurse with shoulders slumped from exhaustion explained that she'd barely pulled through the night. She had not yet opened her eyes or given any indication that she could hear people in the room. The patient had no identification on her when they found her.

"We still aren't sure she's going to make it. She has gangrene in the leg. We need to amputate, but it's risky because of her already unstable condition. The doctor has her scheduled for this afternoon. It will be a miracle if she makes it through surgery."

Detective Peterson's eyebrows drew down, brooding as he watched the girl for any signs of life. "Do you believe in miracles?"

The nurse nodded. "If you work here long enough, you'll believe anything is possible. The brightest of cases with the most hope might ride out of here in a casket. Then there are cases like this," she tipped her head toward Ashley's bed, "that get up and walk out of here."

"I appreciate your response, but I was talking to my partner," He turned toward the door.

Fran's head poked around the door frame. "We're partners?"

Alec did not answer. He raised his eyebrows, waiting for her response.

Fran's head bobbed up and down. "Absolutely. Miracles happen all the time. You never know! I mean, one time I was working this case with a homeless man and..."

"Great." Alec interrupted. "I guess you better start praying." He gave Ashley a parting glance before leaving the room with the nurse. Fran shuffled along after them. "Has the boy who witnessed it, Brodey, stopped by?" He wanted to piece together whether the two were friends.

The nurse shook her head. "I'd imagine witnessing a murder would interfere with any curiosity he has about her progress. This whole thing is just weird."

"Weird?" Alec asked, making a note to contact Brodey with a few more questions.

"Well, yeah. After looking at her leg more closely, we could see patterns of healing, meaning it had been injured for a while. Not only that, but the healed sections had indications that she'd reinjured it over and over. Almost like," the nurse rubbed her arm against an unseen chill in the air, "she walked on it for days."

"People walk around injured all the time," Alec said dismissively.

No. Not like this," the nurse replied. "It would have caused such extreme pain that she should have passed out when she tried."

"Interesting." Alec pivoted on his heels and said, "Well, thank you for your time."

The nurse rubbed her eyes and said, "No problem." She stuck out her hand to shake his but realized he'd already made a beeline for the elevator. She mumbled under her breath.

"It's ok," Fran whispered over her shoulder, a few steps behind him. "He's kind of an ass sometimes, but you get used to it." She gave the nurse a departing smile and tucked a stray hair back into her bun before ducking into the elevator after Alec.

In the lobby, Alec's phone rang. "Peterson," he answered.

Fran waited, studying his face. He'd been gone for a while, chasing down new leads before popping back into this investigation, and the chief told her he wanted her to keep tabs on him. The department in Chicago confirmed that he was investigating a case that they suspected was related to this one, but the chief had a gut feeling.

Alec hung up and returned the phone to his pocket. "How 'bout I drop you off at the precinct and go grab us some lunch? It's on me."

"Nah, we can get some on the way."

"On the way to the precinct?" He played dumb, and she could tell.

"On the way to wherever you're headed." She stated plainly.

Detective Peterson gave the keys in his pocket a few rattles. Fran could feel the satisfaction of knowing she had read him right. She tried to hide a smirk. She hadn't spent a lot of time with him, and he tried to keep people at a distance, but she knew his tell. The jingling keys.

"Have it your way." He turned and walked through the revolving door.

Fran froze for a moment, shocked that he'd come to a decision to allow her to tag along so quickly. Convinced he might still try to shake her, she hustled after him, making for a clumsy exit from the revolving door right into another woman.

The woman cursed, "Watch where you are going!"

"Sorry," Fran put up both hands apologetically.

"You scuffed up my shoe. Just one of these shoes probably costs what you make in a month eating donuts and drinking coffee behind that pitiful badge!" The woman's furious red face made her streaky hair stand out even more. She raised her foot to show a small black mark on her bubble gum pink heel.

Fran glanced over her shoulder at Peterson. He reached for his keys, approaching the car. She whipped her head back around to face the woman. "Listen, I'm really sorry." She yanked her card from the front breast pocket of her uniform and half tossed it at the woman. "Call me and let me know if you need me to pay to have it fixed. My name is Fran." She rushed after Alec, leaving the woman no time to respond.

~~~~~

Simone scowled and whispered through clenched teeth. "If I didn't have more pressing matters, Fran, I'd take more time to deal with you." She placed the card in her purse, composed herself, and glided effortlessly through the door.

Simone stepped off the elevator, still seething about her Gucci pumps. She approached a deflated nurse.

"Excuse me," she said.

"How can I help you?" the woman said without looking up.

"I think my niece is here. She's been missing for a few weeks, and I've been calling hospitals every few days to see if anyone matching her description had been admitted. I spoke with a woman downstairs who said I might find her here." Simone wrung her hands in front of her summoning the most desperate demeanor she could.

"What's her name?" The woman asked, clicking away at her keyboard.

"Ashley."

"Do you have a *last* name?" The woman asked.

"It doesn't matter because I think she was admitted as a Jane Doe. That's why I said I've been calling to see if anyone matching her description has been admitted. She has a track record of using fake IDs and credit cards. She is, after all, just a kid." Simone struggled to say 'kid' in an endearing tone.

The nurse continued to plunk away on the keyboard. "Yes, there is a Jane Doe in room 337. I'm sorry, but no visitors for now. Even if she were your niece, she wouldn't know you were in the room."

Simone placed her hand on the nurse's desk. "I understand." She wiped a nonexistent tear from her eye and sighed. "I'm so close to finally finding her. I hate to think I'm completely helpless in this matter. Is there anything I can do to help you? Maybe I could assist with her medical history."

The nurse finally looked up at Simone, her expression skeptical. "Do you have her primary physician's information and permission to request her records?"

"Oh," Simone said curtly. "I didn't realize I would need all that. I'm not sure if I have the permission to get that information for you from her doctor or not." She pulled out her cellphone and started scrolling through contacts. "Let me call them and check, okay?"

The nurse nodded. "That would help."

Simone half-turned from the nurse's station before stopping. "Wait, this is silly," she smiled easily. "I don't want to go to all of this trouble if I'm not even sure she's the Jane Doe you have. I understand there are no visitors, but may I just look at her through the door to make sure it's my Ashley?"

The nurse paused and searched Simone's face a moment longer. Simone resisted the urge to tap her foot while she waited for the nurse to make up her mind. The Master would not be pleased if she walked out of here empty-handed. And for her own satisfaction, she planned on discretely killing Ashley.

The nurse puffed out another sigh. "Alright, but I'll have to escort you." She heaved herself out of her chair.

Simone resisted the urge to roll her eyes. "I'm *so* sorry for the inconvenience this is causing." Her shoes clacked down the corridor after the nurse with practical shoes, passing a series of rooms before stopping at 337.

Simone looked at the nurse, a wordless expression asking for permission to take a peek. The nurse nodded, so she took one step into the room. The girl was on the far side, but Simone got the confirmation she needed.

She glanced at the palm of her hand to assure herself that the rune she'd drawn was still there. While she would never call herself a slave of practice like a witch, Wiccan, or spellcaster — runes suited her needs in situations like this. The ancient language had power that she could not deny.

She turned to the nurse and smiled, "You've given me what I need, love." She placed her hand on the nurse's arm to thank her and said, "You have a lot of work to do, and you want me to stay here and visit with my niece."

The nurse's eyes shifted out of focus as she slipped into otherworldly control. Without blinking, she stiffly turned and walked back toward the nurse's station. She passed by two doctors who were talking outside another patient's room, but they didn't seem to notice her. Simone only needed a few moments, and with a little luck, no one would notice the nurse's unfortunate disposition. Even if someone spoke to her and she did not respond, which she wouldn't, they would hopefully interpret her silence as rudeness. She would float without purpose like a lost buoy in the ocean until Simone released her.

Simone turned to Ashley. "I've been looking for you," She couldn't hide the excitement in her voice.

She slid into the room and closed the door quietly behind her with a click that solidified Ashley's fate. Simone glided to the bed and placed her purse on the end near Ashley's feet. She drew her index finger up along Ashley's immobilized body to the top of the bed, where she rested her elbow. Ashley's dark canvas of hair made her face stand out like the moon in a starless sky. Simone reached up and brushed it away from her face.

Simone clicked her tongue. "Such a pretty little thing." She pushed away from the bed, scanning the room. She expected to find some sort of bag with Ashley's belongings. A quick survey of the shelves, the chair, and the table revealed nothing. She bent over and pulled the blanket away from the bed to see if they had been stored underneath.

"I didn't know you were going to make this difficult," she seethed. "Even immobilized, you are a thorn in my side, child." She replaced the blanket and half stood before stopping cold.

Ashley was sitting straight up in the bed, her oily black eyes fixated on Simone. She robotically reached up and removed the oxygen tube from her face, then inspected the IV stuck in her arm before deciding to leave it.

Simone's heart fluttered. She fell backward onto the floor, her heels making a scraping sound on the tile. She scooted quickly until her back hit the wall, eyes wide and terrified. She sounded small when she spoke.

"You — you are not my Master," was all she could manage to sputter out in her shock at finding Ashley clearly possessed by something she did not recognize. Demons, although difficult to identify to an outsider, had a way of reaching into the soul with a wordless pull. Simone felt no pull.

Ashley grinned. "You search for the kenasai? You will not find it here. Nor will you find the harvested souls. They do not belong to Tyrannus. They belong to the king. You've chosen the wrong master, and now you will pay for the wrongs you have committed against our kingdom."

Simone's mouth had gone dry. The king? She served a demon who called himself a king. Did more than one king exist? She tried to swallow with great effort, chancing a glance at her purse on the end of the bed.

She looked back at Ashley, whose gaze had also landed on the purse. Simone might as well be made of lead. No way would she beat a demon to it. They could command human bodies in ways that defied nature.

Just when Simone thought she had lost, Ashley jolted. She rigidly threw her body back into the pillows, thrashing wildly. The purse fell to the ground as an inhuman cry escaped her mouth. Coughing and sputtering overtook her, and her eyes darted wildly about. Through gritted teeth, she uttered, "It cannot be."

Simone wasted no time. She darted across the floor, clumsily grasping for the purse and dumping the contents. She fumbled through the items on the ground as Ashley continued to scream. Any minute someone would surely come through the door, startled by the chaos in the room. Simone's hand pushed the syringe she planned to use on Ashley to the side, knowing it would no longer work. After what felt like an eternity, she found the object she needed.

She stood, still shaking, pointing a knife at Ashley's writhing body. The rune on the handle of the knife began to burn as Simone spoke, half laughing and half out of breath. "Fortunately for me, someone has begun praying for Ashley's soul." She quickly stabbed the girl in the chest, leaning in to gaze into the eyes of evil. "Prayer stings, doesn't it? Don't worry, you won't have to endure it much longer."

She removed the knife, and the darkness disappeared from Ashley's eyes. Her body relaxed, and for the remaining moment in her life, she returned to her human state. A single tear ran down her cheek as she let out one last breath.

"Sorry, dear," Simone said, feigning sympathy. "I don't think you're going to make it." She gathered the contents of her purse, slung it over her shoulder, and touched Ashley's forehead. She whispered words in Latin and backed away from the bed just as nurses burst into the room.

"I don't know what happened!" Simone cried. "She just started seizing, and I couldn't stop it. I thought you said she'd be okay!"

A nurse pushed her out of the room as they pulled out the paddles to shock Ashley. Simone walked down the hallway lazily, knowing the charm she'd spoken over the girl would hide her true death for the time being. Stepping onto the elevator, she released the desk nurse from her spell with a single word.

~~~~~

"You're quiet," Alec said.

Fran pulled her gaze from the passenger window. She finished her silent prayer for the girl in the hospital by mouthing the word 'amen' before replying. "I guess I'm just wondering where we're going. I figure asking isn't going to get me anywhere since you're hell-bent on being all mysterious."

"You don't like surprises?" Alec asked.

"It depends on the surprise. Chinese food would be nice right about now."

Alec pulled into a dusty parking lot and drove slowly to an old, repurposed warehouse. A flea market, an antique store, and oddly enough, an insurance agent all advertised on a small sign underneath a banner that boasted 'Space Available.' By the looks of things, Fran guessed plenty of space was available.

"Let's go," Alec said, stepping out of the car.

Fran followed him up the stairs and into a small open lobby area with signs for the different vendor locations. Newly constructed walls stood out against the worn brick that formed the old industrial building. They walked down the hallway until they came to a door with no label or sign.

Detective Peterson knocked. Fran could hear someone shuffling around on the other side of the door before shouting, "Who is it?"

"Graham, it's Alec. Just open the door."

Fran could hear a female voice say, "Leave him out there unless he brought food."

She smirked at Alec and said, "I told you Chinese food is a good surprise."

He raised his fist to knock again, but the door opened, leaving him with his hand in the air. The boy, who Fran guessed to be in his early 20s, took one look at Alec and turned back into the room without acknowledging her. A light electronic buzz filled the air as they stepped into what she could only describe as a nerd fortress.

Computers and tablets laid open, running some sort of program that looked like decryption software. Two tables sat across from each other. One table had wires neatly clamped and color-coded notes organized into orderly rows. The other had wires that looked like poorly packed Christmas lights. Wads of paper piled around the outside of an overstuffed trashcan. A girl, also young, wheeled her desk chair around the chaos and said, "I don't see food."

The boy walked over to his clean workspace, plopped into his chair, and took off his glasses to rub his eyes. "Kelsey, I'll go get us some burgers after this, ok?"

The girl sat up, hopeful, red hair dangling over her eyes, "Or maybe Chinese?"

"Whatever." The boy replaced his glasses and returned his gaze to Alec.

Alec held out his hand toward Fran. "Fran, this is Graham and Kelsey. Guys, this is Fran." He turned to Fran and said, "They are working for me on the computer aspect of this investigation."

He turned back to Graham and said, "What do you have for me?"

Fran approached the pair slowly. "Why aren't they stationed at the precinct?"

Graham ignored her and said, "Well, you were right. I used Brutus to obtain her password and used it to login to the site. We had a stroke of luck because the site administrator hasn't deleted her account yet due to her..." he searched for the right word.

"She's dead," Kelsey finished for him.

He looked at her, expression annoyed. "Yes. Anyway, I was able to pull some of the communications she had with several other users. Group conversations were hit and miss, but I thought you'd want to see this." He pulled up something as Alec leaned in.

"They're hackers?" Fran spat. "Alec, what are you doing? We can't have hackers working with us on this! We have to get warrants for this stuff, or it's not admissible in court." She took a step back to avoid the air of incrimination. She now understood that the chief's suspicions were right.

Alec looked up from the computer; his expression had changed to innocent. "They're not officially working on this with us. Right, guys?"

"If you don't bring me food soon, I'm going to amend the terms of our agreement," Kelsey chimed in.

Alec shot her a look.

She rolled her eyes and sighed, "Yeah, yeah, we don't officially exist."

Fran crossed her arms. She peered at Alec. "This isn't ethical."

He walked over to her, showing feeling for the first time since she'd met him. "Fran, I can't tell you how long I've tried to play with these creeps by the rules. It's gotten me nowhere. We don't have enough evidence to incriminate the website itself. But I've got a gut feeling about this. I really think we need to pursue it. I just need a leg up on this case because right now, I'm grasping at straws.

"You don't have to stay, and if you don't want to, I understand. But for the record, you're the one who wanted to come. I've done everything I can to keep any of this from falling onto the precinct. The chief is clueless, and that's the safest bet for him. I want him to be able to say he had no idea what was going on if we're caught," he finished.

"Which we won't be," Graham added, tapping his pen on the desk. "We're too good." He smirked at Kelsey, already back to typing behind her screen. She held up a peace sign.

Alec searched Fran's eyes, waiting for her response. Fran could feel the heat in her cheeks and hoped it didn't show. She wanted to catch the killer, too, but she played by the rules. How could he show her this and expect her to keep silent? And now that she'd seen it, she had her own ethical dilemma to deal with. Should she tell the chief and risk losing a possible lead? Or should she trust Alec Peterson?

She turned her back to him and put her hand on the door.

"Please don't go," Alec said, sounding a bit desperate. "Just give this a chance."

Startled by the sudden soft side of the detective, Fran paused. She looked over her shoulder. "I'm not going anywhere," she mumbled. "But I have a granola bar in the car I'm going to get for that skinny girl before she dies of starvation."

Erica Darnell

Chapter 14

Simone paced back and forth outside her car, playing back her confrontation with Ashley's unexpected tagalong guest. She knew she would have to pitch Ashley's death as positively as possible.

"So, as you can see," she said into her phone, "this small blip has actually helped us. I was able to eliminate the girl and, therefore, the threat." She hoped she sounded more confident than she felt. Torture was not something she ever wanted to endure again. Her stature and service meant little to her master.

"Now, we cannot even coax the whereabouts of the kenasai out of her! How does *that* work in our favor?" An angry voice replied.

"I truly had no choice. It was me or the girl."

A low laugh rumbled through the phone. "You're going to wish it were you dead in that hospital bed when I'm done with you. I enjoy helping you learn your lesson."

Simone leaned against her car to keep her legs from giving out. Begging for forgiveness would not save her. She decided to forgo useless pleas and try diversion.

"Teaching me a lesson is going to be a low priority considering the news Ashley delivered. If our movements have truly been discovered, it's only a matter of time. Do we have enough souls?" She asked.

"If demons in Lucifer's kingdom are aware of Tyrannus's work, we either have an informant among us, or the detective knows more than we think. Perhaps the detective even works for Lucifer. His reach is far. The souls that we gather are to no avail if we cannot keep our work secret from the King of Hell."

Simone rubbed her head, saying, "I don't understand how we will convince all of the souls to fight for us. If we procure some against their will, why would they do as we ask?"

"We will offer freedom to the souls who fight. The souls who choose not to fight can serve as examples of what happens to those

127

unwilling to help us with our cause. I don't think we'll need many examples to prove our point," the voice said.

"But with a new ruler and a new kingdom, won't you need them to stay?" Simone asked.

A long sigh came through the phone. "You ask too many questions."

"I have long been faithful to you, my lord. I only ask to understand why I fight a battle we may not win. It becomes more dangerous for me by the minute. There is no honor amongst demons. Hence Tyranneus planning the uprising against Lucifer. I am merely human, so who is to say I have any stake in a battle amongst traitors?" Simone knew she walked a fine line, but what did she have to lose? He already planned to do unspeakable things to her.

"I said we would offer freedom — not give it. Once they have fought the battle, they will no longer be able to obtain the freedom they seek. No soul who fights for us can ever leave."

Simone wondered if the master remembered that he had made promises to her many years ago. In not so many words, he had just inadvertently informed her that their contract was null and void. He no longer needed to torture her because he just stole all her hope. For years she had faithfully served in hopes that her part of the bargain would be honored. She mourned the loss of her own soul for a moment, wondering if she ever honestly believed he would fulfill his end of the bargain in the first place. In a way, her newfound knowledge of her eternal bondage made her a better ally. All these years, she restrained herself, hoping to preserve a bit of her own humanity for the day she walked away. Her master knew this.

She now had nothing left to lose. The last fragile remnants of love drained from somewhere deep inside her. She had harbored it in a safe place like a small lifeboat in a stormy sea. But there was no reason to keep bits of herself locked away anymore. She would never see her daughter again.

He finally spoke again, "Find the detective and lure him someplace private. I would like to have a word with him." He hung up abruptly.

Simone returned the phone to her purse with a sigh. "Oh, sure," she said to herself. "Detective Peterson and I are on great terms. Let me just call him up and ask him to dinner in a private area." She rolled her eyes and crossed her arms, stewing.

When she began recruiting young people for their cause, she took them to eat to discuss joining The Gathering. Most of the kids she ran into hadn't eaten a good meal in weeks. Sometimes she played the sympathetic ear to a teen who just needed a friend. Other times she outright used manipulation or blackmail. The blackmail was easy. Catch a street kid stealing and use it against them. They would do anything to stay out of the system.

When Peterson found connections between a few of her mentors and suspicious deaths, he eventually landed on her doorstep. He showed her pictures of herself with her recruits in various public areas. She knew he wanted her to think he had won. She'd felt him observing her over the photos with his self-inflated smirk. Most people would squirm and say something incriminating at that point. But Simone knew how to keep her mouth shut, and so did her mentors. They played the part of grieving friends. Simone played the part of helping teens that no one else cared about. She even volunteered with an organization that provided housing to homeless teens.

Her connections with people in high places didn't hurt, either. His speculative evidence meant nothing. He tailed her for a few weeks, and instead of escalating the matter as harassment, she took advantage of it. She spent those weeks showing off her special friends. A few golf scrambles and benefit dinners later, he lost interest in her.

She had to give him credit. He had an impressive knack for digging. She admired and hated him for it. Thanks to Peterson, they had new preventative measures in place for public areas with cameras.

How could she get him alone? She batted away the thought of him working with Lucifer. Being alone with a friend of her enemy gave her spine a tingle. She knew that working through the police department would lead to some lucrative possibilities, but she didn't have any connections in the local precinct. She considered pulling some strings in Chicago. Maybe she could isolate Peterson if she filtered some false information down the chain of command. He was desperate. He might act alone.

She suddenly remembered running into the policewoman at the front of the hospital. Grinning, Simone reached into her purse and pulled out Fran's card. Perhaps coercing someone between a rock and a hard place would help her gain access to Alec Peterson.

~~~~~

129

Kelsey licked the wrapper for any last remains of the granola bar as Graham explained the way the forums worked to Alec and Fran.

"So," he continued, "although the face of the website boasts independent thought and decisions, the belly of the beast offers no such thing. If you look at these posts here, some of the members of the Gathering are feeding off of each other's doubts. Read this one by one of the female members." He pulled up a post from the week before:

Our mentors aren't here to support us. They're here to keep us on the website! I met with a friend of mine and had a good time. She is looking for a roommate and offered to let me move in with her and pay her back once I get my feet under me. I told my mentor about it, but she said my friend was just being fake. Why tear me down like that? What kind of mentor tells you not to take an opportunity to help yourself?

He continued to scroll down, "And look, she got a bunch of responses. Some were supportive of the mentors, but many felt the same as her. Unfortunately, many of the comments were either edited to look less agreeable or taken down altogether. But the point is, there were lots of people who supported her suspicion that the mentors weren't what they seemed."

Fran stood a few steps away, still not completely committed to aiding in their investigation. She spoke up without moving closer, "What is a mentor?"

Kelsey stood and picked up a few print-offs that were strewn about her desk. She walked over to Fran and held out the stack to Fran, who shook her head, refusing to take them. "I'm still not sure I'm a part of this."

Kelsey shrugged one shoulder. "It seems that anyone who becomes a member is eventually assigned a mentor. We aren't sure how the members are prioritized, though. Some newer members are immediately assigned one, while some of the veteran members don't seem to have one yet. I think that means that some of the veteran members are phishers. Each mentor helps the member through their journey to take their own lives in a way that is comfortable to them. My current theory is that they might even offer to do it alongside the member as a kind of comradery.

"But I don't understand how they can offer to do that and still have mentors readily available for incoming members. They're essentially killing off their staff."

Fran squinted, thinking aloud, "Do you think any of the mentors come back after leading a member to commit suicide? Wouldn't other members notice?"

Kelsey shook her head, "No, because all of the mentor/member conversations are private. So other members wouldn't see the pictures or usernames of the mentors until they've been paired with them. I was able to hack into the back door and print off pictures of a few people I think may have been mentors." She held up the stack of papers she'd gathered up for Fran again. "You know you wanna look," Kelsey grinned.

Fran scanned the picture of a smiling young man on the top of the stack of pictures. Her eyes had gone misty. "They're so young and normal-looking. But if what you're saying is true, they're killers. They're leading these people to their deaths under the ruse of friendship." She looked up at Alec, not sure if she was ready for the answer to her next question. "Alec," she swallowed, "how long have you been investigating these deaths?"

Alec answered without looking up from the computer screen. "Three years." He shifted a bit in his seat.

"If the mentors don't really take their own lives, why even bother to make a suicide pact with the members? What do they need to be in the same room for?" Fran asked.

Alec offered, "I don't think the mentors ever intend to take their own lives. That's why there was a gun with blanks in it at the Molly Gregory scene. It wasn't Molly's, it was the mentor's. Maybe they are in the room to offer support but never follow through on their end of the deal?"

"That's the million-dollar question," Kelsey added in response to Fran.

Graham cleared his throat, "Anyway, the girl who posted her doubt about her mentor is no longer an active member. If you go to this tab," he clicked the words 'success stories,' and found the girl's username, "she supposedly boarded the train early just a few days later."

Kelsey answered Fran's quizzical glance. "She killed herself."

"Supposedly." Alec inserted.

"Yeah, well, that's where you come in. All I do is provide the information," Kelsey inspected her fingernail. "Anyway, they seldom use the term 'suicide.' It's not kosher."

Graham snorted, "That is not what kosher means."

Kelsey drew her eyes slowly from her fingers to Graham. "You get the point."

"Alec..." Fran's voice stopped short in her throat.

Alec looked up to see a very pale partner. Her hands held the stack of papers she had been sifting through, but her shaking hands made them rattle like leaves. Unable to take her eyes off the photograph on top, she carefully passed it to him.

Alec stared unblinkingly. "It's our Jane Doe from the hospital."

~~~~~

Kate stood outside a rugged-looking mobile home. Talismans hung around the outside of the door and several pendants dangled from the overhanging that appeared to be protecting its own position on the trailer. In the background, Fin complained under his breath until he finally freed his bike from her trunk. Jake sniffed around a chalk drawing on the front doorstep.

"Why did you insist that I bring Jake?" Kate bent down to run her fingers lightly along the surface of the chalk.

"Animals come in handy when dealing with dark spirits and demons," Fin replied. "They seem to sense evil."

Kate cupped Jake's face and looked into his big brown eyes. "How do you know if an animal senses something weird?"

Fin chained his bike to a nearby tree. "Well, I guess it depends on the animal. I would say any behavior that's out of the ordinary. You know Jake best."

The woods. Kate stood, quickly releasing Jake's face, afraid to continue touching him. She took a timid step back. "He has always loved the woods behind our house, but since the break-in, he won't go back there anymore. I've been brushing it off."

"Well, that's why we're here," Fin said. He walked up the rickety stairs and opened the door, oblivious that the overhang may decide to give way to its sag and squish him like a bug.

"What is all of this stuff?" Kate asked. She ducked through the layers of pendants, wind chimes, and strange beads. She chose her path carefully to avoid shuffling piles of papers.

"Protection," Fin said, pointing to the hanging objects. "Once you've seen what I've seen, you'll feel like you can't get enough of it."

Kate tried to keep herself from imagining what could be worse than what they witnessed together. She rubbed the backs of her arms with her hands to stop the chill in her body. The small room had a bed and a half kitchen. The stove looked like it served as a desk strewn with open books and notes. She also noticed books stacked inside the microwave, probably due to space issues and the sheer amount of reading material Fin seemed to keep on hand. On the opposite wall was a door that she figured led to the bathroom, and a small board was hinged on the wall to drop down for use as a table. Aside from the books and trinkets, the trailer seemed well kept.

Fin reached into a wooden chest to the side of the door and pulled out an amulet. Holding it up into the sunlight, he nodded to himself.

He held it out toward Kate and said, "You should wear this."

Kate took the amulet in her hand, inspecting the symbol carved into the metal. It was a beautiful swirl with a green gem in the center. "What does it mean?"

"It is meant to be protection against evil spirits."

Kate squinted. "If this works so well, why do you need all of your protection outside?"

Fin glanced around his small home with a sense of pride. "I might not have much, Kate, but what I do have is invaluable. The amulet would only protect the wearer, not the space around the wearer. I hope no one ever comes to know the treasures I have in here, but it's protected just in case.

"Plus, it seems like no matter how much information I acquire, I don't know everything. This is more of a learn-as-you-go profession. As you saw, my extensive research only scratched the surface of understanding the kenasai."

Profession? Kate glanced out the window, wondering if she'd involuntarily embarked on a journey that would lead her to live like Fin. She let her finger trace the amulet's smooth surface. Somehow, she felt that if she placed it around her neck, it would solidify her fate. She looked up at Fin, who had his arm half-buried in a giant tin of cheese puffs. *I'm not sure I want to go down this road,* she thought.

He nodded to her, clearly waiting for her to oblige. She did, lifting her shirt and dropping the amulet inside so wouldn't be noticeable. "So," she said, "now that I have the amulet, I'm safe." That wasn't so hard.

Fin scoffed. "Safe? Heavens, no. I said it protects from evil spirits. It's not invisible armor."

Kate wrinkled her eyebrows, thinking back to Ashley and their eerie encounter in the parking lot. "If—if an evil spirit wants to take over my body, can it?"

"It depends," Fin said. "From what I can understand, people who have faith in God are impenetrable to a certain degree. For the most part, though, I think demons need to be invited in. Unless, of course, the person has already opened themselves up to evil. Then the door is already open."

Kate could feel goosebumps returning to her arms. She quickly placed her purse on the table. The kenasai inside made a clunking noise. "The person who gave me that thing wasn't normal. She had, like, inhuman strength. And she didn't speak like a young woman would speak."

Fin nodded. "She may have been possessed. Who knows?"

Kate held Fin's gaze. She knew. And after everything she'd seen, she was all too happy to leave the object with Fin.

"Is the person still in their body? I mean, when the spirit leaves, is the person's mind ok?"

Fin shrugged a little too nonchalantly for Kate's question. "Ah! Perfect." He exclaimed. "We'll need this," he said, holding up an old book. His fingers left cheesy dust remnants on the tattered binding. He hurriedly brushed them off before opening the book. "We're going to use a binding rune."

"A spell." The words came out of Kate's mouth unnaturally. "Are you a witch?"

"Don't be absurd. Of course I'm not. It's not a spell. It's a symbol with power."

"With power..." Kate trailed off, sounding like Fin's personal parrot. Her legs wobbled a little under the weight of her emotions. Or maybe she needed something to eat. Her mind wandered to the last time she had food. She should be honest and tell Fin that she had no interest in this supernatural world he seemed infatuated with. How could she explain that she couldn't believe something she'd seen with her own eyes?

She couldn't. Furthermore, if she pushed him away, she would not have anyone else to turn to.

Chapter 15

Alec had stepped away to call the hospital to ask about the girl's condition. He really hoped she would wake up so they could ask her about her involvement on the website. The nurse did not have good news.

He stormed back into the room, stuffing his phone in his back pocket. Fran jumped as he slammed the door behind him. She only took a moment to search his face before she spoke.

"She's dead, isn't she?" She asked matter-of-factly.

Alec pinched the bridge of his nose and drew in a long breath. He felt like he finally had an advantage that his foe did not anticipate. He stopped playing by the rules. Sure, it compromised his own integrity, but he needed ground to stand on.

Graham spoke without looking up from his computer. "Well, isn't that just great? I'm so glad we did all this work to get a dead lead." He ran his hands through his hair and added, "I'm going to need more money for this gig so I can get some life insurance."

"How did she die?" Fran asked, looking a little suspicious.

"Her heart failed. They said the infection must have spread through her blood, and it was too much on her system," Alec replied morosely.

"That's convenient that she died right after we made a connection that could have changed the case," Fran said. "This is so frustrating."

"I haven't followed up with Ms. Gregory lately," he said, dropping his hand from his face. "I think I'll call her."

Fran nodded. "She left you several messages while you were away. Or I guess you were only pretending to be away?" She added, looking around the room.

Alec didn't respond to her jab. "I know. I just dragged my feet because I was hoping the other suspicious deaths would bring me more than a higher body count. The cases that I investigated cannot be linked to the cases in Carbondale, but they are remarkably similar.

"We also need to call the witness to the murder. Brodey may have more information that we can use."

Fran nodded. "I read over the notes from his first account of what happened. We might be able to help him recall small details that he overlooked."

"Did you say Brodey?" Kelsey asked. "As in Brodey Hill?"

Fran pulled up some information on her phone and scrolled for a moment. "Yeah, that's him."

"He was a member of The Gathering." Kelsey's fingers deftly glided over the keyboard. She turned her screen so they could see it. "He hasn't been a member for very long, but he had a mentor. They're the communications we hacked into and tried to intercept without any success."

Alec leaned in, excited about the prospect of a new lead. "What was the mentor's name?"

Kelsey continued typing, biting her bottom lip. "I don't know, but with some digging, I might be able to find out.

"I can tell you that he planned to kill himself yesterday morning," she added.

Fran continued to scroll through the document in her phone, nodding. "That corroborates his statement."

"If I can get into his account, I might be able to..." Kelsey cursed.

"What?" Graham asked.

"He's already deleted it," Kelsey opened her drawer, pulled out a pack of gum, and shoved a piece in her mouth. "All of his old posts are here, but if he deleted his account, it's possible his communications with his mentor were also deleted." She bent back over her keyboard, chewing her gum ferociously as she typed. "If there's a way to find it, I will."

"Why don't you invite the FBI in?" Fran suggested, changing the subject. "If the murders are happening in more than one state, they would have access to make those connections. It only makes sense with a website like this that other states would also have increased suicide rates."

Alec sighed. "It's all speculative right now. Until I have something more concrete, they aren't going to step in. I have no proof that the murders are connected to The Gathering. Furthermore, the weapons and methods are different each time. Without a pattern, it's just wild accusations.

"What we are talking about here is an entire group of serial killers. It's almost like a cult mentality. Clusters of killers working together are statistically rare. I'm more inclined to believe that there is one suspect who is leading the flock.

I also have no idea how many cases have been written off as suicides because of the history of the victims. My gut tells me there are more murders linked to this case than the ones I've been able to put together."

His phone rang, interrupting his train of thought. "Peterson." He answered.

"Detective Peterson," a woman said. "I'm calling from the hospital. We spoke a moment ago on the phone about your Jane Doe."

"Yes," he replied.

"I didn't realize it, but the nurse who is working the main station said she may have had a visitor. I thought you would like to know."

Alec furrowed his brow. "What do you mean she 'might have' had a visitor?"

She hesitated. "I'm sorry, but we're overworked and exhausted. Most of us are at the tail end of a long shift. I don't want to make excuses for her, but she didn't follow protocol, so the visitor's log was not filled out. I don't know who the woman was. And the nurse —well, she seems a little confused. She can't seem to remember if the woman confirmed that she knew the patient after seeing her."

"The nurse is confused. Well, that's just great," Alec said, letting his emotions get the best of him.

Fran and Graham exchanged looks. Kelsey continued typing, oblivious.

"I am going to file the appropriate paperwork and have it sent over, but while we're waiting, can you let security know that I would like them to pull video from the security cameras?" Alec nodded at Fran, who pulled out her phone to call the chief.

"Yes, of course," The nurse said.

"Great. We're also going to want to talk to the nurse who was at the station. What's her name?"

"Okay. Her name is Melissa."

Alec wrote the name in a notepad he'd pulled from his back pocket. "Tell her to stick around. We can be there in fifteen minutes or so," he added before hanging up.

~~~~~

Kate could hear a familiar creaking that made her feel nostalgic. She stood from the chair where she'd fallen asleep watching television. The creaking continued rhythmically. It took her a moment to realize it was coming from her grandmother's old swing in the yard. Sometimes wind gusts on the side of the house brought life into the old remnant from her childhood.

She walked to the back door, remembering warm, sunny days on that swing with her grandma. She and Molly used to help make homemade lemonade and put on big sun hats from grandma's closet. She smiled at the thought of the time she and Grams had with Molly before she died. Her smile dwindled quickly with the realization that they would have no new memories to make.

She opened the back door, but to her surprise, no wind gusted through the house. How was the swing moving in this still air? She walked out into the late evening sun and listened. Creak, creak, creak. It was moving. Her heart lifted. Could Molly have come to visit in her dreams? Like a child, she darted around the corner of the house, anticipating the welcoming image of her sister.

She slowed when she saw a stranger in the swing. Trying to temper her disappointment, she raised her hand to wave. "Hi. I'm Kate. Can I help you?"

The girl looked up, and a flash of recognition swept through Kate. She instinctively took a step back. "You! You ruined my life!" she yelled.

Ashley looked up at her, full of innocence and wonder. Her pink dress laid perfectly across her lap and the swing. White lace trimmed the bottom that tickled at her knees. She continued to push with her feet and appeared to be trying to feel the creaks of the wood with her hands on the seat. Her hair fell in a loose braid down her back.

"This is such a lovely old swing," Ashley said, her smile genuine. "I can tell it's been used a lot."

"Get off of it. Get out of my yard. Leave!" The tainting of something she and Molly had cherished brought heat to Kate's cheeks. Remembering her last terrifying encounter with this stranger in her dreams, she raised her hand to her neck to search for the amulet Fin had given her. She searched far to the right of her collar bone, then her numb fingers gave up the search on her left. The amulet was not on her neck.

Ashley waggled her thumb over her shoulder. "It's back in the living room. You took it off as soon as you got home. You don't need it, though. Come sit down." She patted the old wooden seat.

Kate took a step toward her, still wary for obvious reasons. "How did you know I was looking for the—"

Ashley interrupted, "The amulet? It's a nice little trinket. I'd keep it around if I were you. Not everyone has protection against things unseen." Ashley turned her eyes to the ground and shivered slightly at a memory. She carefully smoothed out her dress a couple times.

Kate took another step toward the swing trying to muster the courage to get closer. She wanted this to be over while simultaneously hoping it would go on so she could glean more information about Molly. Against her better judgment, she confessed, "When I heard the creaking, I thought maybe you were Molly. She loved this swing so much." Speaking about Molly in past tense drove a knife through her stomach every time. She swallowed hard.

Ashley clicked her tongue. "Sorry to disappoint."

If Ashley meant her harm, she would have done something by now. Ashley's demeanor had completely changed from their last encounter. She seemed like a different person. The tug of her heart won and Kate did what any dumb lemming would do in a dream. She ignored all rules of common sense and followed Ashley's request for her to sit down, albeit on the other end of the swing. Just in case.

"Do you know what it's like to be a puppet?" Ashley asked.

Kate shook her head. "If you're talking about what I think you're talking about, then no."

Ashley nodded, thinking quietly for a moment. "I think a big mistake most people make is assuming that the only spiritual war is between the realm of demons and the realm of angels. It was my mistake, too. Apparently, demonic realms don't exactly get along." A humorless smile touched her lips. "We are nothing to them. Simple pawns as they fight amongst themselves.

"I'm not sure if they know that we can remember some of what happens when they take control of our bodies," she continued. "I remember snippets here and there. Most importantly, they spoke of an angel."

Kate searched her face. "An angel?"

Ashley nodded. "The old ones, they said an angel follows you. I remember that part clearly. I think they want you to stop the demon army that is rising to take over Lucifer's kingdom."

Kate scoffed. "I don't know which is more ridiculous. You telling me there is a rising demon army, or you saying that I am going to stop it." Perhaps both were equally unbelievable. Kate didn't exactly own a cape.

"Your humor is much like Molly's." Ashley pulled her braid around to the front and lightly ran her hands down it, twirling the bottom. "I don't have much more time," she said, her voice filled with regret. "They're coming for me."

Kate leaned toward her, less out of sympathy and more out of curiosity. "Who? Who is coming for you?"

"That doesn't matter right now. We have an important matter to discuss. My second gift to you." Ashley said. "You know, the one I promised you last time we met."

Kate sat up rigidly. She forgot that part of her dream. Her head shook before her words came tumbling out. "No, thanks. I don't think I need any more presents from you. Like I said, you ruined my life. I don't even know what's real anymore. I can't talk to my friends about it, and I would seriously consider becoming an alcoholic if I thought it would help me cope with what I've experienced in the last week.

141

"The only person who understands all of this is a deranged old man. So, there you have it. That's my new life. I've lost my sister. I have a new bestie who lives in an old trailer that looks like it was decorated by gypsies. I have a strange necklace that I apparently need to be wearing around town to protect me from impending doom. And according to you, I'm tasked with stopping a spiritual war."

"Kate," Ashley said, leaning in. "This is not something you can prevent. I already gave you the other gift. Where is the kenasai?"

Kate smiled, feeling satisfied. "I knew that thing was trouble. I gave it to my deranged friend."

A shriek came from the street. Kate peeked around Ashley toward the front of the house. A light orange glow flickered. The sun had nearly set, and the glow looked almost like fire as it grew more and more intense. "Did you hear that?" she asked. Her mind told her to get up and run, but her legs didn't respond.

Ashley didn't look over her shoulder. Her face remained steady, white and unwavering as the moon. She reached out and grabbed Kate's hand. "You have to get the kenasai back. Kate, please, you need to keep it."

Kate held her gaze, feeling more courageous now. "No."

Another shriek came from the street. Kate jumped. It sounded closer this time. She looked over her shoulder to confirm she still had a clear path to the door. She didn't want her own shriek to join the loud chorus rising from the street. If she made it to the house, would she be safe?

Cracking and popping echoed around them. Small bits of ash began to fill the air like dark snow. Ashley reached up and brushed some of the ash from her face, leaving a smear on her cheek. She wiped her hand on her dress, leaving a black streak there, too.

The smell of smoke drifted to them. Finally, Ashley looked over her shoulder. "You cannot run from your destiny," she muttered. She quickly snapped back to Kate and squeezed her hand, her eyes fierce. "Promise me."

Kate could see tears pooling in Ashley's eyes. But fear trumped her empathy. She tried desperately to free her hand from Ashley's. "Promise you what?" she asked.

A tear fell from her dark lashes, leaving a white streak through the smear on her face. "Promise me you'll get the kenasai and keep it with you."

"Why would I do that?" Kate whispered through her teeth, hoping whatever lurked in the street would not come down the side of her house. She continued to tug her hand, wishing she hadn't sat close enough for Ashley to grab her.

Ashley pleaded. "It's not a promise for me. It's a promise for you. Molly loved you more than anything." She stood, still gripping Kate's fingers tightly. "She talked about you all the time. You saved her from taking her own life before. You got her to go to counseling." She sniffed and wiped her nose as steady tears came now. "I wish I had a sister like you."

Kate heated. She rose to her feet with Ashley. "You have no right to talk about my sister that way. You led her to her death, didn't you?"

She looked at Kate again. "The old ones have come for me now. Don't let the rising army use Molly's soul. I think you can find a way to save her. I don't know what it is," Ashley pressed her lips into a hard line. "I think Molly knew you had it too. Something inside you is special."

Kate gave up her efforts to get free. Molly's soul? Her brain began to mush together pieces of the puzzle she'd been working on. She shook her head, hoping her feelings weren't true. "Is Molly's soul in the kenasai?" she asked.

Ashley nodded. "I'm so sorry. It's time for you to go. Run!"

"I don't understand!" Kate yelled as the commotion grew louder. Ashes gathered around her eyes, stinging them. She squinted, trying to see through the tears. "Come with me. I have so many questions. Please come with me! How do I save her?"

"This is my fate, but it doesn't have to be Molly's," Ashley crouched and curled into a ball, balancing on her heels with her dress over her knees. She looked like a child.

Grasping for anything that might make this impossible, Kate defiantly shouted, "I don't believe you."

"Run," Ashley replied without looking up. Then, she whispered barely loud enough to hear above the approaching flames, "You will believe me soon enough."

Fire bent around the house, and Kate turned, sprinting toward the backyard. Her legs ached, and her lungs burned. She chanced one last glance over her shoulder, her hair slapping her face. Ashley hadn't moved, but the flames gathered closer. The ashes mottled her dress in black and gray. She had her hands folded and clasped behind her head to tuck herself further into a tiny ball.

Kate rounded the house to the back door just as Ashley screamed. The scream went on for what seemed like ages. It was longer than any human breath should endure.

Kate sat straight up in the chair, her heart racing. The pulse flamed in her ears, drowning out any other sound. She looked around in a desperate attempt to anchor herself. She still couldn't hear over the rush in her ears, but the TV glowed in the corner. The sun had nearly set. She tried to shake the images of the dream by taking some deep breaths and letting them out slowly.

This room wasn't enough to settle her. She stood and marched to the door, determined to prove she had nothing to fear. She could walk outside and see that the world was not on fire. She stared at her hand on the cold doorknob, reconsidering.

Something brushed her leg, and she jumped, turning to face the threat with her back against the door. "Jake! Oh my God." Her heart thumped wildly in her chest. Jake's tail swished on the floor behind him at the prospect of going outside. She had been so focused that she didn't notice him approaching.

She turned back to the door. This had to settle her nerves. "Let's get this over with, boy."

She stepped into the dusky air. To her surprise, Jake accompanied her. Of everything she doubted, she believed Fin's explanation about animals sensing the spiritual world. If her dream really happened, Jake wouldn't set foot outside the back door. She allowed herself to relax a little as she crossed the backyard to the side of the house.

She could smell ash and smoke. She took another deep breath through her nose, just to be sure.

She looked down for Jake. He sat several strides behind her with his head down as he gazed past her. He didn't seem

144

threatened. Using him as her litmus test, she slowly stepped to where she would be able to see the side yard. He didn't react.

Satisfied with the results of her little experiment, she turned, peering into the forming shadows of dusk. She couldn't allow uncertainty to give her pause, or she would have to search the darkness with a flashlight. She took quick strides to the lifeless swing.

She carefully ran her hand along the seat, not sure what she expected to discover. Really, she wanted to find peace of mind. The swing offered no answers, but she could feel the ominous dream unraveling with each moment that passed.

Something on the ground caught her eye.

A perfect dark circle covered the area where she had left Ashley in her dream. She bent, running her fingers over the remaining black pieces. The tiny remnants of grass turned to dust, crumbling when she touched it.

Kate stood, the black covering her fingers. She didn't owe this girl anything, but she owed everything to Molly. Not caring about the future her words would unlock, she spoke to the ashes, "I promise."

Chapter 16

Fran and Alec waited patiently at the nurse's station. Well, Fran waited patiently with her hands folded in front of her while Alec paced every few moments. When they brought Melissa around, the head nurse lingered within earshot. Alec wondered if she intended to provide moral support or if she wanted to make sure Melissa did not say anything that might incriminate the hospital itself.

He approached Melissa as gently as possible. Her eyes kept darting back to the head nurse. Peterson stopped a bit further away than he needed to, hoping she would appreciate the extra space between them. "Why don't you start from the beginning?" Peterson asked.

Melissa looked at the head nurse before starting. "I was sitting at the station." She picked at the hem of her scrubs.

Alec allowed a bit of time to pass before prompting her. "And?"

"And a woman came through the elevator doors. She said she'd been looking for a particular Jane Doe." Melissa reached up to her hair, trying to smooth the unruly surface leading up to her ponytail. She glanced again at the head nurse, who had taken a step closer.

This isn't going to work for me, Peterson thought.

A patient ambled by, pushing a squeaky IV stand in front of him. He gripped the dotted hospital gown in a feeble attempt to cover his backside. Alec seized the opportunity, turning to the head nurse. "I think we need to go somewhere a little more private. I really don't want to alarm any of the patients."

She nodded and showed them to an empty room. She stood to the side as Fran and Melissa walked in. As Alec entered the room, he grabbed the handle and pulled the door closed before the head nurse could follow. He watched her shadow dance in the crack between the door and the floor for a few moments before it disappeared.

Fran smiled at him, mouthing, *thank you.*

Letting out a sigh, he turned to Melissa and said, "Please, go on."

Melissa had visibly relaxed a little. "May I sit down?"

"Of course," Alec said, arranging the chairs in the room for her to sit facing him and Fran.

Melissa cleared her throat. "I need to be honest with you. I'm upset. And yet I feel like I shouldn't leave anything out, or it could interfere with your investigation, right?"

Alec nodded. "Just try to tell us as much as you can remember. The head nurse said you were a little hazy on the details, and that's okay. We'll try to ask questions that will help you remember, too. That's all we are here for. You aren't in any kind of trouble with us."

Melissa nodded and began again. "This lady, she said she was looking for someone. Her niece, maybe? Anyway, I told her that she couldn't visit Jane Doe. She tried to come off all helpful and said she might be able to assist with some background information if she knew it was the girl she was looking for. The whole reason I didn't log her was because she only wanted to look in to see if it was her niece before going to the trouble of gathering information and patient history.

"That's when it happened." She looked down at her hands before continuing. "I — I lost time."

Fran leaned forward as Alec asked, "What do you mean you lost time?"

Melissa held her hands up helplessly. "As much as I try, I can't remember anything that happened after I showed her to the room. I never would have left her there! I don't think I did." She clicked her tongue as a teacher would, chiding a student.

"What is the next thing you remember?" Alec asked.

"I was at the front station again. I heard them calling a code for Jane Doe's room, so I got up and rushed back to see if they needed help," she said.

Alec folded his arms. "Have you ever lost time like that before? Maybe due to stress or exhaustion?"

Melissa shook her head. "You know, when you're tired, sometimes you misremember or think you may have said something when you didn't? It's not like that. Whatever happened is just completely gone. It's so strange."

Alec unfolded his arms, running his palms along his pants. "It's ok," he said reassuringly. "Do you think you can give us a description of the woman?"

Melissa looked up at the ceiling, probing her own mind. "I remember she was tall. But I don't really remember what she was wearing or much about her appearance. I was working on the computer when she came in, and I only barely glanced at her because I was busy. Her hair was down, maybe blonde and brown?"

Fran broke her silence and interrupted, "You had a whole conversation with her, but you didn't get a good look?"

Melissa flushed. "I'm sorry. I was just so busy, and I expected her to leave because I told her no visitors. I didn't even stop typing while she was talking to me," she bowed her head, looking ashamed.

"Don't worry about that now," Alec said, shooting Fran a look. "What about other details? Do you remember how she smelled? Was her voice high or low?"

Melissa looked up, nodding enthusiastically. "Yeah! She smelled like perfume. I don't remember much about the way she sounded except that she was annoying me."

"Annoying you how?" Peterson asked.

"She seemed like she wasn't used to hearing 'no' for an answer. She kept pressing. And her heels were so loud when I lead her down the hallway. We try to keep things as quiet as possible for our patients, so I remember that."

Fran visibly twitched. Alec glanced her way, but she kept her eyes on Melissa. "Ok," he said. "If you can remember anything else, please let us know." He handed her one of his cards.

A man was waiting in the hall for them.

"Hello," he began, "I'm Mr. Farragat, the public relations officer." He handed each of them a card. "I'd like to be your contact from now on." He smiled.

Alec put his hands in his pockets, wondering if the head nurse had called him up. Good choice on her part since she clearly attempted to coach their witness. At least she knew how to cover her ass. Alec didn't suspect her, though. It seemed more like she was worried about their liability on the matter of overworking employees than being an accessory to murder. "Thank you," he said. "You could have knocked, and we would have gladly let you sit in on the interview."

Mr. Farragat put his hands up in front of him. "Oh no, that's quite alright. I will be present for any interviews if the press gets involved, of course, but as far as the investigation, I do not want to interfere with your process."

Before Alec could say anything else, Fran interrupted. "Great. Did you receive the request for security footage?"

Mr. Farragat templed his hands together in front of him, looking at the ceiling. "I did, but we are working on a small issue with the footage."

Fran took a step forward, leaning in. "What's the problem?"

Alec cleared his throat, hoping to reel Fran in without touching her. She didn't budge. Something Melissa said about the visitor set her off. Was this about the heels? The noise? Whatever the reason, Fran couldn't reset her usual composure.

"Ah — well, the quality of the footage is subpar. We're trying to clear it up so you might glean some information from it," Mr. Farragat explained nervously.

"Sir," Fran continued, "if your security cameras do not work properly, how can you ensure the safety of the patients? Furthermore, you have visitors, nurses, administrative staff, and cleaning crews." She held out her fingers, counting down each one for visual emphasis. "How do you think they would feel knowing that your equipment is...how did you put it? Subpar?"

The man took a step back, Fran's attack pushing him into defense mode. "Actually, the footage before and after our unknown visitor was fine. There was some sort of outside interference, and we cannot see any of the footage from the entire floor. This sort of thing happens sometimes. Our new cameras are wireless, and the signal can be interrupted for a variety of reasons."

Alec stepped closer to Mr. Farragat, cutting Fran off from whatever else might fly out of her mouth. He held out his hand, signaling for the man to walk with him to the elevator. "We'll take the footage regardless," he said. "I know some people who might be able to work with what we have." He looked over his shoulder to check on Fran. She followed tensely with her arms stuck stiffly to her sides. Alec nearly told her to take the stairs, not wanting to share an elevator ride with her.

Once the elevator doors closed, he snapped. "Fran! What in the world? That man is our ally. We cannot afford to burn bridges right now."

"He has to provide us with the footage. I didn't burn any bridges. And you interrupted me! I was going to ask for footage of the hospital entrance. Maybe if we narrowed down the time that she arrived and left, we could pinpoint the suspect from that entry point!"

"First of all," Alec began, trying to keep his own anger in check, "she is not a suspect. She is a person of interest."

"Alec," Fran stopped him, taking a deep breath, "earlier when we left the hospital, I..."

Alec cut her off, "I wasn't finished. Secondly, we can't chew him up and spit him out, and then ask for a favor!"

The doors to the elevator opened, and Alec stepped out stiffly.

Fran's anger had depleted significantly. "I'm sorry. I need to tell you why I reacted that way. When we were leaving earlier, I was rushing to catch up with you and I..."

"No, Fran," he hissed, trying to keep from making a scene. People lumbered around the lobby with pagers as they waited for loved ones to come out of surgery. "This is not the time or place for this conversation. Take some time to pull yourself together before you ruin everything we're working for."

He handed her the keys, adding, "I'll call a cab."

~~~~~

Kate pulled an old yellow sundress out of her closet and a white cardigan. She slipped into some comfortable flats, checked her outfit in the mirror, and rushed down the stairs. She felt like such a bad friend when Marcy called asking her if she still planned to come to the cookout she'd told her about weeks ago. Kate played like she hadn't forgotten but cradled the phone between her shoulder and ear, doing a quick scan of her pantry.

She needed to get groceries.

She needed to start keeping better track of events on an actual calendar.

She needed to go to Fin's to get the kenasai back.

And, apparently, she needed to stop a demon army.

Kate told Marcy she would bring potato salad. She grabbed an empty bowl from the cabinet, stuffing it into a bag. She had just enough time to get dressed, grab the bag, Jake's leash, and run out the door.

"Wait for me here, boy," she instructed Jake. She hustled in the grocery store and through the deli section. After a quick scan of the containers, she picked up a potato salad that looked unnaturally yellow but good enough. She turned on her heels.

She nearly stumbled into Detective Peterson. He put out one hand and steadied her by touching her elbow, which tingled lightly at his touch. She felt her stomach flutter when his blue eyes met hers. She couldn't deny he looked charming even in street clothes. "Detective! What a surprise! I didn't see your car in the parking lot." She flashed a smile, felt like it was too big, and toned it back to a grin.

"Oh. I came here in a cab. I'm sorry, I didn't mean to sneak up on you. I wasn't sure it was you until I was close, and then you turned and caught me off guard," he said. "You are wearing a dress," he stated plainly. "I mean, of course, you know what you're wearing. I just haven't seen you in anything outside of your running gear."

She smiled at him dumbly before realizing she should probably respond. "Yes. I'm wearing a dress." *What is the matter with you?* She scolded herself. *This is the man in charge of investigating your sister's murder. You're swooning like a schoolgirl!* She couldn't help but notice that his hand lingered on her arm.

He noticed, too, jerking it back down to his side. He glanced at the cold salads. "I'm just here grabbing lunch."

"Right," Kate said. She held up the potato salad. "Well, I better go. Fran said we are meeting soon. I put it on my calendar, but I can't remember the date," she lied, remembering marking it. She didn't want him to know she was looking forward to seeing him again, even though she was.

His face lit up. "Yeah, I'll see you then. Looking forward to it." He made a face that told her he felt silly for saying he was looking forward to it, so she broke off their awkward exchange, heading to the checkout.

Marcy didn't say anything about Kate's late arrival or her store-bought potato salad. She knew Marcy would notice, though. Kate's homemade version looked nothing like this store-bought counterfeit. She graciously took the bowl, setting it on the table outside with the other dishes.

Jake bopped over to Jasmine, and the two did a circular romp with each other. Kate smiled at how happy Jasmine seemed with Marcy's family. Brenden had given her a new collar and name tag, and she had purple bows on her ears. It would have meant a lot to Molly to know her dog received such special treatment.

Molly, whose soul was trapped in a container amongst other souls.

Kate reached up and squeezed her temples. She could do this. *Just be normal for a little while and get this out of the way,* she scolded herself. Even though her life resembled nothing remotely close to normal anymore.

"So," Marcy interrupted Kate's thoughts, "how is work?"

Kate hadn't noticed Marcy standing right next to her, arms folded. Fail number one in pretending to be normal.

"Oh. Um. I actually resigned," Kate responded, trying to sound casual.

"What?!" Marcy said, her hands immediately coming up to Kate's shoulders. "Why did you resign? You didn't even tell me you were thinking about it."

"I know," Kate looked at the ground. "I think I need more time than they were able to give me. I felt like they were very accommodating, but I didn't want to take advantage of their generosity. Because of my absence, they were running behind. I tried working part-time. You know, just doing what I could from home, but I didn't feel like I was efficient enough," she recited different sections of her resignation letter almost verbatim.

The concern in Marcy's eyes didn't falter. "Kate. I need you to know I am here for you. I am not sure what to do, though. I think you need some space, and I don't know how much to give you. I want to reach out to you every day. I miss you. Please, promise me that you will call me more. I'll do the same."

"I—uh, I promise," Kate had a hard time saying the words that changed her life just the night before. This seemed like such a trivial promise compared to the last one she made to a circle of ashes on the ground. Call Marcy more. No problem.

"Kate?"

"Yeah?"

Marcy took her hands from her shoulders and folded them again. "You spaced out on me there for a second."

Kate added spacing out in the middle of the conversation to her second fail in pretending to be normal.

"Sorry," Kate tried to paste an easy smile onto her face.

Marcy gave her a sideways glance. "Right, no problem. So do you have another job lined up?"

153

"Not yet," Kate answered, grabbing a plate and dumping a spoonful of baked beans onto it.

"I see." Marcy followed her lead, grabbing a plate behind her.

"Molly had a really good life insurance policy. I found out last week that I am the only beneficiary. I guess Molly figured Grams wouldn't be around anymore by the time she—" Kate's voice caught in her throat. She cleared it. "Anyway, I need to talk to Grams because I feel like I should give her some of the money, too. I also don't really know what to do about our parents. They didn't come to the funeral since they were out of the country. We really haven't been in touch with them in so long."

"Oh, Kate, I'm sorry," Marcy smiled. "Please know that you aren't alone. I think what you're going through is completely normal."

Kate had to stifle a laugh. Marcy's kind eyes waited for her to agree. "Right! Yes, you are so right. This is all so normal. I don't even know why I feel like it's changing my whole life." The last words came out bitter and sarcastic enough to make Marcy's shoulders slump.

"I'm sorry," Marcy said. "I didn't mean it that way."

Fail number three. Kate put down her plate, trying to think of a quick escape. She immediately gave up on elaborate plans like feigning illness or getting an important phone call. Marcy deserved better than that, so Kate landed on a direct approach.

"Marcy, I shouldn't have come today. I'm the one who should be sorry. I came because I know I've been an absent friend and I feel bad about it. I really want to talk to you about what's going on, but I don't know how."

"I will understand, Kate," Marcy said, her face confused.

"I know you would understand. I just — I don't think *I* even understand what I'm going through. More than anything, I just want to be done with it all. I want to be done selling Molly's house and car, done deciding how to distribute her belongings and insurance money, and just done with everything else that is looming over me." She felt like 'everything else' was a good way to describe demon armies, dead person ashes, and soul catchers. "Until I'm able to get out from under all of it, I really don't know how I'm supposed to move on.

"So that's why I resigned. I have a lot to do, and once I can get it all taken care of, then maybe I can take care of myself."

Marcy took Kate's plate and turned to continue filling it up for her. She turned back to Kate and handed her the full plate. "Arthur will be out here in just a second with some plastic wrap for you to take this home with you. When I saw you pull up, I knew you wouldn't be staying long. I could tell by looking at you that you needed a to-go plate.

"You're my best friend, Kate. I know you better than you think I do. How about next time we get together and just do a paint night or something? No talking about issues or problems. Just good ol' girl talk and wine." Marcy smiled, filling Kate with hope.

Kate could feel her bottom lip beginning to quiver. "I would like that," she said, trying to keep her voice from cracking.

Right on cue, Arthur walked up behind Marcy with some plastic wrap and a bag with two frozen casseroles. He smiled broadly, "Marcy said you'd be needing this." He took her plate, wrapped it, and placed it on top of the casseroles.

"I baked those a few days ago," Marcy added.

Kate felt a tear fall from her eyelashes. Before taking the bag of food, she hugged Marcy fiercely. She whispered, "You are the best friend anyone could ask for. Thank you so much."

She turned to Arthur and took the bag, smiling at him. It was her first true smile in days. She whistled over her shoulder for Jake to follow.

Marcy waved goodbye to her, shouting, "I expect your homemade potato salad next time!"

Chapter 17

Kate and Fin had their noses stuffed in books for days trying to figure out how to open a kenasai. When his books turned nothing up, they switched to the internet, which also turned nothing up. Fin did pull out the drawing he had seen years ago, though, and it had an uncanny resemblance to their object. Not that Kate needed any convincing. Fortunately, Fin believed in the reality of the dream world, so he also had no doubts.

"Maybe you have a gift," he said.

Kate continued scrolling down the page she knew would end in disappointment. "How's that?"

"Well, everyone has gifts. Even the Bible talks about different gifts. And dreaming in the Bible was significant, too. Not only that, but dreams have considerable meaning for different tribes and peoples dating back as far as history records."

"Right," Kate said, still disinterested.

"Maybe you are one of those people who can use dreams to your advantage. It seems like there is a correlation between what happens in your dreams and what happens in reality sometimes, right?"

Kate thought back to her childhood, a smirk on her face. "Well, then I guess I really do need to be afraid of what's under the bed."

Fin squinted at her. "I really don't know why we're friends."

She closed her laptop. "What's your gift?"

"Intelligence, persuasion, and people skills," he smiled.

"Those sound like fine-tuned characteristics, not gifts. And that third one is questionable."

Fin shrugged, changing the subject. "You know what day it is?"

Kate pressed her hands down to her sides. "No, Fin."

He smiled, batting his eyelashes. "Helping Hands! Alright, let's get ready. I hope Pat brings her lemon cookies. You know, the ones with the homemade frosting?"

Kate rolled her eyes. "I know what day it is. When I say 'no,' I mean I don't want to go. I haven't seen Kyle since all that weird stuff happened, and frankly, I hate that group."

"That group is the reason we met!" Fin gasped, feigning offense. He stood and plopped his feet into his boots. "Let's go. Who knows? Maybe we will get some new information."

Kate rolled her eyes, knowing her choices were to drag herself along with Fin or sit in his trailer searching for something she thought they might never find. She picked up the kenasai and placed it in the bottom of her purse. "We really need to find a safe place for this," she muttered half to herself. The idea of walking around with her sister's soul in her handbag gave her goosebumps but leaving it in the trailer seemed disrespectful.

She drove to the meeting after Fin put his bike in her trunk. While his habits struck her as odd, she could not say she blamed him. Plenty of times, she'd gone out on girls' nights that she had wished she had driven to herself instead of carpooling. Kate might not be antisocial, but she knew when her social muscles reached their limits. If she had her own car there as an escape route, she always felt better about going.

She also had a natural inclination to say what she really thought. Through the years, she'd come to realize that as much as people glamorize the 'great friends' who will give it to you straight, very few people actually appreciate that trait. Kate had learned to keep her mouth closed and tiptoe around to keep from offending people. As if that wasn't exhausting enough, she had her facial expressions to deal with. They betrayed her time and time again. She wished she had a poker face.

After a few hours of hanging out with groups of people, she typically started feeling strained because of her efforts to keep everything in check. Marcy seldom took offense at anything, which made her an excellent friend. She also did a good job covering for Kate when she let something loose from her thoughts that she shouldn't have.

Kate and Fin hopped out of the car and started for the door.

"Kate? Is that you?"

She turned to see Kyle slowly ambling up, assessing Fin. "Yeah," she replied feebly. "Fin convinced me to come."

Kyle raised his eyebrows dubiously. "Fin. He convinced you to come." His gaze shifted between the two of them. He gave up on waiting for a punch line and continued, "I haven't seen you since that weird thing happened." His voice dropped to a whisper, "Are you ok?"

Fin turned dismissively and walked ahead of Kyle and Kate. She purposely didn't answer. Mostly because she wasn't okay, she didn't want to admit it out loud, and she sucked at lying. As they got to the room, a few people waved and smiled at her.

"Did you hear about that girl?" Kyle asked her.

"What girl?" She asked, pouring water into a cup.

Kyle stooped his shoulders a little. "You know. The one that we — uh — met in the parking lot."

Kate shook her head, choosing to keep her opinion about his choice of words to herself. 'Met' hardly came close to the term she would have used. She could sense Fin drawing closer. She tried to ignore him but rolled her eyes. For someone who ran a self-proclaimed intelligence operation within the group, he sure lacked the ability to be discreet. He had the advantage of coming off harmless.

"Anyway," Kyle continued without confirmation from Kate, "she was involved in a suspicious death in Carbondale at the school. She's some kind of freak!"

"How did you hear about that?" Kate asked.

He rolled his eyes at her. "The news. Geez, do you live under a rock or what?"

Kate tugged a stray hair behind her ear. "Kind of."

"Well, she died," he reiterated. "The police had her picture in the news saying if anyone knew anything about her to come forward. I went down to the station to tell them that was the girl we saw at the pet store. Did they call you?"

Kate shook her head. "When did you go in?"

"I don't know," he said, popping a cookie in his mouth. "A couple days ago. I don't know for sure if they're even going to contact you because we didn't really know who she was. They wanted a name, which I couldn't give them. But I wanted to at least tell them."

Kate nodded. She glanced at Fin just long enough to catch his *I told you so* look. She sighed. He would make the ride home insufferable.

"Kyle," Kate said, placing her hand on his arm. "I feel like I owe you an apology."

"Don't worry about it, Kate. I was being pushy, and I knew it. You aren't the only one healing from a loss and making questionable decisions because of it."

"I—uh." Kate laughed lightly. "I guess we can move on from it even though you just called me a questionable decision."

Kyle laughed with her. "You know what I mean."

Fin used the universal sign for gagging before finishing off the last lemon cookie.

Joe stood ceremoniously. "Hello, everyone! I'm happy to see Kate back tonight." His statement was followed by some nods amongst those in the circle. She smiled her thanks at them.

He continued. "We also have a new visitor. This is Brodey Hill. Brodey, would you like to say anything before we get started?"

The boy shifted in his seat before deciding not to stand. Joe sat next to him to put him at ease. "Hey, I'm Brodey. I guess he already said that. I'm kind of nervous." His gaze fell to the floor. "No offense, but I don't really know if this is going to work for me. My girlfriend and I have been looking for a non-counseling outlet..."

Joe nodded toward the group, "We're not that into counselors either."

That's for sure, Kate thought. At least with a group of people the conversation doesn't die into awkward silence like a one-on-one session.

"Right." Brodey folded his hands. "I know this group is technically for people who have lost loved ones, but my story is a little different. It was my suitemate, and I thought I knew him, but it turns out I didn't. He died tragically, and I saw it all." He started to lean back into his chair but remembered to add, "Oh yeah, and he tried to make me kill myself."

Kyle stiffened and pulled out his phone. Kate tried to glance nonchalantly at his phone to see what had him typing so furiously, but she couldn't get a good look. Her phone vibrated, causing her to jump because it was in her purse, and for a moment, she thought the kenasai had moved on its own.

Kyle shot her a sideways glance that told her she needed to check it immediately. Joe continued in the background, explaining a little about each person to Brodey. She reached down into her bag and tried to grab the phone without making the kenasai roll around.

She pulled up the text:

I think this kid saw the murder at the school!!! The police
mentioned a witness but never showed his picture. How
many tragic deaths could there have been? I'm sure it's him.
Man, that sucks.

She responded with a frowny face, but before she could drop her
phone back in her purse, Joe stopped and said, "Oh! And here is
Blanch."

Blanch, arriving late, grabbed a chair and pulled it up next to Kate.
Looking down, Kate realized her purse still laid wide open from
grabbing her phone.

She looked up just in time to see Blanch staring down at her. "May
I sit here?" she asked.

"Of course!" Kate responded a little too eagerly, forcing a pleasant
expression. She stashed her phone back in her purse and zip it closed.
The phone made a clanking noise as it hit the kenasai.

Kate could feel Blanch's inquisitive stare as Joe picked back up
with introductions. Had she seen the kenasai, or did she just hear it?
Even if she saw it, would it matter? Probably not. If it was so obscure
that they couldn't find references, someone recognizing it off the
street seemed improbable.

Kate finally brought herself to meet Blanch's gaze. It made the
Arctic seem like a summer vacation spot. Blanch blinked, looking
down at her purse. Kate tried to look a bit ashamed. Then she
concocted the best story she could think of. "I've not had anything to
drink, don't worry. But I just feel better having it with me." She hoped
Blanch would buy that she had a hidden drinking problem. People
carried flasks, right?

Blanch paused for a moment, a look of doubt crossing her face.
Then, she whispered back, "You don't have anything to be ashamed of
here, dear. I'm sure plenty of these people sip the sauce."

~~~~~

When the meeting finished, Blanch watched as Kate and Fin left
together. She helped Joe clean up the chairs, said her goodbyes to a
few other people, and turned out the lights. Before stepping out
herself, she pulled out her cell phone and made a call.

"Hello, this is Blanch. Turns out you were right about Ms. Catherine
Gregory. She's acting a bit off."

The impatient voice on the other end said, "Get to the point. I don't have time for this."

"Well, for one thing, she's made an odd friend in Fin."

"I don't care for that idiotic man. He presents no threat to me," the voice interrupted.

Eager to offer something good, Blanch continued, "She's also drinking," and then quickly added, "but she acted strangely about it. And don't ask me where she found a cylinder flask. Putrid habit." Blanch investigated her fingernails.

"Tell me about the flask. Was it metal? Are you sure it was a flask?" The voice finally sounded interested.

"I only saw it for a moment. It was metal, yes. I intended to speak to her more about her drinking problem, but she left with Fin before I had a chance." Blanch waited, glad that she was able to provide juicy gossip.

Her 'friend' would, in exchange, provide her with cash. The arrangement made her feel important, too. Joe had tried to convince her to leave the group several times, telling her that she didn't need it anymore and she had healed. She knew that, of course. But if she left Helping Hands, the money would stop. So, she explained to him that they needed someone who had healed to continue to support the members of the group. It was a point of contention between the two of them.

Blanch heard a click at the other end of the line before it went dead.

~~~~~

At the precinct, officers mulled in and out, working on various cases, filing reports, and getting some much-needed coffee before heading back out. The office coffee didn't have any bones to it, and the bottom of the pot had a permanent lining of coffee tar from continuous use. Most police officers prided themselves in knowing the best places to buy coffee and breakfast, anyway, leaving the office carafe as a last resort.

Small's, a local meat market, bested everyone else when it came to breakfast sandwiches. Alec stopped by almost daily. The first time he walked in and asked what to order, the clerk responded with, "Nobody beats our meat." Alec raised an eyebrow at the kid, wondering who hired a smartass before the clerk pointed up at a sign

161

that proudly displayed the saying as their motto. They even sold shirts that people wore around town with the double-meaning motto. Now it made him smirk.

He chewed his last bite of breakfast, licking his finger, opening the hospital video in his case file. He pressed a puff of air out between tight lips as sixteen minutes of nothing but grainy fuzz played. Resisting the urge to bang his head on his desk, he pressed his palm to his forehead, wishing he could push out answers. He would send the video to Kelsey and Graham, but he knew they couldn't fix something that wasn't there. If he merely needed them to clean up a grainy picture, they could do it in a flash. But no picture at all? No way.

"Everything ok?" One of the younger officers asked, passing by.

Alec looked up. "Yeah. Just one of those cases that has a lot of slamming doors, you know?"

The officer nodded his understanding. Then, looking at the screenshot, he asked, "Are you working that pet store case? I don't think we're looking into it anymore. Sorry, man."

Alec shook his head. "No. This is the security footage from the hospital."

The officer tilted his head to the side. "Can you play it for me?"

Alec wondered why he seemed so interested in bad footage, but he pressed play anyway. Why not? After their argument, Fran had taken some vacation time, and he had not seen her in two days. He didn't mind an extra set of eyes on it.

After seeing the first minute, the officer nodded. "Yeah! That's exactly what happened to our parking lot footage from the pet store! Technology sucks."

Alec smiled before joking, "I know. Maybe we need to make a public announcement to stop buying Wi-Fi cameras.

The officer laughed. "Like they'd listen. It's weird, though."

Alec looked up at him curiously.

"The security cameras at the pet store weren't Wi-Fi." The officer shrugged and ambled away.

Alec opened a new window on his screen and shot an email to the chief asking if he could send the footage and information about the pet store incident. The thought of finally making a connection between two cases sparked just a bit of hope in a journey of dead ends.

Chapter 18

Kate heated up one of Marcy's dishes in the oven and put on a pot of coffee. Grams always liked coffee right after dinner. Kate had a limit. She couldn't drink coffee after 2:00 pm because it kept her up all night. But not Grams. That woman could sleep through anything.

When she called Kate asking to get together, Kate welcomed the idea and invited her over for dinner. She knew it would push her to make an effort to tidy up her house, too. She walked through the living room, giving it one more quick inspection before letting Jake out into the backyard.

She stepped out with him to make sure he didn't wander too far. Since her final dream of the girl, he had started slowly making his way back into the woods now and then. He did so cautiously, but his return to semi-normal routine put her at ease.

"Katherine?" her grandma called from the front.

She rolled her eyes; her grandma never called her Kate. At this point, if she did, it would be weird. "I'm out back, Grams!"

At the ripe old age of 75, spunky Grams still mowed her own lawn, tended her garden, and played a mean game of dominoes. She even walked with confidence and strength, though the years had slowed her down a bit. Kate and Molly used to say they kept Grams young since she raised the two of them.

"Hello, darling!" she beamed.

"Grams! It's been too long." Kate hugged her firmly, breathing in the scent of peppermint that Grams always dabbed behind her ears.

"What on earth happened to your yard over there?" Grams asked as they walked together to the door. "I saw that part of your grass

164

died off in a patch. Did you spray it with something? I told you that all-purpose weed killer would kill your grass too. If you have weeds, you need to pull them by the roots."

Kate laughed. "It'll be fine! It'll grow back eventually, right?" Kate hadn't thought of an explanation for how a dead girl's ashes singed her yard, so she just rolled with Grams' reason.

They walked into the kitchen with Jake close behind. The smell of Marcy's casserole filled the room, and with Grams there, Molly's absence felt heavier. She and Molly cooked nearly every evening with Grams in the kitchen.

"That smells delicious! What are you making?" Grams asked. She grabbed two plates from the cabinet and began to set the table.

"Marcy made it for me, so I thought I'd share." Kate picked up the foil with a label reading it aloud, "Chicken Paella."

"Speaking of Marcy," Grams started, "she called me just the other day."

Kate kept her back to Grams so she couldn't see a reaction. Her body stiffened a bit, though. She had anticipated that Grams had an underlying reason for wanting to get together but also hoped that maybe they could just enjoy each other's company before getting down to business.

She pulled the dish out of the oven and turned to face Grams. "Oh?"

"Dear. You never had a poker face. I know you probably don't appreciate her reaching out to me on your behalf, but she's worried about you." Grams sat up a little straighter with a stiff upper lip, adding, "She's a good friend, you know."

Kate let a sideways smile touch her lips. Grams always made that face when she said something that she thought Kate might disagree with as if her body language alone could persuade Kate. "I know," Kate conceded. Grams looked surprised and relaxed a little as Kate brought the hot dish to the table. "Listen," she said, "She's probably right to worry. I haven't been acting myself since we lost Molly. But I'm trying to work through it the best I can. I'm sure you're doing the same."

Grams waved her hand dismissively and placed her napkin in her lap. "Katherine, I have no concerns about you getting over Molly's death. You were always the resilient one."

I guess now isn't the time to tell her that I'd like to curl up into a ball on the floor every day, Kate thought. *That is definitely not resilient.* She waited for Grams to continue while she served them both a helping from Marcy's dish. She smiled when she felt Jake's nose on her leg. He knew better than to beg or put his head on the table, but he never ceased in his efforts.

Kate decided to bring up the other topic she thought Grams might have on her mind. "Did Marcy mention the insurance policy?"

Grams nodded. "I don't need any of that, Katherine, but thank you for considering me."

Kate furrowed her brow. She expected more discussion about both topics from Grams, but neither seemed to be a topic of interest. She took a bite of the paella. "Mm, this is so good!" She said before even chewing. She hadn't eaten a decent meal in a while.

Grams made a face, reminding Kate that, even as an adult, she could be admonished for speaking with food in her mouth. "Yes, Marcy has always been quite the chef."

"So," Kate said after swallowing her food, "I guess the only thing left to discuss is my parents." This topic usually passed by quickly in all conversations growing up. Grams kept tight lips about their parents. Kate assumed it was because she held a grudge after they abandoned their only children. She looked forward to getting every tense topic behind them and just talking about life in general.

But Grams furrowed her brows before gently placing her fork on the edge of her plate. Kate immediately wished she could leave the table. She knew by Grams' body language that she'd rather drive through a thunderstorm on a bicycle than hear what Grams had to say.

"Darling," Grams began, "we need to talk about your parents, but not because of the life insurance policy."

Kate's mind raced through the possibilities of Grams' news. Did her parents die? If they did, she would have to assess how she should feel or react. She did not have any standing relationship with them, so she didn't think she would cry. Did that make her calloused, or was it an understandable response?

Or maybe Grams planned to tell her that her parents might visit. Probably not. She hadn't seen them since her early grade school years. In a sad way, death would be the least awkward news, and therefore the most preferable. Kate felt a little dark for landing there and abandoned her internal guessing game.

Grams continued, "I need to begin by telling you that I've never lied to you." Tears gathered at the bottom of both of her eyes. She lifted her gaze to the ceiling, trying to keep Kate from noticing.

"Grams! Please! Whatever you have to say, I could never ever be upset with you. Molly and I may not have had 'normal' parental role models, but we were lucky to have you. There were plenty of times that I wondered why people pitied us. They had no idea how amazing our lives were with you. I can't say I'd ever change it." She surprised herself with her own eloquence. Typically, when people cried, Kate only offered awkward responses and canned phrases to play it safe, but this was Grams. She simply could not allow Grams to beat herself up over anything she had done in the past. She was a saint.

Instead of taking heart in Kate's words, Grams shuddered like a building undergoing demolition. "Just let me finish." She picked up her napkin and dabbed her eyes. "You're so fierce, Katherine. Just like your mother was. But like her, you have no idea how strong you are."

Kate balked at being compared to her mother. Grams had never said anything bad about her parents, but she never compared the girls to them, either. "I'm nothing like her," she responded resolutely.

Grams let out a weak smile, "Oh, yes. Yes, you are." She patted Kate's hand. Then she let out a breath. "I can see it in your tired eyes. And it's time you know the truth before it gets worse."

Before Kate could open her mouth to argue, Grams continued. "You remember growing up how you and Molly had such terrible nightmares?" Acknowledging Kate's affirmative nod, Grams sailed on into uncharted territory. "They manifested in both of you very young, younger than your mother's did." She removed her hand from Kate's and tightened her grip on her napkin, pulling it. "She tried everything I did for her as a girl. Dream catchers, charms, prayers, and different juices to help you sleep soundly. Nothing worked. Finally, she convinced your father to try a rune that would help to bind your gift of dreams while you lived in my house."

Runes. Either Grams had an excellent grip on Kate's new reality, or Grams had clearly lost her mind. How could she possibly know about those? And if she really did, how could have Kate lived oblivious to it all these years? Kate's stomach stirred apprehensively with the anticipation of more unwelcome news.

"They decided to combine it with a rune for protection, too. In their line of work, family members are the most delicate and fragile aspects of life. I feared when you girls grew up and left my home that your gifts would resurface. It only made sense." She blotted another tear from her eye. "Molly's did. It drove her into depression. By the time I finally told her that she had the gift for dream walking, it was too late to help her learn to control it. She had already started down a path that I couldn't pull her back from. She tried to fight it. She tried so hard." Grams dabbed her eyes again. She shook her head.

A flood of childhood memories washed over Kate, but now she had a new lens of revelation to peek through. Growing up, she didn't think much of the protective nature her grandmother had. Her biggest trigger point as a child now made the most sense. Her words droned out low and soft as pieces of a long-neglected puzzle assembled in the fringes of her mind. "We were not allowed to sleep at friends' houses, but people could sleep at ours."

"I couldn't risk it," Grams confirmed.

"I don't understand what you meant when you mentioned mom and dad's line of work," Kate heard herself say. Her mind bubbled with what seemed like a ceaseless list of questions, and that one just happened to boil up to the top first.

"Kate, you come from a long line of incredibly special people. We carry a deep burden that most will never understand or know. They are hunters and seers of the spiritual realm. Some of us have special gifts, too. Your mother passed her gift for dream walking down to you girls."

"Dream walking." Kate meant to ask a question, but instead, she defaulted to parroting her teacher again. Except this teacher she knew very intimately. This teacher had withheld valuable information from her for her entire life.

Grams could sense her pain. She gave a compassionate look before continuing. "Most of our children know very young that we are hunters and spiritually gifted. The Bible mentions angelic languages, although not in detail…"

"What does any of this have to do with the Bible? You're talking about *spells*, Grams. I might not have a church background, but I know what a spell is." Kate couldn't stop herself from interrupting. Her anger bubbled into her face as it turned hot. The one person she could trust had betrayed her all along.

Grams shook her head emphatically. "A rune is not necessarily a spell, although there are other types of runes that can be used as such. It's simply a command written in Enochian, or in other words, angelic script. Sometimes it's also referred to as the Alphabet of the Ark. It is a powerful language and not to be taken lightly.

"Your mother and father were very gifted in using Enochian. Despite the good that came from their skill, they lived a dangerous life." Grams made a face of disapproval.

Kate was feeling more and more emotional about being lied to her whole life, but she couldn't speak. The new information Grams offered about their parents stunned her into silence.

"But their lives are even more complicated than that, dear." Grams pursed her lips, considering how to continue. "Most hunters stay single and have no family because of the obvious dangers it could bring. But there are many times in life when they cannot face the perilous nature of their work alone, so they have guardians who help keep them on track. They understand the life of a hunter, and they also have a trained education in Enochian, although they have no gifts of their own.

"When your mother, Alice, met her guardian, they were teens. Dean Gregory was handsome and charming, and she fell in love with him. Most guardians are much older than their charges, and therefore this is not normally an issue. I disapproved of their relationship, but once I realized I couldn't stop it, I gave up trying to convince your mother otherwise. She was so headstrong. And they brought you girls into the world, such precious gifts, not only to us but to the world.

"We had to keep your lineage a secret. Never before have children come from both a line of hunters and a line of guardians. We didn't know which you would turn out to be. The day finally came when your parents had to leave for your safety, and we bound your gifts. Alice was especially torn, knowing that her love for Dean and her love for the two of you had created a war. I don't think any of us will ever be able to forgive ourselves, but we had no choice."

On one hand, Kate felt relieved to know that someone could explain what was happening to her. Fin had mentioned that perhaps she had gifts, although she doubted he realized the depth of the gifts. On the other hand, she felt cheated. They had taken something from her without her permission. On top of that, she had to deal with an onslaught of realizing she might never have a normal life again. A double blow.

She tried to imagine what her much younger self would say if given the option of binding her with a rune. She shook her head. It didn't matter what she would have said. Contrary to Grams' opening defense, they lied to her and Molly all those years. The sting of knowing that Molly had dealt with so much more than just depression pushed Kate to her next response.

"Molly never told me. Neither did you! *You knew*," pain laced her voice.

"Katherine, please. Without having experienced the past few weeks, would you have ever believed either of us? Molly was always so sensitive, and I can only conclude that her gift manifested because of it. You guarded yourself much better than she did," Grams reached out to touch Kate's hand.

Kate reeled. "It's not Molly's fault that she was lied to and unprepared to handle it." She pulled her hand back from the woman she'd admired all her life, the knife of betrayal still stuck in her heart. "You can't possibly know what I've gone through the past couple weeks."

"I'm afraid I know all too well what you're going through." Grams looked down at the table, her face slightly ashamed. "Like I said, your mother passed dream walking down to you. Dream walkers can communicate and reach out to each other. It's a honed skill that I can teach you. It is often how our guardians find us when we are ready to begin our lives as hunters. We can also bring other people into our dreams..."

"Wait," Kate put her hands flat on the table. They left steamy prints when she lifted them. "Have you been in my head?"

Grams put up a defensive hand. "Normally, I would have to be invited, but you have no idea how to control it, so our dreams overlapped a few times these past weeks. Because you don't have any training, I couldn't hear much detail. What I've seen is blurry, but the circle of ash in your yard proves to me that I've seen some of what you're experiencing." Her eyes filled with empathy. "I'm so sorry, Katherine. It is terrifying, I know."

Kate breathed deeply, trying to process both the sense of betrayal and the relief that washed over her with the answers her Grams provided. She tried to pick the most important question from the myriad of curiosities bouncing around in her head.

"Who is my guardian?" Kate asked.

"Guardians don't have the power to enter your dreams without permission. I am a dream walker, so it is a little bit different. But I don't know that you have a guardian, dear," Grams responded with a sideways glance accompanied by even more bad news, "They usually present themselves much earlier in a hunter's life. We've not been able to find any documentation on binding gifts of hunters in the past. Really, we have no frame of reference to guess what will happen to you now. We just have to trust that our decision will serve the greater good."

Kate felt like an experiment gone wrong. She envisioned her lab rat self in a cage, oblivious that soon she would be tossed in the ocean and told to swim when all she knew how to do was run in a toy wheel. She took a stab at another question. "So, mom and dad -- they didn't want to leave us? Why couldn't we have just stayed together?"

Grams sighed, appearing just as hurt over the conversation as Kate did. "I've dreaded this day for many years. I've tried to imagine how you would react and how I could explain why we did what we did." She shook her head. "But I can't even convince myself that we did the right thing. Coming from our lineage is both an honor and a burden. Alice and Dean did the only thing they knew for sure would protect you. They practically erased you from their lives in order to keep you alive."

"When Molly's gift began, what did you do for her?" Kate asked. Still grieving for her sister, she wanted reassurance that the one person who could have helped did everything she could.

Grams hesitated, fidgeting with her napkin. "She asked me for some solutions I couldn't provide."

"Like what?" Kate inquired.

"She asked me to rebind her gifts. But I couldn't."

Kate cocked her head and asked a daring question. "You couldn't, or you wouldn't?"

Grams drew a quick breath. Kate's newfound mistrust wounded her. "I couldn't," she whispered. "Although it wasn't for lack of trying. I really think that Molly's desire to continue suppressing her gift is what drove her depression. She resisted accepting who she really was. Fighting it became a battle she wouldn't walk away from but couldn't win, either."

"I'm older. Why didn't my gifts come out first?" Kate asked, standing with her dish. "Did you use something different for me?" She walked to the sink, not wanting to make eye contact with Grams upon hearing the answer. She couldn't bear the weight of being spared while Molly suffered.

171

"I believe your gifts did come out first," Grams said with a bit of pride in her voice. "But you resisted seeing them. You are strong, and Molly was spiritual. She searched herself and asked questions about the world and universe. She had a very free spirit.

"Like I said, I can see some of your dreams. I have been seeing them for a long while. But only recently have you become more aware and active during your dreams. I accepted years ago that, without being more open to spiritual possibilities, you may never have even realized what you are capable of."

Kate relaxed a little with that answer. Molly had a free spirit. And Kate was, well, admittedly rougher around the edges. She wondered if she overcompensated for Molly's nonconformity, and that caused her somewhat serious demeanor. Whatever the reason for her emotional stiffness, she couldn't deny the clear difference between her and her sister.

They washed the dishes and wiped down the kitchen in silence. As they finished, Grams awkwardly put her arm around Kate and gave her a sideways squeeze, whispering, "I'm so sorry we lost Molly. And I wish your struggles would end with the understandably traumatic loss of your sister. I'm afraid things will get worse before they get better. I'm here to support you, whatever you need."

She walked to the door and hugged Grams goodbye before plopping on the couch with her legs tucked up, resting her elbows on her knees. Grams had mentioned her dreams but not the kenasai. She wondered if Grams had any clue about the artifact being in her possession. Probably not, she surmised. If Grams didn't know about the kenasai, then she most certainly didn't know about Molly's soul.

They had spoken off-handedly a few times about the investigation and Detective Peterson's progress, or lack thereof. Grams knew that Molly hadn't killed herself, but she still acted as if Molly played some part in her own death. Kate pressed her forehead to her knees, trying to understand. She should have asked more questions. She probably should also tell Grams about the kenasai, but she now felt that the trust was gone.

Chapter 19

Fran's eyes glazed over as she perused more news stories coming through her feed online. Since her spat with Detective Peterson at the hospital, she took a few personal days. He was right to tell her that she needed to reel herself in. But Fran could not shake the feeling that the woman she bumped into in the front of the hospital may have been the mysterious visitor to their Jane Doe. She only had a hunch to go on, but it felt right. The timestamp for the security camera supported her theory that after their altercation, the woman had ample time to make it up to the nurse's station.

Fran swallowed another bite of stale Krispy Kreme donut, nearly choking when her phone sliced through the silence in her apartment. She fumbled for it, silently hoping that the person on the other end wasn't Detective Peterson. She'd embarrassed herself, and she knew it. The man already made her miserable in varying degrees; she did not want to know what his *I told you so* face looked like. She climbed the mountain to his good graces, just to watch it crumble when her emotions got the best of her.

"This is Fran," she answered.

A huff of frustration puffed through the phone. "Well, I can't say you're the easiest person to get a hold of. I've tried the precinct all week. I thought perhaps you were purposely avoiding my calls, but someone finally informed me that you were on vacation."

Fran instantly recognized the degrading voice on the other end of the phone as the woman from the hospital. She had been praying that she would finally call. Fran hoped that if she had a chance to meet with her, then establish a bit of comradery, she might inconspicuously glean a bit of information about her reason for visiting the hospital. Her emotions may have pulled her down a few notches under Peterson's scrutinizing gaze, but with the right information, she could restore herself and validate her gut feeling.

Not wanting to give herself away, she played dumb. "I'm sorry, I'm not sure who this is. How did you get my number?"

"How did I get your number? That's the least of your worries. It cost me a pretty penny to fix my damaged shoe, and I plan on sending you the bill. You did offer, after all. Or is your address as difficult to give out as your phone number?" The woman scoffed, clearly too important to be wasting her time on this.

"Oh, yes," Fran said slowly as if jogging her memory. "I remember you! In front of the hospital? I missed your name."

"Don't hurt yourself thinking too hard. My name is Simone. How do you propose we work this matter out?"

Fran cradled the phone on her shoulder and searched her desk for a pen. "I would be happy to take care of the bill. Do you want to meet somewhere? I'm not too keen on giving my address to people who insult me," she retorted, taking a calculated risk by responding negatively. She wanted to throw Simone off her game a little bit. She guessed that most people didn't challenge someone with an ego this big.

Irritated, Simone shouted, "Meet you? What on Earth makes you think that I would subject myself to..."

"Listen," Fran interrupted. She knew she poked the beehive in the right place. "Either you want the money, or you don't. Where can we meet?"

A long pause drifted from the other end of the line. Fran held her breath, hoping that her classes on profiling had paid off. If she pushed the right buttons, Simone would want to meet in person to further subjugate Fran. It would stroke her ego.

Finally, Simone's icy voice trickled through the phone. "I'm a realtor, and I have a showing tomorrow afternoon at one of my clients' homes."

Fran jotted the address and time down before Simone abruptly hung up. She peered down at the address, digging in her memory. It sounded familiar. "Oh my God," she murmured aloud. "It's Molly Gregory's house." This couldn't be a coincidence, could it?

She quickly did some online digging and found that although the agency had pictures of Molly's house, it made no mention of a specific realtor. She pulled up the page with pictures with descriptions and qualifications for each realtor within the company. None of the pictures resembled Simone, and none of them shared the name, either.

Fran tapped her pen on her chin, thinking. She picked up her phone and called the agency to ask for herself.

"I'm sorry," the young man on the other end of the line replied, typing in the background. "It seems we don't have a realtor assigned to that house."

Fran's shoulders slumped. She licked the end of her finger and dabbed it onto her donut crumbs while she contemplated her next move. She had hoped to obtain more information about Simone before meeting her. "Thanks for checking," she mumbled.

"We did have a realtor previously assigned," the man offered, "but he unexpectedly resigned."

"He resigned?"

"Yeah, we were all really surprised, actually. Nice guy. Then one day, he just emailed out of the blue and said he was retiring early. The house is still on the market, obviously. Even though we don't have a specific realtor assigned to it yet, we can still show it. Would you like to see it?"

Fran could feel the hair on the back of her neck prickling. "No, thank you."

Simone had not been completely forthcoming with her. Why? She scrolled to Peterson's number and held her phone for a moment, wondering if she should tell him. She shook her head, deciding against it. She could meet with Simone at the house and see where that led. Why would she choose Molly Gregory's address?

She sent an email to the chief letting him know she would be back the day after she met with Simone. She omitted the information about her meeting, though. She did not want to make her gut feeling official yet. As of now, she simply needed to resolve a personal matter.

~~~~~

Kate walked in her front door and removed Jake's leash. She paid the price for running this afternoon instead of the morning. She grabbed a towel from the kitchen, wiping sweat from her face and arms, and then filled Jake's water bowl. He lapped it up before flopping onto the ground, sprawling his legs in an attempt to cool down.

Kate grabbed her phone from the kitchen table, checking for missed calls. Fin had called, but still no call from Grams. Knowing Grams, Kate fully expected her to reach out any day now.

She had a lot of questions built up for Grams now that she had time to mull over their conversation. Rather than draw inspiration from the most recent revelation in her life, she hoped to squander the 'opportunity' it presented. She had all but convinced herself that if Grams and her parents could find a way to suppress her through childhood, then they could do it again. She much preferred that over the alternative of becoming a demon hunter.

She also did not like the fact that Grams seemed so unsure about her future. And who did she have to talk to about these matters? No one. She remembered how she instantly thought Grams might be crazy. Even Marcy would probably think Kate had lost her mind before she had a chance to explain the dream walking part.

The doorbell rang, pulling Kate from her thoughts. Jake barked his surprise and danced circles around her while she walked warily to the front door. She peaked through the side blinds before opening the door.

Detective Peterson stood with his hands in his pockets. He wore more casual clothes than his usual blazer and dress pants. His jeans had a tailored appearance, and his polo shirt matched his blue eyes.

"Detective Peterson! I nearly forgot we had a meeting today! I'm so sorry, please come in." She stepped to the side, allowing him to pass by. He smelled good. She did not.

"Hello Kather...uh, Kate. How are you?" He asked.

"I'm good, thanks." She couldn't help but smile, though she was anything but good. Detective Peterson offered a much-needed distraction from her present predicament, even if the distraction meant talking about Molly's murder. He had grown on her throughout the investigation. Her last encounter with him at the grocery store made her blush every time she thought about it.

He cleared his throat, pulling her back from her thoughts. "Oh, give me a minute, ok?" Remembering that he didn't like animals, she ushered Jake out the back door. "Do you need anything to drink?" She asked.

"Actually, a water would be great," he said, standing near her mantle. As Kate rounded the corner back into the living room with a glass of water for each of them, he pointed to the mantle, asking, "What happened to your pictures?"

Kate felt a jolt deep in her gut. She hadn't picked up the pictures since she and Fin had the strange experience with the kenasai. The shock wave had knocked a few of them over. Hoping the detective hadn't read her face, she responded with the first pathetic excuse that came to mind. "Oh. I started dusting a couple of weeks ago, and I guess I never got back around to putting them up." She squeezed out a smile, hoping that her face wouldn't betray her.

He took the glass from her hand, his eyes never straying from hers. He was deciding whether to probe her with further questions. She met his gaze, trying not to notice how handsome he looked while waiting and hoping he would move on.

Finally, he turned back to the mantle. "I see."

"So," Kate hoped she could change the subject, "did you find anything new in your investigation?"

He turned back to her, his face grim. "I'm sorry, Kate. I wish I had good news, but I still don't have any suspects."

Kate did not make any effort to hide her disappointment. "Oh."

Alec sat in the armchair and held out his hand to invite her to sit on the couch. "I have a couple of questions for you."

Kate sat and put her glass of water on the coaster, handing one to Peterson. "Okay," she responded with a sideways glance, "what do you need to know?" She tried to keep her body as relaxed as possible. The last thing she needed was a detective snooping around her life. She hoped he would keep the questions about Molly.

"Well," he started, licking his lips, "What can you tell me about what happened to you at the pet store?"

Kate sat up a little straighter. Why did he want to know? Did he know something about Ashley? "Well, as you know, Kyle and I called the police. We filled out a report of the accident. But there wasn't much more to it."

He nodded. "And?"

She folded her hands in her lap, treading carefully. "I'm not sure what else to say. I'm sorry if it seems like I'm dodging your question, but I don't know what you're looking for. The police already documented everything." She sucked in a quick breath, remembering her conversation with Kyle. "Is this about the girl's death? Look, I'm sorry I didn't call, but I didn't know it was the same girl or that she even died until Kyle told me. And he said he'd already called the police and told them it was the same girl. So, I didn't think they would need me to call in, too."

Peterson rubbed his chin with his thumb. "Yes, we heard from your boyfriend..."

"He's not my boyfriend," Kate interrupted before she could stop herself. She could feel her cheeks heating up. She thought she saw a ghost of a smile pass across his face. "Sorry. Go ahead." She picked up her water and took a few sips, wishing she had something stronger to drink.

He cleared his throat, amending his statement, "We heard from your friend who was there with you. But my question is actually about the footage..."

"Oh, yeah, it was all fuzzy, so no one could confirm what happened," Kate interrupted again. Her cheeks flushed when she realized she wasn't letting him finish his thoughts. She covered her eyes with her hand and lowered her head.

"I'm sorry, Detective Peterson, I'm just really nervous." She wiped her hand down her face hoping to reset her demeanor from defensive to helpful. "When I saw you standing on my front porch, it was the first welcome sight I'd had in a while. I guess I was hoping this conversation was going to be different."

"You can call me Alec," he said, leaning on his knees to meet her gaze. "And it's okay, Kate. You're not in any trouble."

"Right, okay," she said, wondering if he could tell that she didn't feel reassured. She met his gaze and knew instantly that he could read her like a book. He was a detective, after all. She bit her lip to keep herself from saying anything else.

"Let's start over," he said, flashing a brilliant smile. "No pressure, just tell me what happened."

Kate described what happened, starting with her reason for buying a toy for Jake in the first place. Alec listened intently, waiting until she had finished before asking any questions. She omitted some of the conversation with Ashley, thinking that what was said didn't matter as much as the incident itself.

"So, she just appeared and then disappeared?" Alec asked, his voice laced with doubt.

"I know how it sounds, but that's what it seemed like. I don't know where she came from, and I don't know where she went." Kate sighed, frustrated that she had to revisit the very moment that her entire life changed.

Alec furrowed his brow. "Did she say anything to you, Kate?"

Kate fidgeted with her hair. "Yes."

"The police report just says that the victim was disoriented and that you said she seemed like she was in shock."

Kate nodded. "That's right."

"Well, what did she say that made you think she was in shock?" he asked.

"It was more what she did than what she said. She stood on her leg without even flinching. I know it had to be broken by the way it sounded. It made my stomach turn every time she put pressure on it."

"Did she say anything else?" Alec probed.

"She didn't want us to call 911," Kate recalled.

He perked up a bit. "Well, that's something. If she was severely injured, why wouldn't she seek medical attention?"

Kate shrugged.

"Did she say anything else?" he asked, pulling his keys out of his pocket.

"Yeah," Kate said, pausing. She couldn't remember if it was at the actual pet store or in her dream, but she remembered something about the way Ashley addressed her. "She called me child."

"*She* called *you* child?"

Kate nodded. "I don't know why or what it means. It was just weird. Like I said, she was definitely in shock."

He thanked her for the water and for taking the time to talk with him, promising to call if any new leads came up. Kate watched him walk to his car before going to the back door to let Jake back in the house.

She picked up her phone to see a text message from Fin. *Where are you? Come to my house ASAP. Someone broke in.*

~~~~~

Detective Peterson waited for Kate to walk away from the window before strolling casually to her car. He pulled out a tracking device that Kelsey had given to him. Checking the street first, he quickly ducked and planted it on the underside of her vehicle. When he stood back up, he saw Kate staring at him from the porch.

"Uh, what are you doing, detective?" She had tucked her hair into a ponytail and thrown on a new shirt. She had her keys, phone, purse, and water bottle stowed beneath her arm. He surmised that she had grabbed them hastily on her way out the door.

"Oh!" He smiled. "I thought you might have a flat tire, but it looks like it's just low on air."

She rushed down the sidewalk, unlocking her car and piling her belongings into her purse with a clank. "Ok, thanks for checking. I'm just on my way out to...see a friend."

"You should probably get the tire looked at. If it's a slow leak, it will..."

"Yes, that's nice of you to check," she said, shoving past him. Their hands brushed for a moment, and he quickly retracted his. "I'll totally have it checked by someone. Thanks." She tossed her stuff into the car and climbed in, slamming the door behind her.

Well, at least I won't have to wonder where she's off to, he thought to himself. He shot a text to Kelsey. *It's in place. Activate.*

His phone bleeped when she responded. *Oh, Alec, you have such a way with words. So eloquent, so inspiring. It's activated.*

He rolled his eyes and sat in his car, turning on the AC. He had hoped that the video from Kate's incident with the same girl would turn up some evidence. But as the officer said, the camera mysteriously cut out at the same time. Just like the hospital camera. He had been in this line of work too long to believe in coincidences. Originally, he and Fran had discussed having Kate followed for a few days after the break-in at her house, but nothing came of that. They pulled the tail off her.

He felt a pang of guilt when Fran crossed his mind. He might owe her an apology, but he hadn't reached out to her yet. The chief told him that she would be coming back in, so he decided to stop and grab some donuts and coffee for her. He knew food was the way to her heart, and if she needed some time to heal, he understood.

Chapter 20

Kate pulled up to Fin's trailer and slammed her car into park before she'd completely stopped. She jumped out of the car and ran to the door. It hung crooked and bent with one hinge completely disconnected.

"Fin! Where are you?" Kate called, completing a semi-circle around the door, trying to see past the darkness inside.

"I'm fine, hang on. Did you bring a flashlight?"

"Yeah, I always have one in my trunk. Let me go grab it." Her feet crunched on the gravel with each step. She walked purposefully back to her car and popped the trunk. Ashley's army jacket was perched on top of her trunk's belongings, chipping away at the walls in Kate's mind that held her together. Frustrated, she tossed it aside and dug deeper for a flashlight.

"You're taking forever. Don't you have a car caddy or something?" Fin asked, poking his head out of the trailer like an animal from its dark den. Several of his belongings laid organized in front of his steps. He had pulled those out before the sun sank too low.

Kate rolled her eyes. "My trunk is like a disaster zone. Just give me a second." She fumbled around her box of desk belongings that she'd packed on the last day of work, through dog toys, a frisbee, a blanket, and an emergency first aid kit. Her hand finally landed on the cheap plastic flashlight. "Ok, I got it," she announced, holding it up.

"What is that? A Barbie flashlight?" Fin blinked. "Are you sure it even turns on?"

Kate put a hand on her hip. "I *told* you that you can just use the flashlight on your cell phone like a normal person. If this doesn't work, you're going to have to resort to using the technology you already have at your disposal."

"It's unnatural for a phone to have a flashlight in it," Fin objected, marching back to his trailer. "Shine it in here while I look around."

He disappeared into the darkness as Kate lit his path. She could hear his feet swishing through all his belongings that had been tossed through the trailer. He began lifting and pulling out different chests, checking sketches, and surveying his amulets. "Odd. None of my amulets have been moved or taken." He pulled a piece of paper off the bottom of his boot, filing it back in its place.

"I don't think that's what most people are on the market for," Kate joked.

"Look at my house, Kate. Do you think anyone in their right mind would choose to break in here by chance? It's not my first time to be looted. And it's always when the wrong people find out what I'm into and come poking around..." he trailed off.

"What?" Kate pressed.

"Have you told anyone about the kenasai? Where is it?" He reached back into the trailer, pulling a few ornate pieces from the floor.

"I've been carrying it with me. But I haven't told anyone about it, no." She thought back to when Blanch had possibly seen it in her purse. And to Grams, who said she'd seen parts of Kate's dreams. Grams hadn't mentioned the object, but perhaps she meant to if Kate had responded well to the other information she provided. Kate shook her head, thinking twice. It seemed dangerous. If Grams knew she had it, she would have said something. As much as Kate hated admitting it, everything Grams had done thus far, even deceiving her, was for her own protection.

"I guess it's possible someone may have seen it. But even if someone chanced a glance at it, how could they know what it is? I mean, you have been doing this for years, and you barely know what it is, right?" She looked to him, hoping he would agree.

He didn't.

"Kate, we have to put that thing someplace safe. You can't just cart it around with you. It doesn't belong to us, so it's reasonable to assume that whoever owns it will be searching for it." Fin started placing his amulets, maps, and books back into their designated boxes before pausing, a file open in his hand. "That's what I thought. The rendering of the kenasai I had...it's gone."

"Why would they take a drawing?" Kate pondered. "If it's theirs, they should know what it looks like."

Fin pointed to all his charms and runes hanging around the trailer. "Maybe because they had to use someone else to get in. If someone had charms or runes of their own, or if they harbored a spirit, they wouldn't be able to pass through my veil around the trailer."

Kate played with her ponytail, thinking. "So, they sent someone else in. Someone who couldn't be traced back to them, maybe?"

"That's what I would do if it were me," Fin said, standing. "Let's go see if we can get my electricity hooked back up."

As Fin tinkered with the wires, Kate continued to think out loud. "Fin, if they saw it in my bag, why would they ransack your trailer?" As soon as she said the words out loud, she realized her home could be next. "Oh my God," she whispered.

"Woo hoo!" Fin shouted as his lights flipped back on. "There's just something about the light that makes a bad circumstance less bleak." He wiped his hands on his pants, surveying Kate's worried face. "You were saying?"

"They're going to break into my house next! It only makes sense. What time is it?" Kate grabbed her phone from her back pocket, "Oh my God."

"You have the kenasai with you. What are you so worried about?" Fin asked.

"Besides someone ransacking my home and going through all of my belongings," she shot him a heated glare, "Marcy is meeting me at my house, like, now for a girls' night. What if they waited for me to leave, and they're there?" Kate started pacing. She quickly dialed Marcy's number. It rang through to voicemail three times. "Pick up the phone!" she shouted, exasperated.

She turned abruptly to her car, running to the driver's side and climbing in. Fin followed wordlessly, getting into the passenger seat. He held onto the door as she peeled out of his driveway. "It's going to be okay, don't worry. She will notice your car isn't there, right? You usually park on the street."

Kate bit her lip, trying to keep herself from crying. "If she gets hurt, it will be my fault, Fin! It's not like I took this kenasai on purpose, okay? I don't even want it. As a matter of fact, if I didn't know Molly's soul was in it, I would gladly give it back and ask them to brainwash me back into normalcy!"

Fin had anchored himself with both hands, trying to steady himself with Kate's stunt driving. "It's just one dilemma we can work through. Try not to stress out…"

"It's not just one dilemma, Fin!" Despite Kate's best efforts, tears stung her eyes, and her voice came out thick. "There's more to it than that." She pressed the gas pedal to the floor, flying through a yellow light. She wiped her tears with the bottom of her palm, trying to clear her vision.

"We haven't had a chance to talk, but my Grams, she…" Kate cut off. She didn't have time right now to recap that conversation. She peeled around the corner and onto her street. Marcy stood on the sidewalk and looked like she was warily approaching the house. Kate slammed to a stop, her screeching tires startling Marcy.

"Kate! You scared me to death." Marcy took a deep breath and then turned back to the house. "Did you realize you left the door wide open? I was just about to call you."

Kate ran up to Marcy, hugging her tightly. Her front door stood wide open, inviting anyone to enter. Kate pulled away from her, her hands on her shoulders. "I'm so glad you are okay! I was worried when you didn't answer my calls."

Concern etched Marcy's face. "Have you been crying? What's going on? Who is that?" She pointed over Kate's shoulder to where Fin stood, leaning on Kate's car.

"I, uh, yeah. I've been crying." Kate fumbled through her thoughts, trying to figure out what she should tell Marcy. "Fin is one of my friends from Helping Hands. We were, uh, out for coffee, and I just lost track of time. Sometimes when I talk to him about what's going on in my life, I get caught up in the moment because he's been there, so he understands." She was getting better and better at lying on demand. Kate wiped her nose on her sleeve and ran her fingers under her eyes, trying to clean up her appearance.

Marcy eyed Kate. "Wait a minute…that's," Marcy lowered her voice, "*weird* Fin? The guy you said shows up just for snacks?" She glanced again in his direction, giving him a once over. "When did you start hanging out with *him?* I thought you said he gave you the creeps." Her animated hands started flapping like birds that needed to be freed.

Kate smiled. Marcy's mannerisms always gave her a chuckle. She looked back at Fin, who was giving her the evil eye. She smiled at him, too. Despite the fact that she faced yet another home invasion, she felt slightly uplifted at finding Marcy safe and sound. She had to take moment to be thankful. "Come on," she pulled Marcy by the elbow, "I'll introduce you."

She tried to keep her mind off the house and hurried through an awkward introduction between the two of them. "...so anyway," she went on, "we've been hanging out about once a week. Fin is really helping me work through some stuff. I'm still good to hang out tonight, but I need to take Fin home. And apparently, I need to check the house since I somehow left my door open." Kate shrugged a nonchalant shoulder. "Good thing Jake is in there to ward off any intruders."

Marcy nodded, kindly regarding Fin. "Thank you. Kate's my best friend, so anyone she knows and loves is a friend of mine." She reached into her purse for her keys. "Kate, let's just reschedule. I wasn't going to be able to stay very long anyway because Arthur's mom needed some help, and he can't take Brendon with him. Is that okay?"

"Of course. Call or text, and we'll work out the details." Kate tried not to sound too eager to get rid of her. Marcy plopped into her car.

"Marcy?" Kate called, signaling for her to roll down her window. She did. "Yeah?"

"Do me a favor and don't mention this to Grams?" Kate tried to keep her face friendly, but it was a little bit of a jab, and she knew Marcy would take it that way.

"Oh, yeah. I never meant to..." her eyes shifted before landing on Kate's, full of apology. "I was just worried."

"I know," Kate managed a sincere look, empathizing with her friend. "She just doesn't process things the same way I do. I need space."

Marcy, still looking guilty and remorseful, nodded and rolled up her window.

Kate turned on her heels as Marcy drove away. "I have to go check on Jake. You coming?"

Fin nodded. "Do you want to call the police?"

Kate cringed. Thinking of how she probably already cast herself as suspicious earlier in the day with Detective Peterson. "Did you call them for yours?" she asked Fin.

He shook his head. "They aren't as effective in the kinds of things I deal with. You know, *weird* people like me don't like calling the authorities."

"You heard that, eh?" Kate said with a grimace. "Sorry. I didn't know you when I said those things."

His head bobbed. "I understand. People need to get to know me, and they'll realize I'm perfectly normal."

She searched his face for sarcasm and found none. She smirked. "Right."

She slowly approached the door with Fin behind her. "Jake?" she let out a quick whistle. The front door yawned before tilting back toward her. "Jake? C'mon, boy," she called again, clapping. She waited for the sound of his paws on the ground but heard nothing.

She rubbed her sweaty palms on her legs, working up the courage to press the door open. Suddenly, Fin pushed her to the side, strong-arming the door so that it hit the wall behind it with a loud thud. If they had any chance of catching someone by surprise, it was gone now. He stood defiantly in the foyer, both hands on his hips. "Is anyone in here?"

Kate used one arm to stabilize herself on the door frame and motioned with her other, "Fin." She kept her tone low, though Fin had already announced their presence. "Please don't ever do that again. You gave me a freaking heart attack." She reached over and flipped her light switch, hoping they hadn't taken the same measures with her house as they had with his. Her stomach sank when the lights didn't come on.

"I can fix that for you, don't worry," Fin said, still speaking at an abnormally high volume. Apparently, he did not mind that someone else might be hiding in her home.

"Fin!" His name barely passed her teeth as she made a motion across her throat, indicating that he needed to cut it out.

He shrugged a shoulder and sauntered in like he owned the place. Fin circled casually through the living room while Kate slowly crept up the stairs. At the top, she checked behind her to make sure Fin was not going to boldly push past her and parade loudly down the hallway. He stood at the bottom of the stairs, making a motion that the living room was clear.

Someone had closed all the doors. Placing her hand on the knob to her bedroom, she slowly turned it, and the hinge creaked, slicing through the silence. Her eyes hadn't adjusted to the darkness yet, so she pulled out her phone and turned on the flashlight, sending the beam down to Fin as proof of its usefulness.

He responded by narrowing his eyes at her sorcery.

Her bedroom had been turned inside out. She stepped in, still wondering where Jake had gone. Maybe he fled through the front door as the thief went through the house, disheveling all her things. Her drawers laid on the ground like empty coffins. The askew mattress teetered on the side of the bed, and even the trash from her bathroom now littered the floor like confetti after a party. She did a quick survey of the shower and closet to make sure no one lurked there before stepping back into the hallway.

Fin gave her a questioning look, and she let out a puff of air while motioning with her hand that the room had blown up. She crept down the hallway and stopped before opening the guest bedroom door. Through the gap between the door and the floor, a paw stuck out sideways. Her heart stopped. *Please be alive, buddy,* she thought to herself. She turned the handle and pressed the door against the resistance of Jake's arm.

He whimpered, and relief flooded through her. She knelt, realizing that his paw got stuck when someone slammed the door shut. He must have been fighting them. She shut off her flashlight so it wouldn't shine in his eyes while she worked. "Good boy, Jake." She whispered, lightly caressing his head. She eased his paw out sideways, and he laid his head on her knee. "It's ok, boy, just a little further..."

A door down the hallway creaked. Kate stood quickly, jumping into the hallway. Jake let out a rumbling growl. She squinted, peering into the darkness, trying to see more than shadow. A figure moved. "Fin," she shouted, "someone is..."

The figure lurched, crashing a shoulder into her stomach and knocking the air out of her lungs. She fell backward, scrambling under the weight of someone with a similar build to her. *A woman,* she realized. With a grunt, she rolled over, kicking the assailant off. She stood, catching her breath as the woman also stood with her back to the stairs, facing Kate. She had a hood over her head, and Kate couldn't make out her face.

Fin started up the stairs and made it to the landing, stopping just as the woman grabbed Kate's arm, muttering something in another language. Kate flinched, and the figure stepped back, more relaxed.

Kate stood still, frozen by fear. Slowly, the intruder tensed as if she'd expected something from Kate that didn't happen. The thief put her hands up defensively and took a timid step backward, not realizing how close she stood to the stairs. Losing her balance, she tumbled down, crashing into Fin and landing lithely on top. Kate dashed to the top of the stairs, watching the two scuffle before she delivered a blow to the side of Fin's face, briefly immobilizing him, and took off through the gaping front door.

"Fin! Are you alright?" Kate made her way down the stairs on wobbly legs, still not sure she had her wits about her. She touched the side of his face, and he winced, sucking in a breath.

"Just get me some ice. I'll be okay," he mumbled through a tense jaw.

Jake limped down the stairs, apparently having freed himself the rest of the way, and sat next to Fin. Kate slammed the front door and twisted the deadbolt into place. Normally she just locked the handle, but part of that had been damaged and would not hold the door closed. She peeked through the blinds and saw no evidence of the intruder lingering.

Satisfied, she walked back to the bedroom for her phone, so she could navigate the clutter laying everywhere. In the kitchen, she rummaged through her pantry items strewn on the tile. She found a baggie and filled it with ice, bringing it back to Fin.

"That's going to swell pretty bad," she said, petting Jake and checking his leg. It looked like superficial cuts and maybe some bruising, but the leg didn't appear to have any breaks.

"Who are you?" Fin asked, pressing the bag lightly to his sore jaw. He regarded her with a betrayed look.

She lifted her hand from Jake's head and placed it on Fin's shoulder. "Fin, how hard did she hit you? It's me, Kate."

He rolled his eyes, "I know your name," he slowly propped himself up on the wall, coming to a full sitting position. "But I have no idea who you are. You haven't been completely honest with me, have you?"

Ashamed, Kate averted her eyes. She had purposely neglected to share her conversation with Grams, not due to mistrust, but because she just needed time to chew on what happened before talking about it. She knew, though, that he would interpret her secrecy differently. She would feel the same way in his shoes. She slipped into defense mode. "Fin, I've told you everything. I've told you things that I haven't told anyone else, even Grams and Marcy."

He shook his head. "No. You haven't." He reached into the front pocket of his shirt and pulled out the necklace he'd given her weeks ago for protection. "You aren't wearing this. I found it on the end table in the living room when I walked through."

Still unwilling to admit she had not revealed everything about her past, she shook her head. "What does that have to do with anything? I'm sorry I wasn't wearing it, Fin. I hope it doesn't hurt your feelings, but this is all new to me, and I guess I'm just trying to avoid getting in too deep. I want to be in control of my own life."

"You're in control. Don't play me. What do you have? A tattoo for protection?" He threw the necklace, and it bounced across the foyer.

Kate raised an eyebrow. "Um, I have no idea what you are talking about."

"You don't have a tattoo?" He asked, giving her a wayward stare.

She shook her head; pieces of her hair that had fallen from her ponytail danced in front of her eyes.

He pushed forward, grabbing her shirt. "I don't believe you!" He began tugging at the bottom hem, meaning to pull off her shirt and check for himself. "Show me!" He sounded crazed and malicious.

Jake's nose was on his face in an instant, a snarl seeping from his lips and baring his teeth. Fin froze.

"Let go of my shirt, now," Kate demanded.

Fin slowly released his grip on her and held up his hand to let Jake sniff. Jake sat back on his haunches next to Kate with his head low, no longer snarling but still at full attention.

"Fin, what the hell? Why would a tattoo be so important? It's me. You have to trust me like I trust you. But I do have a few things to share," she admitted. "I'm sorry we haven't talked yet. But my Grams stopped by a few days ago."

He searched her face for a long time. Then, relaxing against the wall again, he said, "That woman, she was speaking Latin in the form of a hex or a spell. At this moment, you should be doing what she wants you to do. Like a puppet." He looked her up and down again. "But clearly, you're fine.

"If I hadn't found the amulet, I would have assumed it protected you against her attack because its power comes from angelic writings. Since you proclaim you are not a Christian, the only other way you could ward off an attack like that without an amulet would be a permanent etching on your skin, which you claim not to have." He held out a hand, supporting his evidentiary statements. "So why weren't you affected?"

That explained the intruder's pause and fear after she touched her. She thought she had the upper hand and planned to use Kate's submission somehow. Kate pinched her brows together. "I don't have a tattoo." She rolled her eyes at the thought of him inspecting her body. "Sorry to disappoint, but I'm not going to prove that to you, either."

He stood slowly and began to pace the foyer, gathering his composure. "This is the second time you've surprised me, Kate. The first, I'm certain, was an accident. But now it's becoming a trend. I need you to be more open and transparent with me."

She tightened her lips, summoning bravery where she felt none. "Fine," she said, standing and firmly planting her feet and crossing her arms. "I'm a demon hunter."

A few moments passed, and with each one, Fin's face changed from surprise to incredulous and back to angry. He looked her up and down, finally settling his gaze on hers, and a huge smile cracked his face. "That's funny. Oh—that's hysterical," he slapped his leg as his playful smile turned to a mixture of uncontrollable laughter and winces from the pain in his jaw. Wiping tears from his eyes, he pointed one finger at her. "You. Katherine Gregory. A..." another fit of laughter ensued. "Demon hunter!" he spat between chuckles.

Her shoulders slumped, and her arms fell to her sides in defeat. She wrestled with whether she should take offense or find solace in the fact that he considered 'demon hunter' an impossible title for her to bear.

Fin continued to carry on, animating his own imaginary conversations:

"Who are you?"

"Katherine, slayer of demons that I didn't even believe in until mere weeks ago." He batted his eyes.

"No! We cower in fear at the sound of your name!" he faked on.

She put both of her palms in the air in front of her. "Okay, you've had your laugh. I'm done, and I'm starving. I'm not going to try to clean this house on an empty stomach." She shouldered her purse and pushed past him. He continued his antics, following her onto the porch. Locking the door, she realized he'd fallen silent behind her.

She turned, trying to hide the pain he'd caused with his jests. "What, Fin?" Her voice cracked angrily.

"You're — you're serious!" His eyes opened nearly as wide as his mouth. "You think you're a demon hunter?"

"No, Fin. I don't *think*, I know. Remember that conversation that I mentioned between me and Grams that upset me? Well, she broke the news to me and shattered my already crumbling world. So, excuse me if your jokes don't rub me quite the right way." She couldn't look at his face anymore, so she dropped her gaze to the ground, wondering how to proceed. The ground offered no answers, either.

"Kate." He put his hands on her shoulders, giving her an encouraging look.

"What?" She asked, trying to keep from sniffling.

"My dear," he said, shaking his head, "you're the worst demon hunter I've ever met."

Despite her fear and her anger, she cracked a half-smile.

Chapter 21

Fin shook his head and shoved another mouthful of Chinese takeout into his mouth, reflecting on everything Kate had just relayed to him. She poked at her food with her fork. "You don't believe me," she stated bluntly.

"Oh, I believe you," he said.

"But?" Kate popped a piece of chicken into her mouth.

Fin snorted. "But? But look at you, Kate! *You* even have a hard time believing you're a demon-hunting dream walker." He shoved more food into his mouth and spoke around it, "For the record, I was right. You have significant dreams."

She conceded with a nod. Then she asked a question that had been bouncing around in her head. "Fin, are you a guardian? I mean, could you be my guardian?"

"I think I'd know if I were." He said, twirling noodles around his fork, looking a little amused.

She felt disappointment sink her small boat of hope. "Oh. I just figured since you know about angelic writings and stuff..." she broke off, not bothering to finish the rest. She never did well with expressing her emotions, especially if she cared about someone. As much as it surprised her, she cared very much for Fin. He had taken her under his wing even though it brought danger into his own life. She would have invited the idea of him as her guardian with great relief. Of course, he had worked on this information and this case for years. She wondered if that meant he would go his own way if they ever figured out how to stop the demonic uprising. Then she would truly be as alone as she felt.

Her thoughts gathered back around her own future. She looked around her house, still a nasty mess. If she could figure out how to get Molly out of the kenasai, would she continue to fight like her parents fought? What would that even look like? Fin had mentioned that people had ransacked his house multiple times. Did she want that in her life? Did she have a choice?

Fin interrupted her inner turmoil, "I have a confession." He looked up under his bushy white eyebrows. "I actually knew you were a dream walker."

Kate sat up a little straighter. "It seems that everyone else knows more about me than I know about myself. Maybe you should start a club." She rolled a piece of broccoli around, deciding not to eat it. "How did you know?"

"That night that I showed up at your house unannounced, I saw parts of your dream with the girl. I recognized the kenasai. I understand a little bit better now that you were probably reaching out without realizing it. It only makes sense if you don't know how to use your gifts."

"But even if I did unintentionally reach out, why would it be to you? Wouldn't it make more sense that I would accidentally dream-lasso someone I am close to?" Kate picked up her leftover dinner and put it in the fridge.

"I don't really know how it works. I think you need to talk more to your Grams about it." Fin stayed seated at the table, most likely to keep it as a barrier between them since he knew how she felt about her Grams at the moment.

She began picking up items off the kitchen floor and stuffing them into a trash bag. "Pass." She knew she would eventually have a list of questions to approach Grams with, though. So she added, "For now, anyway."

He folded his hands and tucked them under his chin. "I don't really think she did anything wrong."

Kate began shoving the random pantry items more forcefully into the kitchen bag. "Well, she didn't do everything right, either. You have no idea what it's like, Fin! I'm a freak. I'm a freak, and I didn't know it."

"Oh, I know what it's like to be a freak. It's no big deal, really." He scratched his chin. "You kind of get used to it."

"Great," she said in a tone that didn't match the word.

Fin held both hands out, continuing his thoughts. "Anyway, I know you said that you are part guardian, part dream walker. I don't know much about the demon-hunting community because they're shrouded in secrecy, but I can tell you that they wear talismans. Or, as I mentioned before, tattoos for protection. Something is different about you, Kate. If you don't need any form of protection, then your Grams may have more information about your lineage."

Kate grabbed a broom to sweep up the remaining mess. "Is it possible she just doesn't know? I have to say to her credit that she was heartbreakingly honest with me. She knew the things she said would probably destroy a piece of our relationship forever, but she definitely didn't hold back."

"I suppose it's possible she just doesn't know." Fin replied dubiously.

"Plus, how am I supposed to ask her about that without telling her what happened? Then I'd have to explain that I have the kenasai."

Fin rubbed his temple with his fingers. "That is one thing I'm going to have to agree on. The less people who know about the kenasai, the better. We're in deep enough, and we don't want to put anyone else at risk."

Kate tied the trash bag and tossed it by the back door, grabbing another from the closet and moving to the living room. Fin followed her, picking up items from the floor and setting them on the couch for her to look through. "I don't suppose you have any idea who that was," Kate said.

He shook his head. "I didn't get a look at her. Definitely a woman."

She smiled. "So, you were beat up by a woman?"

He put a hand on his hip. "I'll have you know I'm trained in krav maga. She just caught me off guard."

"Krav maga?" Kate asked. "What is that, like, karate?"

"No, not really. It's focused on self-defense more than fighting. The emphasis is on counterattacks and neutralization. I would be happy to teach you a little bit," he offered.

Kate allowed herself to giggle a little as she pointed to his swollen face. "Yeah, it seems like it's really working for you."

He pressed his lips into a thin line. "Very funny. I believe the assailant was also trained. Even falling down the stairs, she managed to take advantage of the situation by landing on top. And she wasted no time with an offensive strategy." He reached up, gently running his fingers down the side of his face to test the soreness and swelling.

"It's settled then?" Kate asked. "We don't tell anyone else about the kenasai until we're out of danger." She plopped on the couch for a quick rest before tackling the upstairs rooms. Drawing her knees up and wrapping her arms around them, she asked, "We will eventually be out of danger, right?"

Fin's eyes filled with sympathy. His expression told her that he chose his next words carefully, wrestling with how much truth to give her. "If you mean to think they will give up, I don't think so. Let's just get this kenasai business out of the way, shall we? One battle at a time."

"I've been trying to think of a good place to hide it," Kate said. "Maybe Molly's clinic behind her house?"

Fin thought for a moment before responding. "Maybe."

"We can go out tomorrow and take a look to see what you think," she added. "I need to check on her property anyway to make sure the people I've been paying to take care of the yard are doing a good job."

Fin nodded his agreement before standing. "It's been a long night. Try to get some rest."

Kate stood with him and followed him to the door, locking it behind him. She turned, leaning her back against the door, knowing that a good night's rest would not come for a long time.

~~~~~

Fran pulled up to Molly's house and checked the clock. She had purposely arrived early, and after a quick scan of the street and driveway, she deduced that she beat Simone.

She meandered up to the front porch, checking the door. It was locked, of course. A realtor lockbox dangled on the handle, mocking her with its contents. She peered inside but didn't see anything out of the ordinary. Tucking her hands in her pockets, she turned and checked the street again before walking around to the backyard.

Fran glanced toward the clinic. She smiled at the thought of first meeting Detective Peterson. It seemed like so long ago. She never expected to sympathize with such a distant person, but she had come to know him better than she thought she would.

She shaded her eyes and peeked through the back window, not sure what she expected to find. She had made attempts to research Simone, but she couldn't find any information on any woman named Simone that matched her appearance within a 60-mile radius. She'd even searched some of the smaller counties for landowners. She combed through boat registries, thinking that perhaps the woman lived near or on one of the region's lakes. Everything came up empty. She simply didn't exist, adding fire to Fran's suspicions.

Not really sure what she should be suspicious of made her task especially difficult. She didn't have any of the basic information that police needed to establish a firm hypothesis with which to investigate. She didn't know who Simone was, where she came from, what her purpose was, or why it tied in with their investigation. Rather than allowing the answerless questions of who, what, where, or why to deter her from her focus, she determined that she might need to interact with Simone in a more unconventional manner.

She had learned from Detective Peterson. He did not allow roadblocks to throw him from the case. She would pursue her lead off the clock until she could solidify her suspicion. The possibility of Simone's innocence also hung in the air, but Fran had more confidence in her intuition than to allow a lack of information to cast a shadow of doubt.

She caught a glimpse of movement behind her in the reflection of the window. She turned in time to meet a blow with her face. With a crack, her head rang, and she felt herself falling to the ground. Trying to move felt impossible. She sensed another blow coming, and her heart filled with regret. Her pride had now been shattered twice in the span of weeks.

Just before the looming strike landed, a lovely pair of candy apple red heels came into focus. She could feel a trickle of blood rolling from the gash they had administered to her face. Fran resolved herself to scratch these too, given the chance. Then her world went dark.

~~~~~

Kate awoke on Molly's front porch, seated in one of the wicker chairs. She stood slowly on the creaky wood. She laid her hand on the worn railing and absently wondered if the yardman had watered the hanging ferns.

Thump.

Kate pivoted quickly toward the house. She held her breath, listening. She tip-toed across the porch as it continued to creak in protest. Holding her hand over her eyes, she peeked in the window. The house was empty. "No!" she whispered. Someone had taken all of Molly's things.

This can't be! Who would take her things? Surely a neighbor would have noticed people stealing furniture. She reached into her purse to fish out the keys. A sudden gust of wind blew her hair across her face. She made several attempts to pull it behind her ear before it whipped right back around. Looking up, she noticed the ferns tilting back and forth on their hooks like ocean buoys. The limbs in the trees danced wildly, losing some of their leaves.

Placing her hands firmly on the rails, she leaned out to take a peek at the sky. Turbulent clouds swirled in a circular pattern. Leaves now riding the wind's coattails struck her in the face. It felt like sticking her head out the window of a moving car.

She backed against the house, fearing she might become an involuntary passenger on the wind like the debris from the yard. She could hear dirt and rock pelting the windows and covered her mouth with her shirt, hoping to protect her lungs. She cautiously inched sideways one step at a time, reaching until her hand finally hit the door handle. She grabbed it, surprised to find it unlocked. She turned the knob, and the wind forced it open. She blew inward with the door like a flag on a pole. Anchored to the handle, she pulled her body closer and made an attempt to close the door.

Thump. *She heard the noise again, definitely coming from inside the house.*

The storm invaded the house, breaking the laws of nature. She fell to her knees, hoping to gain some control by moving closer to the ground. She cupped her hands around the sides of her watery eyes and tried to blink away dirt. Aside from the storm debris blowing through the door, the house was as it appeared from the outside. Empty.

Finally, bits of consciousness trickled into her mind, and she knew. She knew this was a dream. "No!" Kate shouted, trying to grasp for control. The word trailed away, disappearing in the chaos as if she'd barely whispered it. "I'm going to wake up now!"

Thump.

"No!" She attempted to scream again in vain.

She peered through the turmoil and saw a silver object on the ground ahead. She crawled to it, chin tucked down and eyes barely open. She recognized it as the kenasai, but it vibrated with another loud thump. She'd never heard it make noise like that before. She froze in place, deciding whether to reach for it.

Finally, she reached out to grab it, but when her fingers brushed the surface, it began to melt. The metallic liquid spread into a pool on the hardwood floor, giving it a mirror-like appearance. She leaned over it, expecting to see a reflection of herself. She could see the living room ceiling, but she could not see herself. She leaned over further and saw that the other side of the reflection showed a dark but fully furnished room.

Lightning struck outside, and thunder rumbled through the room, causing the image to ripple. Kate looked around the room and back into the puddle. *It must be a window*, she thought. *It did not accurately represent the room or herself because it wasn't a reflection.*

A fist smacked against the puddle from the other side. *Thump.*

Kate jumped back. Seeing that the fist did not pop into the room with her, she reservedly approached the puddle again. Leaning back over, she saw Molly on the other side, prying at the edges of the proverbial window, searching for a way out. Her dark lashes framed intense and desperate eyes.

"Molly!" Kate cried.

Molly's eyes snapped into focus. Her mouth formed Kate's name, but Kate could not hear her. Shadows swirled behind her, causing her hair to toss about. They swirled around her neck and arms, pulling her further from Kate.

"I'm coming for you, Molly! I'm going to get you out of there, I promise!" Kate scanned the empty room, hoping something would appear for her to break through and free Molly. She wished and hoped for it, wondering if she could control her dreams like that.

Alas, she could not. What was the point of being a dream walker if she couldn't control it? Rain began to fall around her, gently at first, but then a heavy downpour ensued. After wiping her hair from her face, she placed
her hands on the outside of the kenasai puddle and leaned over it, shouting, "I don't know what to do!" She didn't know if Molly could actually hear her. She sobbed and whispered, "I won't give up."

Lightning struck, and thunder boomed through the room, once more sending ripples through the mercury-looking liquid. As the ripples subsided, Kate realized that the falling rain had no residual effect on the puddle. Molly screamed, shaking her head, two steps ahead of Kate. Kate still couldn't hear her, but Molly clearly did not want Kate to pursue any effort to release her. Kate ignored Molly's attempts and watched as the rain fell through the image and onto her sister.

"I think I can reach through!" Kate shouted as the thought formed in her mind.

Molly's mouth formed the word "no." She strained against her shadow captors. She made attempts to pull her arms from their grip, throwing her whole body into it.

Doubt crept into Kate's mind. What if Molly knew something she didn't? She watched her sister thrash about, making every effort to free herself. The image of Molly fighting with all of her might ignited something deep inside of Kate. She couldn't just watch, no matter what Molly wanted or knew. Her dreams happened for a reason, right?

Kate lifted one hand and placed it on the puddle. It felt like nothing. She couldn't detect any temperature change or wetness. Cautiously, she pressed her hand down, expecting to feel the pressure of the floor pushing back. To her surprise, her hand continued to glide through the floor and into the room with Molly.

Elated that her plan worked, Kate drove herself on before she had a chance to talk herself out of it. She grabbed Molly's wrist and yanked on her arm. Molly moved slowly through the sludge of shadow. But as her hand crossed the threshold into Kate's room, one of the black swirls engulfing Molly reached through. It slapped around Kate's wrist, burning her with its grip. She yelped at the sting of the shadow. She pulled more forcefully, refusing to let go of her sister, but the darkness stubbornly pulled her back again. Slowly, Kate's strength waned, and she sank down. Her shoulder passed through, and her muscles shook with the effort. She strained to keep her head out of the kenasai, laying her legs flat on the floor to create more traction.

Devoid of options and hope, she called out. "Help! Help me! Can anyone hear me?" She feared that if she could not free herself and Molly, no one would be able to hear her from the other side. Furthermore, if she fell through, she didn't know what would happen to her. Would she be stuck in the kenasai forever? Or would she simply wake up? Her muscles burned with exertion, but she refused to allow her bottom half to pass through. Rain continued to pour and her hair stuck to her face as drops collected on the end of her nose, falling through and onto Molly.

Her palm slipped on the wet surface of the floor, and she fell partway through before she could grab the edge of the puddle again and brace herself with the butt of her hand. Before she lifted her *head back above the threshold, she heard Molly shout, "No, Kate. Please, they won't free me. They'll only trade! You have to let go!"*

Kate lifted her head back out of the puddle and screamed, "Fin! Fin, please help! Come now!" She reasoned that if she could accidentally invite people into her dreams, that perhaps she could purposely invite people in without being trained in how to do so. Did he also have to be asleep for her to summon him? It was her last hope.

She strained so hard that her lungs ached for more oxygen. She began gasping for air and barely pushing it all out before sucking in more air. She knew she could not win this game of tug of war. But deep inside, she could not fight the feeling of injustice. Nobody deserved what these creatures were doing to Molly, and she could not give up.

Like an engine sputtering before running out of gas, she could feel her muscles giving out. Her head and upper body passed back through and into Molly's room. She kept her hand locked on the edge of the floor and curled her toes in her shoes, hoping she could somehow keep the rest of her body from passing through, too.

It smelled like sulfur. Images of underworldly creatures ebbed and flowed through the perimeter of the room. Kate coughed. If she gave herself up, would Molly enter her body and leave Kate's soul behind?

"Fine," she uttered. "A trade. Me for Molly." She couldn't let the unknown consequences hold her back.

Cackling rose and echoed through the room.

"No, Kate. You can't!" Molly shook her head.

"I'm not afraid of taking your place, Molls." Kate smiled.

"I didn't kill myself." Molly cried. "I wouldn't have! I waited for her gun to fire, and I hoped it was over. But she didn't die!"

"It doesn't matter," Kate confessed grimly. She let her hand slip from the edge, preparing to fall in to save Molly.

Before she could pass through, a hand grabbed Kate's ankle. Now hanging nearly all the way in, she looked up to the puddle, water droplets pelting her eyes from the other side. She could barely make out a murky outline of Fin's crazy hair.

"Fin!" She felt a flood of relief and nearly began crying. For just a moment, she felt hope surge within her until she turned back to Molly. The shadows began to collect and swirl around her, lifting her and pulling her away again.

201

Voices gathered from the corners of the room, rising and falling together. "Dream walker!" Terror sent tremors through their whispers and hisses. Molly's hand began to slip out of hers.

"No! I won't let go!" She knew even that Molly was slipping helplessly back into the darkness. "Wait! Don't give up yet! Molly, I need to know. Who is doing this?"

Molly turned her head away from Kate, pained to see her refusal to accept defeat. Her face sank into shadow, joining in the darkness that shrouded the rest of her body.

Kate could feel Fin tugging harder, now with a hand on each of her legs. "Please!" Kate begged. "Tell me!"

Molly's eyes opened, filled with hate. A voice unlike any Kate had ever heard answered, "She doesn't know. She doesn't know." Other voices rose in agreement, screeching and shouting.

The tendril of death released its grip on Kate's arm, and she flew backward into the empty house. The storm instantly ceased. In the now eerily quiet room, Kate drew up onto her hands and knees, staring at the kenasai as it reformed. Her sodden clothes clung to her body, giving her a much slighter appearance than normal.

"No," she whispered. Her tears mixed with her rain-soaked face.

A hand touched her shoulder and squeezed reassuringly. Despite her frustration at being pulled out before she could save Molly, Kate knew Fin had just saved her from a peril she might not even understand. "You came," Kate whispered, standing and wrapping her arms around Fin.

"Of course I did," he said, hugging her back.

~~~~~

Kate woke up in her bed, covered with sweat. Jake had uncharacteristically crawled into her bed with her. She glanced down at his head, laying on her stomach. "You aren't supposed to be up here, boy." He gave her a sad-eyed look, and she put her arm on him. "It's okay, buddy." She wished for someone to tell her it would be okay.

She felt a sting go through her arm. She lifted it off Jake. Holding it up for examination, she gasped. Supporting her weight with her good arm, she sat up, keeping her injured arm in the air.

Burns vined up her arm in the pattern of the dark curled fingers from her dream. She gawked at it in disbelief, walking to the

202

bathroom to run cold water over it. The water felt good on her skin, but each time she pulled it out from under the water, it throbbed again.

Her doorbell rang, followed by rapid beating on the door. She figured Fin might show up. "Coming," she shouted, hoping he would hear her before he opted to break a window.

She opened the door to a very ragged and tired-looking Fin. She walked toward the kitchen and left him in the doorway. He closed the door behind him before he burst into a frenzy of talking while following her.

"Kate! How did you do that? How did you call me to your dream without really knowing how?"

"Fin..." she started, reaching into her freezer for an ice pack.

"I mean, I can't pretend to understand the inner workings of dream walkers, but that seems like a complicated process..." he continued.

"Fin..." she tried interrupting him again.

"...and you just called my name, and there I was, standing on the porch of Molly's house. Of course, you didn't call me directly to your side, which nearly cost you dearly..." he stuck out his finger, preparing to lecture her.

"FIN!" she shouted.

He dropped his finger to his side, noticing the ice pack. "What? Are you okay?"

"We have a bigger problem than my inability to call you right to my side," she replied, holding her burnt arm up.

He let out a low whistle. "It would seem you aren't impermeable to demons after all."

Chapter 22

Fran listened to Simone's heated exchange with someone on the other end of her phone. She could only catch bits and pieces of it, but she could hear enough to gather that Simone wasn't getting her way.

"What do you mean it wasn't at the trailer?" Her voice cracked like a whip. "They both came immediately. Why would they come if he had nothing of value there?"

After a long pause, Simone sighed. "I searched the house entirely before they interrupted. It isn't there. I'm beginning to wonder if you truly saw what you think you saw, Blanch. You will not be paid until we find it." She hung up and tossed the phone into her purse.

Turning back to Fran, Simone rubbed her temples. "Let's try this one more time," she grumbled. "I want to know who Detective Alec Peterson works for. There is no reason for us to go on like this. You merely have to answer my questions truthfully."

Fran struggled against her restraints, grunting through the rag in her mouth. Both of her arms and legs were tightly bound to a chair. Once inside Molly's home, Simone didn't have the option of dragging her up the stairs due to their size difference. She settled for a small kitchen chair stationed in the middle of the living room.

Fran stopped struggling and slumped her shoulders, realizing Simone was no amateur when it came to knots. Plus, every time Fran struggled, it increased her heart rate, sending painful pulses through her concussed head. She blinked a few times, wincing. The swelling on the side of her face pushed her left eyelid closed like a boxing injury. But from what she could tell, the wound had stopped bleeding.

"I'm going to remove the rag from your mouth to give you a chance to answer." Simone raised her eyebrows, waiting for Fran to agree. Fran nodded.

After Simone removed the gag, Fran could still feel pieces of fuzz and cloth in her dry mouth. She coughed before glaring at Simone. "Again," she spat. "I do not know what you are talking about. I've told you he's from Chicago, but you don't believe me. I told you he works for the police as a detective, which you also don't believe. If you're not going to trust anything I say, then we're going to have problems here."

"Who *else* does he work for? Whose side is he on?" Simone prodded.

Fran knew she did not have the answers Simone wanted. In fact, she had no earthly idea what the woman was talking about. She gave up, turning her head toward the floor and closing her one good eye.

She heard Simone march into the kitchen and raise a ruckus rummaging through a few drawers before coming back to the living room. Something cold touched Fran's chin. Without opening her eyes, she knew it was the blade of a knife.

"I guess you don't carry your own, huh?" Fran smirked, finally looking up into Simone's green eyes.

"My weapons are too specialized to use on someone as insignificant as you." She trailed the knife down to Fran's throat. "Now that we understand the severity of the situation, I'd like to know what you know."

Fran couldn't help herself; she had to know the depth of Simone's rabbit hole. "Detective Peterson knows about the website," she led, wondering if Simone would take the bait.

Simone's eyes did not change, but Fran's comment derailed her train of thought. "He has been investigating the website for a while now. I'm sure he knows as much as anyone else knows about it."

So, Simone knew Peterson from before the Marion cases. "Oh. Well, I guess you already know we've linked the Jane Doe that you visited back to the website, too." Fran responded in a bored tone.

Simone's eyes flicked to the knife and back. In that single moment that she took to consider her options, she validated Fran's suspicions about possible connections with the girl in the hospital. Not only that, but she added a cherry on top by associating herself with the website. Fran grinned.

"What are you smiling about?" Simone asked, returning a smile of her own.

"I guess you're thinking about killing me." Fran indicated the knife with a glance. "But it won't stop Peterson. He knows everything." She raised her head a little, feeling victorious despite her predicament.

Simone stowed the knife under the chair and walked confidently to her purse. "Well then, I guess you have me cornered," she replied sardonically, pulling out her cell phone. She held it up, snapping a picture of Fran.

"What are you doing?" Fran asked, embarrassed at the audible rasp in her tight throat. She already knew the answer.

"Documenting. You look absolutely ghastly." Simone reached around Fran and into her back pocket, pulling out her phone, too. "I'm going to need you to make a call for me."

Fran set her face into a stony glare. "There is nothing you can do that is going to make me call Detective Peterson. You're already done for. It'll be better for you if you just make a run for it now."

Simone leaned over the chair. With her free hand, she steadied herself on the arm, leaning in close. She whispered in Fran's ear, "Demons have this thing about them. They don't like traitors. Who knew they have morals, right? And they never run."

Fran leaned back so she could look at Simone. Demons? Who said anything about demons?

Simone's expression darkened. "Stop it!"

Fran jumped at the sound of her voice booming through the room. "Stop what?"

"Stop looking at me like you don't know what I'm talking about!" Simone growled, reaching under the chair for the knife.

"But," Fran blundered, "I don't know what you are talking about." Suddenly, she didn't feel so victorious.

Simone gave her a vindictive smile. "Are you feeling a little less confident now? I suppose if you did know, you wouldn't have shown up alone. Or maybe you're just stupid. Surely you know that Detective Peterson works for Lucifer himself."

Fran's foggy mind couldn't grasp what Simone was saying, or perhaps she misheard the woman. That blow to her head made it difficult to concentrate. "For Lucifer?"

"Yes. As in the King of Hell. The Devil. The Fallen One. Lord of Evil." Simone took the tip of her knife and made little circles in the air. "I could go on and on. The point is, he won't be the King of Hell for long once I have his little band of loyal followers out of the way. Detective Peterson is on the wrong side in this war, and you are simply cannon fodder."

Fran could fight through her fear, but she felt a pang of sadness. Her mind struggled to keep up through the fog of her injuries. Her emotions were losing the battle. "Alec doesn't even like me," she heard herself say. "He won't come." She didn't know if the disappointment she felt was in herself or him.

Simone chuckled. "Nobody cares about you." Shaking her head, she went on, "I don't know if Detective Peterson works for Lucifer willingly or if he is a puppet for the demons working for Lucifer. Either way, you've stumbled across a development in his case, don't you think? You need to convince him to come investigate."

Fran could feel herself fading back out of consciousness. Her vision began to tunnel, and she couldn't focus any longer. That certainly explained the strange conversation. She allowed her chin to drop to her chest, and she closed her eye, welcoming deep, dark sleep.

Swish. The knife hissed through the air, ending with a loud thud that vibrated the chair. Before Fran had the chance to react, a pain shot up her arm like lightning. She screamed, looking down at the handle of the knife sticking up out of her hand.

Simone turned her back, scrolling through Fran's contacts. "I told you I needed you to make a phone call for me. Now pay attention," she mumbled in a detached tone.

~~~~~

Alec stood in the hospital lobby waiting for Mr. Farragut, the man in charge of the hospital's public relations. The automatic doors flexed open and closed each time a patient or family member approached, letting in the dewy smell of morning air.

Mr. Farragut had called earlier that day, explaining that the body of the Jane Doe, who died of suspected blood poisoning, had been tampered with. He couldn't explain the inconsistency in the findings because only the coroner had signed in and out of the log. Furthermore, the autopsy revealed that regardless of the gangrene in her leg, it had not yet spread to her heart, throwing the initial cause of death out the window.

"Detective Peterson?" Mr. Farragut approached him with his hand out in greeting. "I'm sorry for the wait. I got held up in a meeting."

Alec kept his hands in his pockets but smiled at the man. "It's no problem."

Once Mr. Farragut understood that the handshake would not be reciprocated, he used that hand to point in the direction of the morgue. "Please follow me."

They walked down the mostly vacant halls decorated with plants, pictures of flowers, and a couple of art exhibits from the pediatric patients. Mr. Farragut used his ID to access the staff elevator, taking them to the basement.

Alec signed in at the desk before being led to a small room with drawers to refrigerate the bodies. Mr. Farragut stood to the side, allowing the morgue employee to open the drawer. She slid it out carefully and rolled back the blanket from the girl's chest. She stepped back so Detective Peterson could see.

He leaned down, looking at an obvious stab wound. "How deep is this?" he asked.

The woman looked at Mr. Farragut for consent before beginning. He nodded. "It went straight to her heart. She would have died almost instantly."

"And nobody noticed any blood from the wound? Where is the hospital gown?" Alec couldn't imagine how a wound like this was overlooked.

Mr. Farragut folded his hands, saying, "Well, that's part of the problem. She did not die under suspicious circumstances. Our staff couldn't believe she made it as long as she did to begin with. So, when she passed away, we disposed of the garments."

"You disposed of them?" Alec's voice rose.

"I can show you the documentation, but that's the hospital's procedure. MRSA has been a real problem for many facilities and disposing of gowns after patients use them has reduced our chances for infection dramatically. The nurses followed protocol." Although the man was defending himself and his staff, his face remained placid and calm.

"That's unfortunate," Alec said. "When did you notice the stab wound?"

The woman spoke up, "After the body is prepared, we try to autopsy within 24 hours. The autopsy revealed that she did not die of gangrene or blood poisoning, but the stab wound is not mentioned in the report." She pulled out a clipboard, showing it to Alec.

"Do you think they overlooked it? Or was this done after the autopsy?" He asked. Neither looked good for the hospital.

"I really don't know how that's possible," the woman replied. "She would have been covered in blood when they brought her down. Plus, our medical examiner has been practicing for years. We probably wouldn't have even performed an autopsy if she wasn't involved in a murder investigation. But your chief insisted."

"Good thing he did," Peterson mumbled. He placed his hand inconspicuously on the girl's arm as Mr. Farragut droned on about protecting the hospital's reputation but Alec wasn't listening anymore He only needed a moment to search her. *Ah, there it is. A rune was used. Very slippery indeed.*

"...Furthermore, we don't need people thinking that we have employees who mutilate our patients postmortem..." he continued.

Peterson removed his hand quickly and looked up at Mr. Farragut. "I have everything I need, for now, thank you. I'll have the chief contact you." He could wave a hand and make them forget the whole conversation, but humans could be easily convinced and manipulated without supernatural force.

Mr. Farragut stumbled, showing his surprise. "Well, I've already pulled records of employees who have complaints against them. I thought you might take a look at them while you're here."

"No, I'm good. Thank you for your time. Can you please take me back to the lobby?"

Mr. Farragut and the technician exchanged wary glances. They'd expected more drilling from Alec. "Sure, sir. Let's go."

As soon as they stepped off the elevator, Alec's phone vibrated on his hip. He saw Fran's name before answering. "Hey, Fran. Chief says you're coming back in today?"

There was a long pause at the other end of the line. Finally, Fran's thick voice cut through the silence. "That's right."

"Are you okay?" He asked. She sounded downright awful. "Don't come into the office and get everyone sick. We'll be just as happy to see you tomorrow if you need another day." He tried to sound genuine. He needed her back to help him now that he knew where to look.

She grunted. "I am fine, Alec. I just tried calling a few times and was worried when you didn't answer. It was going straight to voicemail."

"I was in the basement at the hospital. Bad reception."

"Oh. Well, I am calling because I decided to come to Molly Gregory's house before heading into the office." She breathed shakily, adding, "You know, to see if being at the crime scene helped me think."

Something was off. Her voice sounded like it had been dragged over gravel. Alec responded carefully. "Uh-huh."

A scuffle happened in the background, followed by another grunt. "You should probably come over here." She breathed heavily and slurred the last few words.

"We can talk about it when you get to the station," he said, keeping his tone even. He needed to know more about what was happening on the other end of the line. He hoped if he stalled long enough, he could glean more information.

"Alec," Fran said, allowing fear to seep into her voice. "I have to tell you I'm sorry."

"Sorry for what?"

"I'm sorry for the way I acted at the hospital. And I'm sorry I got myself into this." A commotion happened, and it sounded like Fran dropped the phone. He could hear her in the background yelling desperately. "Don't come! Alec, stay away!"

The call disconnected.

Alec looked at his watch. From the hospital to Molly's house would take him about twenty minutes. It didn't sound like Fran had that kind of time, and she certainly couldn't spare him the luxury of thinking before acting. He sprinted to his car. He would have to think on the way.

~~~~~

Kate turned onto Molly's street, carefully driving with one hand. While her other hand didn't hurt too bad anymore, Fin's bulky bandage made it difficult to use her fingers. "Was this really necessary?" She complained to Fin.

"You're lucky I already had a salve made up in my trailer," Fin retorted, still fuming at her for trying to jump into the kenasai in her dream. "What if you'd gotten stuck?" He asked for the umpteenth time. "Now that we know you are vulnerable in your dreams, you're going to have to be more careful, Kate. You can't just do whatever you want."

"It does feel better," she admitted. "Thanks." She put the car in park, adding, "Let's just get this over with so we don't have to store the kenasai in that tree by your house forever." After her dream, they took extra measures to hide the kenasai until they could find a better place for it. They reasoned that no one would go back to the trailer again, but even so, an old tree nearby had a hole just the right size.

"The rune I drew on the tree will help protect it for now, but you're right," he agreed. He rubbed his shoulder.

"What's wrong with your arm?" Kate asked.

"I'm okay, but you could probably afford to lose some weight before asking me to pull you out of another supernatural portal." He began to open the passenger door.

"Wait," Kate said, stopping him. "I know that car." She pointed to a car with Chicago plates, waiting for her memory to catch up with the recognition. "It's the realtor for Molly's house."

"Does she have an appointment to show it?" Fin asked.

"If she does, she didn't tell me." Kate made no move to get out of the car.

"Well," Fin led, staring at her, "are we going in?"

Kate sighed. "I don't really like the realtor. She gives me the creeps."

"At least we're here so you can see if she's any good at what she does," Fin offered.

"Yeah." Kate hesitated. She had a bad feeling about Everly, but her dream made her leery of Molly's house, too. She shook the feeling away, opening her door. "Let's go."

"I'm serious, you know," Fin inserted before they reached the porch.

"About what?" She asked, pushing the front door open.

"You're much heavier than you look." Fin laughed with a twinkle in his eye.

"Fin..." Kate stopped cold. The hair on the back of her neck stood up.

In the middle of Molly's living room, a woman sat strapped to a chair. Her blood-covered head lulled toward the door. The sound of the opening door woke her. Then she slowly turned back, chin resting on her chest.

Kate scanned the room, listened for a moment, and quickly walked over, dropping her purse on the ground next to the chair. She squatted in front of the woman, looking up at her face. It was Fran, the local officer who worked with Alec.

Fran muttered a few words that Kate didn't understand. She did catch "Detective Peterson," though. She leaned closer. "Fran? Who did this?" She glanced over her shoulder, asking, "Are they still here?"

Fin stood nearby, scanning the room. She took her keys out of her purse and tossed them to him. "Go start the car, now," She whispered. He ran out the front door without protesting. She worked to untie Fran. "We're going to get you out of here."

"Well, this is an unexpected surprise." At the sound of Everly's voice, Kate stopped and stood quickly and turned on her heels toward the voice. Everly stood between the kitchen and living room, feet planted shoulder-width apart. "Hello, Katherine."

"Everly." Kate didn't move.

"Actually, my name is Simone. No need to hide behind a pseudonym anymore. It's nice to properly meet you."

"Whatever. I guess you aren't a realtor either." Kate stuck to short responses, still not sure what she'd gotten herself into. She wondered if she should put her fists up to look more intimidating somehow. Soft footsteps told her Fin approached from behind. Without turning to look at him, she shouted an introduction. "Fin. This is Simone."

Simone's eyes moved to Fin. "Actually, we already know each other, don't we, Finneus? How's your face, by the way?"

He didn't respond. Kate turned, checking his reaction, wondering how she could possibly deal with a betrayal from him. "Fin?"

His expression turned to stone. "Yes, Kate, I know her."

Kate's heart dropped. How could he have deceived her so well? Had their entire friendship been a lie? She should have trusted Marcy from the beginning. She already felt guilty for leaving Marcy in the dark, but now finding out that it could have cost her dearly, she regretted it even more.

Finally, Fin added, "She posed as a stand-in funeral director a couple of years ago after I lost my wife. She used the ruse to ask inappropriate and prying questions about my wife's death. I blamed my sensitivity on my emotional state." He clenched his jaw, jeering at Simone. "The real funeral director turned up dead a few weeks later. Suspicious, right? It's the reason I started attending funerals in the area if the deaths were suicides. I wanted to know who she really was. She disappeared, and I couldn't track her down, but I kept going to funerals, hoping I would find her again." He directed his gaze at Kate. "That's why I was at Molly's funeral."

Relieved that Fin hadn't betrayed her, Kate let out the breath she'd been holding. She looked at the ground, ashamed that she'd doubted him.

"It's okay, Kate," Fin said softly.

Simone cut in. "You've come a long way since then, Fin. Taken up some new hobbies like Blanch and Joe suggested, right? Blanch told me she'd seen your trailer, full of – what's the word she used – Satanic stuff." She cracked her knuckles. "People can really be so ignorant, don't you think? If only she knew that most of your renderings and talismans were angelic."

"I guess that's what I get for missing group," he replied, sounding more like his humorous self.

"You broke into my house," Kate said, piecing together Simone's comment about Fin's face.

Simone didn't bother answering and followed up with a demand. "Katherine, I believe you have something of mine, and I want it back."

Kate feigned a clueless look. "I don't know what you're talking about." She now had a long checklist of reasons not to trust this woman: Fin, Fran, and her gut.

"Don't be daft. I know Ashley gave it to you." Simone sneered.

Kate shrugged, sticking to her denial. "I don't know anyone named Ashley."

"You know her. The woman who killed your sister," Simone smiled, knowing her approach would strike a nerve.

It did. Kate's face flushed with anger. She already knew that Ashley had taken Molly's life, but Simone's exploitation of the fact enraged her. She bit her tongue and held Simone's gaze, refusing to respond.

"I don't have time for this!" Simone lifted both hands, pulling a bracelet off each arm ceremoniously. She laid them on top of each other with the opening pointed at Kate. She whispered something in a language that Kate didn't recognize. "I know Fin wears a necklace with angelic writings, but you don't, do you? You've proven runes don't work. Let's see if you can stand up to everything I have up my sleeve."

Kate took a step back, holding up both of her hands as the bracelets began to glow. With her eyes glued to the bracelets, she shouted, "Fin? What's that?"

213

He didn't have a chance to answer before shadows burst from the center of the bracelets. They closed the distance to Kate in an instant and swirled around her, sending pulses through the air. Goosebumps raised on her flesh, but aside from that, nothing happened. The swirling grew more furious, and the pulses intensified. Several shadows broke off from the group, prodding around her chest but seemingly unable to penetrate her body. They wove in and out of her legs. Too afraid to move, Kate stood like a statue -- fists down, her mouth shut tight. Finally, the darkness retreated into the bracelets.

Fin let out an audible breath of relief.

"Impossible." Simone regarded Kate with fear in her eyes. "Who are you?"

Rather than answer the question, Kate did her best to look as intimidating and authoritative as possible. "We're taking Fran with us."

Simone seemed to have regained her composure. "You're going to take me to the kenasai."

"No," Kate answered confidently.

"Yes, dear, I believe you will find that cooperating with me is in your best interest," Simone said, inspecting her bracelets before placing them back on her wrists. "I may not be able to force you, but I have something else you want."

"There is nothing you can say..."

Simone interrupted. "I can show you how to free your sister in return."

~~~~~

Alec pulled up to Molly's house and pulled his gun out. He ran as quietly as possible to the front door, which stood wide open. With his weapon raised, he stepped into the door, checking both sides. He scanned the room as he passed through, noting the empty chair with blood splatter around it.

He checked each room on the bottom floor and then systematically cleared the second floor, as well. Holstering his gun on his side, he returned to the living room.

The chair had a good bit of blood on it but not enough to think that its occupant had died. Was this Fran's blood? He grimaced. Not knowing if she lost blood somewhere before or after this made it a guessing game. How much time did he have?

He noticed a purse next to the chair and squatted down, careful to avoid stepping on any evidence. He took a pen and pulled the purse open with the end of it. He shifted some of the contents around, hoping to find something helpful. The wallet had a window on the outside for the driver's license. Katherine Gregory. "Damnit," he whispered.

He stood and strode quickly to the front door. Looking up and down the street, he confirmed that he hadn't seen Kate's car when he pulled up. "Damnit!" He said again, slightly louder.

He pulled out his phone and dialed Kelsey's number. "Hello!"

At the sound of her voice, he launched into a series of commands. "Kelsey! I need you to go to your computer, pull up the tracking..."

"You've reached the fortress of all knowledge," the answering system continued. "Leave a message for Queen Kelsey at the sound of the beep!"

Alec hung up and held the phone to his forehead in frustration. He sighed. "Damnit."

~~~~~

Graham turned down his music to answer his phone. "Hey, Alec, what's up?"

"Where is Kelsey?" He replied curtly.

"She went to grab some enchiladas at Don Sol. You coming to see us? I can text her and ask her to..."

"Shut up!" Peterson interrupted. "Go to her computer and pull up the tracker on Kate's car."

"Kate? Oh, you mean Katherine Gregory," he said, standing and approaching Kelsey's messy station. "I didn't realize you were on a short name basis with her," he joked.

"Are you at the computer?" Alec asked impatiently.

"I'm working on it," Graham muttered, noting Alec's haste. "Kelsey's going to kill me, you know. She says she knows where everything is in this rat's nest. I organized it once for her, and I barely escaped with my life. She made me swear not to touch it again." The computer screen lit up. "What's the password?"

"What? I don't know the password. Why would she lock her computer?"

"Hello? We're hackers. Do you know what could happen if you walk away from your computer without locking it?" Graham waited for Peterson to shoot him an idea.

In a much softer voice, Peterson responded, "Graham, this is serious. I need to know where Kate is. I think she's in trouble. Please help me."

The door to the room opened, and Kelsey walked in with two bags of food. "What are you doing at my computer? No touchy!" She dropped the bags and rushed over to assess the damage Graham may have caused.

"Peterson!" Graham shouted into the phone. "Kelsey is here. I'm going to give her the phone."

He handed the phone to Kelsey. She gave him a questioning look, waiting for an explanation before putting it to her ear.

"Peterson is sweet on Katherine Gregory, and she's in trouble. He needs you to turn on the tracker." Graham smiled at Peterson's protests about being sweet on Katherine squawking through the speaker.

Kelsey grabbed the phone. "Thanks for pissing him off before handing him over." She rolled her eyes. Her fingers flew over the keyboard. "Alec, I have it. I'm sending the coordinates to your phone now."

Chapter 23

Only a few turns away from the trailer, Kate had no plan of action. She knew that leading Simone to the kenasai posed serious consequences, but she could not pass up on the opportunity to release Molly's soul. Even if Simone took her life, she had to free Molly. Nobody else knew the truth. Therefore, if Kate and Fin died, Molly had no hope at all.

Simone insisted that they bring the mostly unconscious Fran with them. They struggled to load her in the car and had her propped in a seated position. Fin sat sour-faced next to her, partially helping her stay upright. He had ripped off part of his shirt and wrapped it around the wound on her hand to try and stop the bleeding.

His icy glances from the backseat pierced right through her. She knew that anyone who had done such horrible things to a police officer would have no issues eliminating all three of them once they handed over the kenasai. She continued to grind the gears of her mind for a solution, hoping Fin trusted her enough to follow her lead.

She turned onto the gravel road, her tires crunching noisily as they eased toward the trailer. Simone sat a little straighter in the passenger seat. "You must think I'm stupid. I'm not going into his trailer." She turned her sharp gaze to Kate. "You go get the kenasai and bring it back to me."

Kate tried not to let Simone's gaze cut through her. She kept both hands on the steering wheel with white knuckles. She glanced at Fin in her rearview mirror before casually saying, "Fine."

217

Hoping she was doing the right thing, she got out of the car and walked past the trailer. Her gaze settled a tree about 30 yards away. A dark hole in the trunk about 3 feet off the ground marked the kenasai's hiding spot. Her stomach did a somersault.

The passenger door opened, and Simone shouted, "Where do you think you're going? I have your friends in the car. If you're about to try to..."

Kate interrupted her, "If you want the kenasai, but you don't want to come with me to get it, this is the only option."

Taken aback by the new knowledge that the kenasai was not in Fin's trailer, Simone looked in the back seat at Fran. She seemed to be weighing her options. "You," she said to Fin, "come with me."

Fran would most likely remain incapacitated and posed no threat. Kate hadn't heard her utter an intelligible phrase since this whole thing started. She would roll in and out of consciousness, mumbling a few slurred words here and there. Hauling Fran out of the car would only slow Simone down.

Fin moved slowly but unfolded himself from the backseat without protest.

Simone stepped up to him and placed a hand around his neck. Kate's heart leapt into her throat. Could he fight off Simone if he needed to? He looked ahead, steeling himself for what was to come. She pinched the cord of his talisman between her fingers and pulled it up through his shirt collar, ripping it from his neck. "You won't be needing this," she said loudly enough for Kate to hear, then tossed the talisman into the grass.

Kate gasped. She wondered if he accused her of having a tattoo before because he had one as a backup. She held onto hope that he still had a way to safeguard himself. If Simone chose to use her bracelets to summon dark forces, or creatures, or whatever they were, Fin would need more protection than his martial arts.

Turning to lead the way, Kate recalled how she and Fin worked together to put the kenasai in the tree. Though she did not fully understand angelic language, he did explain a bit to her. The rune he sketched around the kenasai would ward off anyone but her and Fin because he knew the counter rune – basically a password that he could draw on his hand. He also used their blood so that only they could use the counter rune. It was genius, really.

Kate admired his work and understood the value of Fin's knowledge. She couldn't fathom how much reading he would have to do in order to obtain such a profound understanding. Even so, he still claimed that he did not know everything. If Simone reached into the protected area of the tree's trunk, Kate didn't know what would happen, but she guessed nothing good. If Simone made her reach in, Kate thought she might be able to reach through without injury because of her immunity to supernatural attacks. Or maybe since the rune contained some of her blood, the rune wouldn't hurt her as badly. Although it wasn't more than a hypothesis, she had nothing better to bank on.

She stopped a few paces from the tree, not sure how far back she needed to stand to keep herself and Fin safe. Pointing toward the tree, she said, "It's in that hole." She turned to Simone, awaiting instruction. She thought if she didn't suggest anything and let Simone decide, it would seem less suspicious. She prayed inwardly that Simone would not make Fin reach in, especially without his amulet.

Simone searched the surrounding trees before turning her gaze back to Kate. "Go get it."

Kate felt her stomach sink in disappointment but kept her face as unreadable as possible. She turned and walked the lonely last few steps to the tree. Her grandmother had used a rune to block her and Molly's dreams, right? So that must mean that some runes would work on her, but how could she know which ones? What would happen to her if this was one of the few that did work? Maybe good runes worked, but bad runes didn't? How could she categorize the two?

She looked into the hole at the kenasai and then back over her shoulder at Fin, who stood biting his lip next to Simone. He did not look too sure of what might happen, either. She closed her eyes, took a deep breath, and reached into the tree with her good hand. Nothing happened. Relieved to be past the first barrier, she confidently moved her hand to the kenasai. As soon as her fingers touched the surface, she knew she had made a horrible mistake.

A blinding white light ignited under the kenasai, and the rune lit up the inside of the tree like a lantern. Kate didn't even have time to suck in a surprised breath before a shock wave slammed into her body, the impact throwing her several strides away from the tree. With ringing ears, she blinked several times, trying to focus. A memory flashed through her mind - playing in the ocean as a child and getting hit by a big wave that left her disoriented. Under the water, she flopped and turned, searching for the surface desperately trying to get her bearings. No matter how much she struggled, her mind couldn't sort out which way was up. She felt that way now. She tried to focus on the tree several times before she finally understood that she lay flat on her back with her face toward the overhanging limbs. The sun poked through the gaps between leaves.

Kate groaned and rolled onto her side, coughing. Each gasp for air felt like glass shards in her abdomen. "Jesus, Fin. Good job on the rune." She struggled to breathe at all. She pushed herself up onto her elbow, hoping to help expand her lungs. Still seeing stars, she turned her eyes to Simone, who had a very amused look on her face.

"Well, I, for one, am glad that I do not have any fractured ribs at this moment." Simone turned to Fin. "Kate isn't so lucky. Give me the counter rune."

"No!" Kate's voice sounded weak and strained despite her effort. She still sucked in less and less air with each breath. "Don't do it, Fin. Please." She winced in pain. Her whole body hurt like hell.

Fin gave her an apologetic look. "Give me a pen," he said to Simone.

She grinned at him mischievously. "You used nature, Fin. Do you think I don't know you need to draw the counter rune with mud?"

Chagrined, he turned his eyes to the ground. Under her watchful eye, he bent down and spat into his hand. He dug enough dirt out of the ground with a nearby stick to make a paste.

Simone held up her hand and said, "Go ahead, draw it."

Fin took the stick and sketched a series of shapes that all intersected with a half-circle. Kate inched over on her butt, trying to inspect the rune. She hoped he would draw it wrong, but he had shown her the counter rune, and it looked exactly the same as the one on Simone's hand.

He must know she's experienced in this subject, Kate thought, dejected. *He cannot fool her with something as elementary as drawing it incorrectly.*

Simone also studied her palm, discerning if he had drawn it properly. She stood and strutted confidently to the tree. Fin kneeled close to Kate, helping her sit up the rest of the way. They exchanged a knowing glance.

Simone couldn't hide her excitement as it spread across her face in a grin. Feeling victorious, she reached into the tree. Her face changed quickly into panic. She tried to lurch back, but an invisible force kept her in place. Part of the tree detached from the bark in a lifelike tendril and sliced into the skin on her forearm before shooting straight through her arm. Kate couldn't tell from the ground, but she guessed it weaved itself right between her radius and ulna, making it impossible for her to free her own arm. Simone yanked on her arm. Her shrill screams filled the air.

"What have you done?" She yelled at Fin before a look of realization crossed her face. "*You...*"

"I used a nature rune and a blood rune together," Fin announced proudly.

"How could someone like *you* possibly have that kind of understanding of the ancient languages?" Simone spoke through her teeth.

Kate turned to him. "Fin, why..."

Fin interrupted. "Your blood was in the rune, so it didn't harm you. But when you reached in without the password, the tree sent you a warning."

"*That* was a warning?" Kate's hand went to her ribs, trying to stabilize them.

"I might have made it a little strong. Sorry." Fin said.

"Uh, yeah," Kate groaned as Fin helped her to a standing position. She was pleasantly surprised to find that standing felt marginally better than being on the ground.

"NO!" Fran cried from the car.

Fin turned a little quicker than Kate, but she still caught a glimpse of Detective Peterson reaching into the car.

"Alec?" she shouted, puzzled.

Fran had a look of terror in her eyes. She shouted, "You work for Lucifer! You are one of the creatures!"

Alec held his arm up and said, "No, Fran, that's not right, I'm..."

Fran hit Alec hard in the face before swinging her legs out of the car and kicking him to the ground. "Kate, you need to run!" She yelled. Kate couldn't believe that Fran had the strength to do anything at this point. Adrenaline must have given her a second wind.

Alec shouted protests from the ground that Kate couldn't understand, but she looked at Fin, and he nodded. She had no idea why Fran thought Detective Peterson worked for Lucifer, and she didn't want to find out. Fran was in no condition to hold him off for very long. The fact that she'd spoken in sentences was a small miracle.

She knelt in the dirt and quickly drew the rune on her hand as Fin had shown her. She had never done anything like this before, and she knew if she wanted to walk away from the tree with at least some of her ribs intact, she needed to get it perfect. She looked up at Fin, who was running back to the car to help Fran. "Fin, is this right?"

He barely glanced at her over his shoulder, shouting, "Sure!"

"Fin!"

He ignored her and continued to the scuffle. Alec tried to restrain Fran in a way that wouldn't injure her further. At least that gave them a chance. She didn't have a choice. She dashed to the tree stopping within arm's length. Simone had manifested a knife from somewhere and was angrily hacking at the tree, trying to free her arm.

Kate didn't know how to reach into the tree without crossing over Simone. She also suspected that if she reached in and freed the kenasai from its hiding place, Simone would also be freed.

Simone gave her a cutting look that said she would stab Kate if she had the chance. Kate glanced back and saw that Peterson had freed himself from his fight with Fran and was running for her with Fin close behind him. She pushed Simone, stretching her arm to reach across. Barely able to fit into the space of the hole, fingers clasped the kenasai as she felt Simone's blade slide into her side under her ribs.

With a thump through the air, the tree released the kenasai, sending Kate tumbling to her knees with the prize in her hand. Simone let out a deep breath as the tree also relented its grip on her, dropping her to the ground with a thud. Simone remained there, momentarily gathering her wits. She had time on her side because the blade had done enough damage to Kate. Gasping for breath and with pain shooting through her body, Kate army crawled away, holding the kenasai protectively against her chest with her burnt and bandaged hand.

Tears streamed down her face. "I won't let anything happen to you, Molly," she whispered.

"Detective Peterson. How nice to see you again," Simone growled under her breath.

Alec slid to a stop, eyes fixed on Simone. "I didn't know you were in town," he replied, widening his stance.

"Lucifer cannot win this battle, you know. Tyrannus already has more than enough to fight." A snarky grin touched her lips. "We're going to dethrone the King of Hell. You can't stop us."

Kate tried to figure out whose side she should be on. Lucifer or Tyrannus? Did she have to choose? If Alec worked for Satan himself, could he help her free her? Would it be worth it?

"Well, Kate," Simone said, eyes still on Alec. "What's it going to be? Will you give the kenasai to me so that your sister's soul has a purpose? Or will you hand it over to someone serving the Dark Kingdom?"

Kate didn't like her options. "Neither. You can both go back to Hell."

"Sorry, dear, I don't belong there." Simone grinned confidently.

"Neither do I," Alec responded with a glimmer in his eyes that made them look like sapphires.

"No. It can't be!" Simone backed into the tree, momentarily frozen. "You still cannot win this alone, half-breed." She barely spoke loud enough for them to hear. Regaining her composure, she removed her bracelets. Quivering hands betrayed her bold words, sending the bracelets tumbling into the grass.

Alec knelt on one knee, planting a hand onto the earth. Gravity gave way, and small pebbles rose from the ground around him. The air compressed heavily in Kate's ears.

Fin finally got to Kate's side as a halo of light enveloped Alec. "Kate," Alec said calmly, "hand me the kenasai."

Kate looked at Fin, hoping for some guidance, but he just stood wordlessly next to her, mouth gaping. She clenched it tighter in her fist, not knowing what to do. Who was Alec, really? What is a half-breed? If he knew what she held was a kenasai, didn't that make him a bad guy? He could emit light, which was new. But the kenasai had both light and darkness etched in its surface, and it didn't have any good in it whatsoever. She shook her head in a feeble attempt to jostle answers to the surface.

Simone had her bracelets locked in front of her, and Kate knew from experience what would happen next. They had to get out of here. Not for her sake, but for Fin's. He had no protection from whatever forces they were about to face.

On cue, Fin helped her to her feet, his face worried when he noticed the stab wound in her side. "Kate, can you run?"

She didn't know if she could, but she nodded anyway, her hair sticking to the side of her face. Fin took her hand and hastily led her in the direction of the car as shadows began to seep from the portal Simone had created.

Between the shadows and the light around the detective, Kate didn't know where to look. She kept her head down, trying to hold on to Fin. She clenched her teeth in an attempt to ignore the pain in her side. She made it a mere five steps. "Fin, we'll never make it to the car. I just can't move that fast. Go without me and take the kenasai." She weakly tried to hand it to him.

Peterson stood and quickly intercepted them with inhuman speed. "You have to trust me, Kate. Give me the kenasai." He put his hand on her arm, and it tingled. "Now." He looked back over his shoulder at the shadows gathering closer.

She jerked her arm away, expecting to see a rune on his hand, but there wasn't one. "No! Who are you?" she asked.

His expression turned from desperation to shock. "Who are *you?*" He asked, his gaze intensified, examining her. He looked back at the darkness coming for the three of them.

She couldn't risk giving the kenasai to Peterson. "You can't have it!" She screamed. He didn't have time to wrestle her for it. The clouds of darkness were moments from slamming into all of them.

Peterson seemed to debate with himself over fighting Kate for the kenasai. His eyes filled with sympathy before reaching out and touching Fin's arm. "I'm sorry, Fin."

Removing his hand from Fin, Peterson turned to face the shadows alone, a small sword quickly slipping out of his sleeve just in time. It seemed to grow in his hand as it emitted the same glowing light that had encapsulated him just moments before. He held it in front of him, and the darkness slammed into it, splitting like an ocean of soot.

Fin turned to Kate with a detached look in his eyes.

"Fin?" She tried to back away. "Fin, what's going on?"

He wordlessly lunged for the kenasai.

Chapter 24

Kate dove to the side as Fin lunged at her. She cried out, rolling to face him. "Fin! Stop! What are you doing?"

Fin did not speak, and his empty eyes struck Kate's core. She realized that Alec had tried to force her to relinquish the kenasai, and when he was left with no other options, he forced Fin to take it from her instead. She threw up her arm to block Fin's foot as it came crashing down into her. Weak from her injuries and trying to protect the kenasai with her good hand, she would never win this battle. She tossed the kenasai out of reach. It rolled to a stop in the grass.

Still on the ground and under her looming friend, she grabbed Fin's leg, pulling him to the ground. He curled, using the momentum of her move to launch into a rolling position. He fell, grabbing her arm, bringing her along with him. They both rolled, following his lead, then he landed crouched over her.

"Screw you and your Krav Maga!" Kate shouted, frustrated. "You're going to have to kill me, Fin. You know I won't stop trying to save Molly! Look what Alec did to you. Do you really want to play on his team if he has to force people into submission?"

He pressed his elbow into her wounded side. She cried out again in pain. She saw stars and feared she might lose consciousness. "Fin, please," she stammered. Through her teeth, she whispered, "I'm your friend."

Satisfied that he'd immobilized her, he rolled and dove for the kenasai. Before he could grab it, a shadow split from the fight with Peterson and ambushed him, sending him to the ground. For the first time, Kate thanked her lucky stars for demon attacks.

She turned her gaze to the battle between Peterson and the shadows. His sword sliced through each one like butter. He moved effortlessly. A small trickle of blood ran down his cheek where the shadows had managed to break through his defenses. She grimaced. He wouldn't last long against the sheer masses of black figures, and she needed an ally. Fin would not be able to fight the supernatural figures off, and Kate didn't think she could find his amulet in time to protect him.

She stood and put aside the doubt in her decision to help Alec. Trying to breathe evenly, she took deliberate strides to the kenasai. She still didn't know what she planned to do with it. Shadows swirled around her, raising goosebumps but nothing more. Her hair swirled in the wake of their movement.

"What do I do?" Kate shouted. She closed the distance between them, standing as close as she could to hand it to him.

"I can't help you. It's too late. Her bracelets are opening a portal," Alec yelled through clenched teeth. He spun and sliced three shadow figures, sending shocks of light through the air. "I have to hold them off, but I'll get us closer. Can you get the kenasai to the portal?"

"What?" She couldn't just throw it into a portal! What a ridiculous idea. Then she remembered her dream, how she reached through the kenasai into the room on the other side for Molly. If the kenasai was a portal, and she threw it into another portal, would it open?

Peterson's blade danced a little too close to her, and she took a step back.

"No," Kate said, her voice resolute. She did not refuse because she doubted that Alec would do it. She refused because she knew she could. These shadows couldn't hurt her, but he didn't know that yet. "I will run to the portal and push it through. Keep yourself and Fin safe."

"You'll die!" Alec tried to reach for her, but a murky shadow slammed into his side, sending him to the ground. By the time he recovered, Kate had already turned away, sprinting towards Simone, who she could barely see laying on the ground.

She didn't know what to expect, but the closer she got to Simone, the more dense the forms of darkness became. Like a negative flashlight beam, it filled the air. The dense shadows didn't harm her, but they slowed her down. Each step became slower. Kate knew her injuries would prevent a second attempt if she stopped. She tried to use all her effort to keep her legs moving.

Simone, suffering from her own injuries, reached for the bracelets. Kate had to force the kenasai through before Simone could separate them.

"Simone!" Alec shouted, grunting with the effort of each swing of his sword. "I know why you serve them."

Simone faltered, giving Alec a wayward look. He had succeeded in distracting her, giving Kate a small window. She pressed harder.

"They have made you promises that they cannot keep." He grunted again and spit blood from his mouth.

"They have her," Simone said, for once looking genuine.

"No, they don't. They cannot return your daughter to you because they cannot access her soul at all. They've been lying!"

Simone shook her head. "No. You're lying."

Just as Kate's hand reached the portal, Alec's words rang out. "She's in Heaven, Simone. Your masters cannot touch her, I promise."

Kate slipped the kenasai into the portal but kept her hand clenched around it for fear of losing it. The shadows ceased, and the metal began to warm in her hand. Tingling traced her arms and reverberated through her.

By the time she realized her soul was leaving her body, it was too late. Suddenly death didn't seem so scary. Instead of panic, peace washed over her, and she let out her last breath. Closing her eyes, she whispered, "Molly?"

"Let go, Kate." Molly stood before her, her soft hair ruffling around her face. "I'm free. You need to let go."

Kate shook her head. "I can't. How will I know you're okay?"

"Trust me. I'm better than I have been in a long time." Molly smiled and slowly took in a deep breath. She let it out and watched her own chest deflate.

"I love you," Kate whispered, afraid that saying those words meant she had to say goodbye. She couldn't keep them, though. She had to tell Molly.

Molly grinned. "I know." She walked slowly up to Kate and put her hand on her shoulder. "I love you too. Now you have to let go."

Kate felt tense. "I can't."

"You can't? Look at everything that has happened to you. I haven't been around for a while, and suddenly you're some kind of warrior. I can see the fire of a fighter in your eyes."

"If I let go, you'll be gone."

Molly's eyes filled with compassion. She hugged Kate and whispered in her ear, "You know how we never got into religious stuff?"

Kate nodded, unable to find her voice.

"I'm pretty sure we were wrong. These gifts we have—I think God believes in us. The least we could do is believe in Him."

Kate mumbled into Molly's shoulder. "You've got a pretty demanding spirit."

Molly laughed and let go of Kate, slowly backing away. "That's more like the Kate I know." Her image began to fade.

Kate's body vibrated.

"Let GO!" Alec cried, pushing again on Kate's chest.

Her eyes flew open, and she sucked in a raspy breath. She glanced at her hand, still on the kenasai in the open portal, before relinquishing her grip.

The kenasai slipped in, sending white bursts of light spinning through the air around them. They swirled from the portal and shot through the trees, rustling the leaves. One by one, they disappeared into the sky.

The bracelets clanked to the ground, separating. The kenasai did not appear when the portal closed.

Fin put his hand on her chest. "Are you okay? You look awful."

She noticed him for the first time sitting next to her. His clothes were covered in blood. She gasped, feebly reaching for him to check for wounds.

For a moment, Fin looked confused. Then he glanced down at himself and said, "Oh! Don't worry, I'm fine. Not a scratch." He lifted his sleeves, showing her his arms. "Angels have healing ability! Did you even know that? By the way, Alec..."

"Is an angel," Kate grunted, still in pain from all her wounds.

Alec leaned in and rested his hand on her forehead. After a moment, he blinked at her in disbelief. "I—I don't think I can heal her." He sat back on his heels, bewildered.

Fin shook his head. "No. You can heal her. She just won't let you."

Kate glared at him. "Fin, I'm sure I want to be healed. Some of this damage is from you, by the way." She could taste blood and began to feel like she might leave her own body again.

He grimaced. "Yeah. Sorry about that." He waved his hand dismissively. "You are special. Alec couldn't convince your mind to do what he made me do. It's the same with the shadows—uh, demons, I guess. You have to find the place in your mind that has that wall up and take it down.”

Kate's eyes drifted to Simone's crumpled body on the ground. “Is she...”

Alec interrupted, “I can't heal the dead.” She thought she heard a twinge of regret in his voice. If he couldn't heal the dead, she didn't have much time.

Fin cut back in, “Kate, I think you can control this. Think about it.”

She remembered running into Alec at the grocery store. She felt something when he touched her. Maybe it was because he caught her off guard. At the time, she hadn't heard from him in a while, and she felt relieved that she ran into him.

“I think you're right,” she murmured.

Alec waited, his hand gently resting on her forehead.

“You have to trust him,” Fin said.

She nodded. She tried imagining an inner switch that she could flip to let Alec in. Nothing happened. She felt herself draining away.

“Stop fighting!” Alec yelled desperately. He pounded the ground in frustration with a clenched fist.

Alec grabbed her wrist and pulled her into his arms. “She's not going to let me in. We have to get her to a hospital now.”

She breathed in his soft scent through one of her last moments of consciousness. He ran so effortlessly to the car, she couldn't even feel the jolt of his feet hitting the ground. It was smooth, like gliding across the surface of glass.

Erica Darnell

Chapter 25

Kate awoke to the sound of Fin's chastising voice. She couldn't quite understand his words over the sound of the beeping. *What is that sound?* Beep, beep, beep. She tried to focus her energy on understanding her surroundings. She realized her eyes were still closed. She painstakingly opened them, and it felt like the first time in a decade.

A stark white room greeted her like shards of glass in her retinas. She couldn't help but remember how it felt to be standing in police headquarters, comparing it to a psych ward. Her eyes shot open wider, fear creeping in. *Am I in a psych ward?*

Fin stood at the end of her bed, waggling his finger at someone sitting down. "I'm just saying, you didn't have to leave me with the car. It took me forever to get here. Next time you go disappearing like that, at least tell me where the hell you're going."

"There aren't that many hospitals around." Kate recognized Alec's voice.

"Well, of course I went to the one in Marion first! It's geographically the closest."

She could hear the smile on Alec's lips. "Yeah, but Carbondale is better."

Fin sounded exasperated. "The point is, I got here. No thanks to you. You can teleport, but you can't send messages?"

Kate tried to lift her head so she could see Peterson. She involuntarily let out a groan. Every inch of her brain hurt. Alec popped up in the corner and came to her side, his blue eyes intense. She whispered, "Thank God I'm not in a psych ward. You guys would be awful roommates."

Alec's face puzzled. "Why on Earth would you be in a — never mind. How are you feeling? Do you need me to call a nurse?"

Fin raised his finger. "I thought you said you wiped her memory."

Kate raised her eyebrows. "What?"

"Oh yeah," Fin jumped on the chance to air his grievances, "you came here via angel express. He appeared in the emergency department and scared the crap out of all the scrubs and white coats. Apparently, angels aren't supposed to do that, so then they have to wipe people's memories clean." He snapped his fingers for emphasis.

Alec reacted to Fin's sarcasm, his teeth clenched. "I only wiped *some* of their memories. They just recall Kate arriving in a different fashion. That's all. Don't make me regret leaving yours intact."

"Why couldn't you just heal me?" Kate asked, yearning for her own bedroom.

"You wouldn't let me," Alec said, his voice saturated with irritation.

"If I'd known you might have taken some of *my* memories, I wouldn't have been so willing, either," Fin said, eyeing Alec.

Alec helped Kate into a sitting position. She grimaced. "Fin, can you get me something to drink?"

"Are you sure you want me to leave you with this guy?" Fin asked, pointing his thumb at Alec.

Kate didn't answer. She just looked at him, pleading with her eyes. Through all his sarcasm and humor, Fin really had a soft side, and she knew it. His eyes twinkled for just a moment, and the side of his mouth curled up. He turned and shouted over his shoulder. "Don't ever do that again. You're my only friend, and you scared me to death."

I love you too, Kate thought.

"I really don't know how you put up with him," Alec said.

Kate shrugged. "He's an acquired taste." Alec looked angry with her for a moment. She didn't really understand why. "I *did* want you to heal me. At least, I think I did. Everything is a little foggy. I definitely wish you had, feeling the way I do now."

"Who are you?" Alec asked her.

She furrowed her brow, looking away from him.

"I'm pretty sure I need to start keeping a running tally for everyone who asks me that question." She picked at the fuzz on her blanket. "According to my grandmother, I'm some sort of dream walker who is meant to hunt demons." She let out a small laugh. "That sounds so ridiculous every time I say it."

Alec nodded. "I've known both demon hunters and dream walkers. You might be those things. I guess time will tell. But there's something else that I've not seen — your ability to keep the spiritual world from touching you."

"You mean like when you touched me? And you tried to get me to do your bidding?" Kate said a little more harshly than she meant to.

Alec smiled, looking out the window. "I'm definitely not used to people saying no."

"Is Fran ok?"

He nodded. "Oh, yeah, she's great. She'll probably be carrying a few more weapons around with her from now on. I expect I'll be experiencing quite the inquisition from her soon."

"So you didn't..."

He interrupted her. "I don't just go around like *Men in Black* erasing memories, Kate. Sometimes people find out about us, and it's okay. It depends on the circumstances."

"Well, look at you!" A stout woman interrupted from the door. "I'm surprised you can even sit up after what you've been through, doll. Let's check those vitals." She bustled into the room, checking this and that while asking Kate to name the current president and year.

"When can I go home?" Kate asked.

"Darlin'," the nurse offered a toothy smile, "that's always the first question. Let's just leave it up to the doctor. You've been through a lot. And don't you worry, we'll catch the fella that did this."

Kate looked from the nurse to Peterson, confused.

Alec interjected, "She, uh, doesn't remember being hit by the car."

"That's not too surprising. Lots of trauma patients can't remember the event that brings them to me. Let's check those wounds, dear." The nurse pulled on Kate's gown, and Alec turned away. She checked the bandages where Simone had stabbed her. "Doc says you're lucky that piece of glass missed your vital organs."

"Uh—yeah, I guess." Kate was afraid to say something that would get Alec and Fin into trouble for whatever lies they'd told.

The nurse checked her IV one more time. Satisfied, she gave Kate a wink. "You get some rest, now. Press the call button if you need anything. The doctor will be in later."

Alec turned back to Kate. "Sorry, it was the best story we could think of."

"Well, it feels like that's what happened," Kate winced as she resituated herself. "What are you going to do about the investigation?"

"As it turns out, The Gathering of Souls is being sued by a young man with a well-to-do father. He claims his mentor planned to kill

233

him. Seems someone interceded on his behalf. The files were wiped from the website, but I happen to know someone who is excellent at retrieving files. We provided the family and their lawyer with the documentation they'll need to prosecute.

"Once that hits the media, the can of worms will be open. The FBI will probably get involved, considering the widespread reach of the website. I'm leaving all my documentation with Fran and a few other local officers that I've worked with in this area. It'll be a good starting point."

Kate nodded. "Good."

Alec sat on the edge of her bed. "I was able to recover a couple more documents for you. Molly tried to leave The Gathering repeatedly. But they wouldn't let her. Finally, it looks like she decided to play along, not realizing that her mentor wouldn't be fulfilling her end of the suicide pact."

"Ashley," Kate added. "That was her mentor."

Alec leaned back a little. "How did you know..."

"I'm a dream walker, aren't I?" Kate pressed her lips into a thin line, wishing she weren't.

"Why didn't you say anything?"

"Alec, all of this is new to me. I didn't know until after Molly's death. I thought I was losing my mind. Then my Grams explained our heritage to me. She said that Molly struggled because she tapped into her gift before I did." She shook her head. "I honestly don't think I ever would have accessed mine if it weren't for Molly's death.

"Molly was a seeker. She wanted more in her life. I don't think she was looking for something like this," Kate held out her good arm, indicating the hospital bed. "But she was never satisfied. I, on the other hand, prefer normalcy."

"Do you still?" Alec asked.

Fin appeared in the doorway, holding a cup of ice water and three bags of chips. Kate shook her head. "No. I don't think so. I don't really have a choice, do I?"

"You always have a choice," Alec said, standing. "And you should give your Grams another chance to explain herself. She went to great lengths to keep you hidden if neither side knows anything about you. She might know more than she's let on."

"How did you know I was avoiding her?" Kate asked, mouth gaping. "Did you look in my mind or something?"

Fin uttered under his breath. "Wouldn't surprise me."

Alec shrugged. "I don't have to read your mind. I'm an angel."

A voice rang down the hallway. "You don't understand! I *am* family."

Kate's eyes widened. "How does Marcy know I'm here?" Kate glared at Fin and Alec. Both simply shrugged, looking innocent as ever.

"Fin, can you tell them to let her in?" Kate asked, pinching the bridge of her nose.

"...and furthermore, if you don't let me in right now, I'm going to barge down that hallway, and you'll be forced to call the police." Marcy's voice echoed down the hallway.

Fin smiled, "Yeah, I like this lady."

"I will be moving on soon," Alec said. "But if you ever need me, here's my card. I specialize in the supernatural, you know."

"I already have that," Kate replied, pushing away his hand. She tried not to let her eyes show the disappointment she felt. She didn't want him to leave.

"No, you don't." He lifted her hand and gently placed a card in it. It tingled her fingertips, and he laid his hand on top of it. "I'm really impressed with you, Kate. People don't surprise me often. No matter what you may think of yourself or where you decide to go from here, you are a fighter."

She smiled, remembering the last words Molly said. "You surprised me, too. I kind of thought you were a jerk at first." Her cheeks heated. "I'm sorry, I didn't mean to say that out loud."

"It's ok. I usually come off that way. Can't let people get too close in my profession." He slowly withdrew his hands and put them in his pockets. "You take care of yourself."

"Do you really have to go? I have so many questions. Like, if there are angels and demons -- is there a God?" she finally allowed herself to ask.

"Kate!" Marcy burst into the room. "You're alive!"

Kate glanced at Marcy and back to Alec. But he was gone. She sat up, ignoring her screaming ribs, eyes darting around the room. "What the—"

"Oh my God, she's *blind*?" Marcy made her way quickly to Kate's bed. "Can you hear me? It's me, Marcy," she drew out her words.

Kate let out a long breath. "I can see. I just — did you see Detective Peterson leaving?"

"He was here? No. In that case, I'm sure the hospital staff would have used him to restrain me," Marcy laughed.

Kate let out a half-hearted laugh. "Yeah, I guess so."

"You look awful. The hit and run is all over the news. I hope they find the guy who did this to you. How are you feeling, hon?"

"I feel like my body was put through a woodchipper and then sewn back together." Kate winced, trying to remain as still as possible. "Every time I breathe, it hurts."

Marcy fidgeted with Kate's hospital gown and hair. "Do you need anything from home?"

Fin came in and handed Kate her drink around Marcy. "I don't think I need..." She gasped, "Jake! Oh my gosh, can you take care of him for me?"

Marcy nodded, "I sent the boys over there to let him out. Anything else?"

Kate shook her head. "I don't think so."

"I'll go pack you some socks and a robe. Do you want any toiletries?" Marcy prodded.

"Geez, how long do you think I'll be here?" Kate laughed.

Marcy glanced over her shoulder at Fin. He shrugged. "I'm not going to tie her to the bed," he said. "Besides, we have a trip planned. I need her to get well soon."

"You do?" Marcy turned back to Kate.

Kate searched Fin's face, playing along. "Uh, yeah. We do."

"We're going on a camping trip up at Devil's Lake State Park. It's a retreat for people who've lost loved ones. I've gone several years in a row," Fin explained, digging into the first bag of chips.

She wondered what attracted Fin to that destination, guessing it wasn't about a camping trip. He continued to carry on about the hiking trails and the home-cooked food in surrounding towns. Remembering the card in her hand, she opened it to see a small perfectly square paper situated in her palm. An ornate rune in angelic language extended to each corner. She closed her hand back around it with the feeling that she'd be seeing Alec Peterson again.

Epilogue

Alec watched from the roof as Kate and Fin left the hospital. His taller companion stood like a mountain, muscled arms crossed. Leather bands adorned with angelic writings squeezed his forearms and biceps. A breastplate etched with runes looked dainty on his broad chest. His glossy, braided beard moved slightly as he flexed his jaw in thought. Alec waited patiently for the general to decide their next move.

"Satan is certainly a sneaky one," the general mused. "I suppose he decided to take on the old adage, 'the enemy of my enemy is my friend.' After all, why fight yourself when you know God sends angels to stop demons who cross the line of those we're sworn to protect. Tyranneus overestimates himself." He reached up, tugging at his beard. The leather armbands made a stretching sound over his muscles.

Alec took an opportunity to add, "I did not know the Fallen One watched me. He used me to quell the rebellion in his kingdom. I'm a fool."

"You're no fool. And you may have slowed the rebellion, but you did not quell it. Tyranneus lives. Tell me about the girl. Who is she?"

Alec hesitated. He already felt responsible for unknowingly helping Lucifer's side of the battle. Now the general, the slayer of demons, asked him a question he could not answer. "That's a good question. I'm not sure *she* even knows who she is." Alec shook his head.

"She has demon hunter blood mixed with guardian blood," the general added without judgment on Alec's ignorance. "How was she hidden from us?"

Alec shook his head again. "I had hoped you would tell me that you knew of her."

A fleeting grin passed across the general's lips. "Our Father tells us what we need to know in time. Perhaps He wishes to keep her hidden for now."

Alec squinted, "She has no guardian. How will she survive?"

The general stared at Kate while she argued with Fin over who would drive the car. He chuckled, "I don't know. She has a fighter's spirit, though. The old man, he'll stay with her."

"How do you know?" Alec asked.

"She is an enigma. He loves enigmas."

Alec placed his palms on the concrete wall, leaning out. "I gave her the rune to call me."

The general made a noise of disapproval. "Be careful, half-born. Just because you stopped following her does not mean the Fallen One will cease as well."

Alec tensed at the general's words. He wondered if God would ever take the derogatory title of half-born from him. "I could continue to follow her, if you wish it."

The general turned clear eyes onto Alec, reading his thoughts. "You should not detest that which the Lord has given you. Half-born angels are needed in the kingdom, just like anyone else. I assure you, I do not use the term in a demeaning way."

Alec nodded, feeling childish.

"You will not follow her. I will assign another if He commands it. You are too close, and your admiration for her may spin into something else." The general turned his back. "You are to follow the grandmother. Find out what she knows and report back. But be careful. She prays fervently."

Alec nodded, knowing that those who prayed in such ways would certainly meet resistance.

The Gathering of Souls

Erica Darnell

Sneak peek into Kate's next adventure.

Chapter 1

Darkness blanketed the quiet school campus as Patty walked through the common space of the elementary dorms. She sipped her coffee, waiting for 5:00am when she would be relieved by the next staff on duty. The Indiana School for the Deaf, despite common belief of hearing people, was a noisy place to be a dorm monitor. Deaf children do not hear the sounds they make by opening and closing doors, or the stomping of their feet on the floors, the slamming of dresser drawers, and sometimes they shouted in the bathrooms to feel the reverberation of sound in the air. They also loved music, especially the kind with a good underlying bass. The poignant silence of nighttime was a stark contrast to the clamorous days.

Nevertheless, Patty loved working with each child as they learned to explore their world. One of the children last year sat behind her and began flipping the pages of a magazine. Patty turned and the student jumped. "How did you know I was here?" She signed. "I was very quiet."

Patty smiled and signed, "When you turn the pages of the magazine, I can hear them."

The student stared at the magazine pages, investigating their delicate lightweight feel. She pinched one between her fingers and very slowly flipped a page, looking up at Patty with her eyebrows raised. Typically, eyebrows are raised at the end of a yes or no question in ASL, but Patty didn't need the question to be signed. She simply nodded to indicate she could hear the whisper of each page turned.

New students had a harder time adapting because many came from homes that did not use American Sign Language to communicate. Most deaf children had hearing parents, and only about ten percent of those parents learned ASL to provide language access in their home situation. Therefore, no one had ever explained that forks make noise when you stab your food on the plate, or that

241

scooting back in a chair sends screeches through the room. Often, students arrived at the school for the deaf with no foundational signing skills at all.

Patty learned sign language through a childhood with deaf parents, although she was born hard of hearing. With the use of hearing aids she could function well enough without signing, but she preferred the Deaf Community. It felt like home. Growing up with one foot in the hearing world and one foot in the deaf world afforded her some advantages, but also had its downfalls. Doctors' offices and hospitals would often ask her to interpret for her parents. Not only was the request a conflict of interest, but she didn't have the training to use ASL medical terminology, especially at 12 years old. Fortunately, her parents understood their rights and advocated for themselves by requesting certified and licensed interpreters.

"Pah-tee!" A scream yanked her from her thoughts. She sat her coffee down in case she needed both hands to sign and console a crying student. Staying away from home for a week at a time was a tough adjustment for the little ones. "Pah-tee!" The child screamed again.

She hustled into the room shared by a few children. Delaney sat hugging her knees and sobbing. She, unlike new students, usually slept through the night with no issue.

Perplexed, Patty placed a gentle hand on her shoulder and signed with one hand. "What's wrong? Are you sick?"

Delaney wiped a tear from her cheek and signed, "No. It was my dream."

"It's okay. You're awake now and it was just a dream. Take a deep breath to help you calm down."

"He was here," Delaney shivered. She shifted her large blue eyes around the room to double check. "He stood over me. He wanted me to give him something."

Patty sat next to her. "It's okay. I'm right here. Let's get you back under your covers, okay?"

Delaney swept the room with her eyes once more before apprehensively laying back down. Patty tucked the blankets around her and sat a bit longer until her breathing slowed into a sleeping rhythm.

"Paytay!" Patty grinned knowing which child said her name that way. Learning to pronounce words and names you couldn't hear was a difficult task.

She shuffled to the other room to find Kenzie sitting in a tight ball just like Delaney. The similarity gave her pause. Neither of these girls were hard of hearing. They were completely deaf. It felt eerie finding them the same way on the same night around the same time. Patty shook the feeling and sat on the edge of Kenzie's bed. "What's the matter?"

"I had a terrible dream! It was so scary and I couldn't wake up. I wanted to wake up so bad!" Kenzie signed frantically. She sobbed and leaned into Patty for a hug.

"It's okay," she signed low for Kenzie to see while she hugged her. "It's over now."

"Can you check on Delaney?" Kenzie signed, turning her tear-filled eyes back to Patty. "There was a dark man. He was so scary. I'll feel better if you check on her."

Patty's stomach tightened. "Delaney?" She tried to steady her hands as she signed, "I'm sure Delaney is fine."

Kenzie tensed. "You have to check. The dark man wants something. Delaney was in my dream and he wants something from her."

Patty stood slowly and backed away from the bed. *What the hell?* She swallowed a little harder than she meant to. "

Of course I'll check if it will make you feel better. I'll be right back." She walked out and pressed her back to the wall thankful for a moment to compose herself. *That was so weird.* She hoped Kenzie would fall back asleep before she went back into the room. She didn't plan on executing her task to check on Delaney because she already knew how Delaney was doing – not good. But how did Kenzie know that?

"Patty!" A new cry rang through the hallway from another room.

Made in the USA
Las Vegas, NV
26 October 2021